Gloria
Mundi

Gloria Mundi

A Novel

Eleanor Clark

Pantheon Books
New York

Library of Congress Cataloging in Publication Data

Clark, Eleanor, 1913–
    Gloria mundi.

    I. Title.
PZ3.C54336G   [PS3505.L254]   813'.5'4
79–1874
ISBN 0-394-50536-0

Design by Irva Mandelbaum

Manufactured in the United States of America

First Edition

To Dorothy Eisner and John McDonald

Sic transit gloria mundi.—So passes away the glory of this world.

—Thomas à Kempis

1

The little plane circled prettily over Boonton, Vermont, no butterfly acoustically or in its purpose, though some were pleased to see it, for various reasons. Practically everybody knew it belonged to Nelco, for New England Land Co., and the regional boss Jim Pace was probably at the controls. He was. Combining business with pleasure was his forte and panorama his favorite word that year. The man beside him was his aerial photographer.

Beautiful; hardly a cloud anywhere. They could see over the whole layout, not quite downriver to Compton, the only place around you could call a city, but that didn't matter. The view they wanted, and got, was from tiny Boonton, over the notch to stodgy old bankrupt Mt. Akatuck—one of the earliest ski areas in the east and where the Japanese had been the latest to lose their shirts; past another one-store village, set however in an eight-mile stretch of trailer camps, motels, etc., to Waterville. Fifteen to twenty stores there altogether, if you counted the hippie joints, plus discos, a couple of real estate firms and, most gratifying to the pilot, the new Nelco office, still without desks or staff but otherwise finalized that very morning.

A few miles south, the long lake was sprinkled with pleasure boats, more sail than stink for once; probably a weekend race. Jim Pace could have gone for a cabin cruiser himself but couldn't see one on a lake and didn't mind admitting the ocean scared him pink; he'd rather it went away, didn't even like seeing it through a car window, and blamed it for the bleeding ulcers that had gone with his fifteen years of spectacular success around Atlantic City. He was a mountain man but didn't want mountains to be too enormous either. Vermont was just right. Besides, he'd been brought up there, if you could call it an upbringing.

His current dream and concern lay in the other direction, north from Boonton center starting with Horton Hill, which he was particularly fond of. Really it was a first low shoulder of the mountain, level on top for a bit before the end of the present road and the big rise. Fine folks there, except for maybe what the Palz setup had become, in one of the

four remaining oldtime farmhouses along the road. The original Horton
farm was still inhabited by Hortons and what's more was still a farm,
not just sugaring, a small herd of cattle too, getting to be quite a rarity
around there these days; Brit Horton, the brother Pace knew better
and liked to think of as his friend, lived in a newer, improvised little
place farther up on the flat. The two or three new weekender dots
between didn't matter, and Mrs. Holloway near where the road
stopped was mainly absentee. From a fork a little past Brit Horton's
house a dead end branched three quarters of a mile uphill to the old
Banks farm, or what had been that until recently.

So much for what might be called home ground, a crucial but tiny
piece in the overall scheme. The plane tightened its circles, especially
over some key spots. Pace's main home now, since he'd found it advisable for more reasons than ulcers to lower his profile in New Jersey,
was outside Boston, and his chief sphere of operations, another phrase
he liked, had been in New Hampshire for some time. Nelco, one of the
oldest and most reputable New England realty firms, fallen on evil
days when he and two associates came to the rescue, had had a number
of assets there that needed playing with. Now he was going to get
Boonton humming, and never had business filled him with more satisfaction. He'd been raised on the edge of it, miserably; French Canadian father, named something like Peysset, drifted down there and at
age thirty-three was killed in a lumbering accident; half Irish, half
Portuguese mother, six kids all told, he the only one she passed on the
red hair and freckles to, made a hard and lousy living at housework for
inns around Akatuck. Now he had her set up in a sweet home of her
own in Phoenix, Arizona, near his two married sisters, and Boonton
Mountain was as good as in his pocket.

He beamed, zipping over it. Room there for the biggest ski area in
the world, in the eastern U.S. anyway, and by God that's what it would
start being when he got the new road through. From the end of the
Horton Hill patch around to the good side, what used to be town road
a century or so ago was now scarcely a jeep track, hard to make out
from the air, but the town lines didn't look as zany as from the ground.
He already had architects' plans for the main lodge and a lot else,
adequate OPEC and other investment, and the town with him. That
last was the icing on the cake, the carnation in his lapel. He'd been
hauled into county courts twice in New Hampshire and lost both

times; a bunch of rockheads in each case, who wanted to go on sticking in the mud, not have him improve the roads past their houses; got him proven a liar in his stated reasons for doing so, accurately enough but progress and squeamishness don't mix. It's one or the other.

He'd laid his plans better this time. "I just love Boonton," was the way he explained having given town residents first crack at the ski area stock before it went up—not that many but newcomers had had the sense or cash to get any—and his promise of a low-interest loan toward a new Town Hall, the old one having burned down a few years before. The only stipulation was that it should be by the new road, half way between old Boonton and the grand new part about to materialize the other side of the mountain. Of course now they'd have to vote the money for the remaining seventy percent of the building costs plus the interest due him, and for the road too. He wasn't going to play patsy for anybody. But the benefits to all the public in the not so long run would be worth every penny, as the sensible majority could see. No wool over any eyes this time. They'd voted for it all, knowing perfectly well that aside from his company's holdings, Jim Pace personally still owned a thousand-plus acres of that ex-farmland, now inferior timber lots just waiting for the magic wand.

Droves of hikers on the Long Trail could be calculated from the jam of cars in the parking space for the Boonton Pond stretch, always a favorite. A very different, compact little gathering the plane skimmed over was visible but of no interest. That was a party at the summer day camp near Akatuck, for the last day of camp as well as the eighteenth birthday of one of the counselors. He was very popular and so was his young snow-white goat, named Lily the Kid, tethered there every day but let loose at 4 P.M. to play racing games with the children. The winner in the treasure hunt behaved badly; he wanted Chip Holloway's goat for his prize. There were whirligigs for the losers and Lily made a marvelous leap over a bunch of them onto a high windowsill, where she baahed and balanced on her clever little hooves, "grinning her head off."

Chip was strung like a coatrack with adoring little boys and girls. They wanted to take *him* home, or go home with him. He was the one they wouldn't go on an overnight camping trip without; who didn't groan at their jokes and knew "everything" about rocks and stars and animal tracks. It was his looks and manners their mothers flipped over; he wasn't rude to them, it was weird, they couldn't account for it; they said he should go into soap or the movies, with that height and muscle and profile, those tangled chestnut curls not messed over his neck but just jaw-length, that big rush of a smile "like he's saying 'I like you!' every time." And oh those gorgeous white teeth, that strange dark burning something in the eyes! The girl counselors agreed he'd be wasting his time in college. The smile would be withheld at appropriate times from the worst of the varmints; urchins, he called them all, good and bad alike, and often felt like one himself. He wasn't sure he felt ready to be eighteen.

Huge cake, out between paddock and swimming pool. "Happy birthday, dear Chi-ip." Hugs and kisses. His school roommate, also for that summer cabinmate and camp sailing instructor, leered, as he'd been doing quite often lately. Things hadn't been ideal on that front. Chip's cabin was going to need a good airing out. The summer before, working around the world on a freighter out of New Orleans, he'd taken a hate on drugs, even pot, also cigarettes and alcohol. That wasn't all. He was a Vermont freak, a nature freak, a freak period, the roommate had decided. Girls after him like ants to honey wherever he went and never yet had an all-out, down to business screw. Retarded; mental, practically. He'd turn off a good rock record to listen to an owl for Chrissake; read poetry, was going to study astronomy and Greek, the other day in some kind of fit smashed all his own pop records, forty at least and good. Roommate leaving for the Vineyard that very night. Couldn't wait. Shyly the birthday boy managed, "It's been a swell summer, being with all of you, thanks a lot," and raced to yank Lily out of the petunias. He'd have had a choice of teams, skiing, hockey, track, to be captain of at school if he'd wanted. He hadn't wanted, preferring to buzz off whenever possible with or without company to his one-room shanty, on Nowhere Hill in No-town as his friend called it. He was the only one at the party scene who could outrun Lily.

A few miles away over the notch, next to the Boonton P.O. right by Route 80, old Thelma Nesbit was pulling up the dry remains of her string bean crop. She'd have liked to stop passing cars and tell them the news, except they mostly had out-of-state plates. The leisure-time labor of her life, especially in her years as a widow, was about to be rewarded. The product was over a thousand photos, starting with daguerreotypes and the earliest postcards, all carefully researched and labeled, covering the town's history, family by family. In the village it had come to be known as The Boonton Collection. For Ebenezer Boon, one of the Green Mountain Boys and the first settler, and a couple of later generations, she'd had to get copies of limners' portraits and sketches when available and fill in with written material; very hard going, that part, kept her on edge for years. She loved telling people the town was not named for Daniel Boone, who spelled it differently and never set foot in that part of the country. And she had not been willing to have the Collection kept by the County Historical Society. Too far off, way down near the courthouse, nearly to Compton; she had no way of getting thirty miles to keep an eye on it, and thought the ladies of the society untidy and ill-informed.

And now it was going to be published—with her name on it! by the Harvard University Press no less! That's what the young fellow who took it away last April said, and he and his wife were living up the hill with Lem and Hannah Palz, as straight-shootin' a pair as you'd find her husband used to say and he'd helped out with their sugaring every spring for twenty years till the diabetes got him, so there couldn't be any monkey business about it. The young fellow said he'd have it gone over by the American History Department at Harvard, where he had what he called a fellowship, and then there it would be! That dumb little Historical Society could go hang. Four months, he said, and that was right now to the day. Thelma's two married daughters and even two granddaughters were calling every day to hear; she couldn't go into the store for a quart of milk without somebody asking.

Her enormous old sunbonnet, tied under the chin with a piece of still older curtain-cord, hid her elation from the passing traffic. Anyway in her excitement she'd left her teeth in the Polident and wasn't comfortable grinning.

As if they'd have had time to notice, those hurriers-by. Last weekend before Labor Day, millions on the move, migratory, swarming, all over the Green Mountains and the Rockies and Europe, by land, water, air. Motels jammed, airports ditto. Like Tartars, a certain Mrs. Philipson on a bus would be thinking a little later: "The Revolt of," by Thos. De Quincey; she'd read that once long ago. This is up in September when the travel graph is on the downplunge temporarily, but just the same. Thousands die on the way and then the slaughter in the river somewhere along the border with China as she remembered, Catherine the Great's Cossacks having chased them all that way; crazed with thirst they staggered to drink what was already more blood than water and in a minute dyed it redder with their own. Some, somehow, reached the other bank and perhaps some version of the new life they had gone for; not many. Still, having Cossacks after you would give point and drama to the flight. Mortal danger better than just fleeing from boredom and yourself.

Travel! what a word! Scrambling in and out of vehicles, everybody looking for a live bear or a peasant on a donkey to get a glimpse or a snapshot of. The awful thought later, waiting for squawk of flight number home, who are we going to show our pictures to? Eight rolls of film and already have ten boxes full in a closet and who the hell's going to sit through an evening like that especially when you never bothered to go sit through theirs.

Margo Philipson was neither in any such pickle nor much of a Tartar, except in having a definite purpose. Occasionally people do. Anyway right now she was still in the same ugly, dun-colored frame house on a side street in Michigan, feeling poorly as usual, without a thought of setting out for anywhere, and a certain southbound pair of hikers were still at the Canadian end of the Long Trail, a long way from the Boonton crossing where a very different couple would shortly be murdered. Not that the two leaving Canada had any particular stopping-place in mind.

"Lily! Lily!" the children cried. But the goat, who loved riding in the car, had leaped onto the back seat as soon as the door was open and now sat there like a nearsighted old lady, impatient to be off. Chip was leaving soon for college and had to take her back to her herd, where she could have a proper goat life and become a mother.

Jim Pace, by a certain leathery puckering around his usually rather shapeless mouth, showed special pleasure dipping over the Banks farm—glad he'd acquired that, great investment, room for a bangup condominium complex up back—and scowled a minute later over a twenty-seven-acre remaining obstacle beyond the Holloway property, but such annoyances were not in the habit of hindering him long. No sign of life around the big Holloway house, apparently closed up as usual in recent years, but on their last pass over it a small car, probably the grandson's, was by the old chicken-coop, and a white dog? some kind of white animal. Years ago Pace had thought of marrying the old lady, some twenty years older than he but a stunning dame still and rich, a bigtime playwright with important movie credits too. He'd have read some of her stuff eventually if it had worked out, he wasn't being insincere; flying over her house even now, embroiled in his third divorce, he remembered how when he first got her bedded down or vice versa he was walking on clouds for an hour, with scarcely a thought of the large tract up the mountain that he wanted from her, preferably for a song. But a bigshot radio character was after her and she turned down the rising young lumberman and realtor-to-be; called him a charming barbarian. And what did she mean by that? With a sweet smile and caress on the cheek, she said ignorant and insensitive. He wasn't then or ever going to forgive that, or her price for the land either, even though he'd made it ten times over within a few months, via father-in-law number one, in Atlantic City. For his original pile, in Quebec, he had to thank Brit Horton who'd taken him along on a fishing trip when Pace was sixteen and lent him fifty dollars, a huge sum to them both at the time, for the first timberland he owned.

Walt Hodge, doing a last useless chore around the Banks barn, at the sound of the plane spat mightily toward where the manure pile had been all his grown life, the actual manure gone now, sold off like everything else. Even from way up the hill there he could hear the traffic humming on the highway and he didn't like that much either. To the man overhead, the rippling stream of cars was more splendid than the beautiful Montglebe River and all its shining tributaries, which he was also getting a bead on. Alongside that river, near Compton where she had been visiting her mother in the nut-house, a female driving alone got a real rewarding encounter going with a trucker on her CB; so glad she got her last meaningful relationship to pay for that before things ground down; trucker tells her there's a motorcycle gang heading north she'd better watch out for. In a camper in Oregon barreling home east a father bawls, "If all of you don't stop that quarreling back there I'm gonna . . ." Cruise ships wedge into this and that little un-spoiled harbor and some big spoiled ones too, Mediterranean, Carib-bean, Asian, South American, hurry hurry, shop shop, only forty minutes at this one.

The suburban limo driver sees so many, two roundtrips a day to whichever airport it is, he stopped noticing a long time ago, except once in a while if one gives him a bad time but there's not much of that, not like cab driving. More chatter going in; never much coming back; they're tired then, sit heavier, weigh more, you could swear the car was actually slower on the pickup with the same number of passen-gers. He used to notice, and even try to tell his wife some of the funny things, like the guy one trip who nearly got killed that morning in a mudslide in California and can't stand nobody wanting to hear about it; see, they're just in from Istanbul or Chicago or something so what do they care. He doesn't care any more either. Once in a blue moon you might get a real doll beside you but mostly it's just more of same, just chickens in a coop, that's all.

And all Margo Philipson was to her various bus drivers all the way from the Middle West. A widow, in her fifties looked like, dumpy figure, poorly dressed, pinching pennies, probably going to visit a daughter or something. Now and then somebody asked, on long trips it helps pass the time, but she didn't encourage it. Only wondered at the sharpness of the feeling of anonymity. So in more innocent times must explorers have felt at moments, aiming to reach the North Pole or the top of Everest before Hillary and Tenzing. Featureless in reduction, beyond personal past, beyond purpose and personality, faceless and nameless before a majesty of peril as in the swarm of so-called travel-ers now. Indeed her purpose escaped her most of the way. Occasion-ally she stared at the photograph in her frayed wallet to remind herself of it but the reminder scarcely penetrated. She continued as on an endless escalator, committed by the mere act of having stepped onto it, for reasons long since hazy. Yet it was not uninteresting to be nobody. Tired as she soon was, it rather perked her up. She realized that for too long, even before her husband's passing away as she called it, perhaps all her life, she had been rather trapped in selfhood, which along with her chronic illness included a near-religion of unselfishness. She was headed for Waterville, Vermont, eighteen miles from Boonton.

She couldn't, of course, know what an unusual string of incidents there had just been and was about to be in the vicinity. Some seasons are like that; in late years with all the drifting and shifting you might say all seasons are. It was the double murder just off the Long Trail early in September that made this one a bit special, and old Brit Horton's being singled out by fate to be more involved in one thing after another than he cared to be; most of his life he'd been pretty good at dodging drama and nuisances, except what couldn't be avoided in public life. Not this time; they came right for him. He was the one who discovered the two young campers' mutilated bodies, boy and girl, eighteen or nineteen; he wasn't alone, another man and a woman were with him, but it was his dog Sam who led them to the spot. And hardly a week before he'd had to snatch Walt Hodge back from his fool suicide, might as well have let him go, to tell the truth, but you can't always be so reasonable. Brit wasn't in the store when it was held up, nobody was but the girl tending it, but he'd been in there when the same motorcycle gang stopped for gas the first time. And so it went. Another sad episode soon to occur, smack in the Horton family, was a direct result of the goddam new road nobody wanted, nobody but the damn fool Nelco faction who fell for the ballyhoo and the loan and rammed it through Town Meeting.

Not quite so locally, a New York to Vermont bus was hijacked, two killed, some wounded, hostages held. Getting to be quite a popular worldwide sport. But a bus! that was a new wrinkle, at least for that neck of the woods.

Mrs. Philipson, though innately timorous enough, never thought of worrying about that on her bus voyage, but then she was half anesthetized at the time, with respect to the worry principle. It didn't upset her to be arriving in a strange place with no lodging in prospect and $3.80 in her purse. If she supposed anything, it was that God would provide. She had been intimate with Him always, her father and husband, though with no other similarity, having both been Protestant ministers, Poppa Methodist and John Episcopalian.

Did you buy that skirt, that rug, that jug? Did you get cheated? Dear God, who can we show our pictures to? Last visit to Momma in the Retreat, the lavender blonde with the CB took up with a well-heeled, redheaded real estate muckymuck at a restaurant in Compton, had quite a night of it but he didn't seem to have kept her phone number.

The trucker sounded more refined so far, not so much in diction; in feelings, that's what counts.

In the bright evening air, tart with the first snap and crackle of approaching fall, Chip Holloway sat in his doorway, feet on the granite slab Brit Horton had helped him haul there several years ago for a doorstep. Some red and yellow strokes had already appeared among the leaf greens, aside from goldenrod. A flock of wild geese flew over, quite low, going to settle for the night on Boonton Pond most likely. Brit's hound barked briefly, a mile and a half away. A bat zoomed crisscross after its supper, poor pickings that time of year, he felt sorry for it having to work so hard. Earlier, he'd flapped a blanket around to air the cabin, and mowed the field out back, down to the small brook you had to strain to hear from up around the house. At Brit's place it wound close, and Brit had had a colony of pet trout in it one time, built a stream-ladder for them and fed them beefburgers, for the fun of watching them congregate when it was time; he'd go to other streams for fish to eat, and the maddest most people had seen him that year was when some summer kids sneaked in and caught his pets. Tomorrow Chip would borrow a tractor and take the hay down to the original Horton farm, Brit's brother's and sister's, for the cows.

"Shall we trot down to Lem and Hannah's and hear some music, Lily? Schubert maybe, or Stravinsky . . ." In that air, he felt strong enough to race the sun west over New York State and on to California if the goat had been willing to keep him company. Summers as a small boy he'd taken violin lessons with Lem Palz and was terrible at it. Never mind. They and the Brit Hortons were more family to him than any of his own; both couples elderly, with children grown and gone, but strong and busy still. He never could be really lonely on that road, in spite of three tacky weekend cabins, ranging humanly from okay to not so good, that had popped up like mushrooms in the last year, fewer though than along the highway and on some other back roads where there was more land for sale. Hannah was getting up one of her cordon bleu dinners for his real birthday the next night. And just that day she had given him back his grandmother's favorite handwoven Greek rug, which he'd been a fool to take from the big house for the summer, mended so beautifully, she having a rug-making business, nobody would ever know Lily had eaten two big swatches out of it. The goat had eaten some of his pants too, and peed on his bed, after contriving a way in via shed roof and transom, and played hell with roses and groceries.

"Bad girl, and I'm going to miss you so!" He'd borrowed her for the summer because he thought he'd get too fond of a dog and wouldn't know what to do with it when he went to college, but the parting a few days off was going to be just as hard. She rested her chin on his knee, one ear up like a huge white tulip leaf, pink eyes on their two horizons, some deep fluffy question replacing the playtime grin; then stiffened in sudden apprehension. That was no owl but the first bear's mating call of the season, from the ledges part way up the dark mass of the mountain over his left shoulder. He told her not to worry, apples were what they'd be after if they came down, and she subsided by his feet, to wait for whatever was to be.

His departed roommate might be right about his backwardness in regard to what the bear was hollering about, though himself sodden in the ass from pot most evenings. And yes, that sharp little tooth at work in there might be lonesomeness. Still, one regret he couldn't muster up was for either of the two girlfriends he'd broken off with last year, after not quite—it was true—losing his virginity with either. Sue, the peach icecream beauty who clung and hung from his arm so tenderly with all her hundred and twelve pounds, wouldn't have cooperated anyway, at seventeen hellbent on marriage in a cute split-level with the successful young businessman she was sure he could be if he tried. So after a sleepless night or two he switched to crazy Jane. No clinger she; could ski Tuckerman's and paddle a canoe down the Allagash almost as fast as he, had already had an abortion, and while intending to stay mad for Chip, planned to sleep around with males or females as fancy might smite. It was what she called first her philosophy, and after her three-week touchy-feelies course at a hundred dollars a week, methodology. She got A's without trying, was a sieve for learning and experience alike, so needed louder music and new and more outlandish dresses all the time, to feel real she said.

A breeze whisked with a hard wild clatter like instant rain through the great tall old maples beside the main house. Being one of the original farmhouses on Horton Hill, all similarly strung out in five or six connected units with an eye to winter's rigors, it was favored by such trees, also a fine dug well of the period. A white half-moon teetered in the sway of the branches. A jogger from one of the new cabins came by, about Chip's age, in all the latest equipment, plodded the short way to the end of the road and back by without a smile or hello. Then two dirtbikes smashed the evening quiet and went on doing so from far up the darkening mountain, pathless but for some old logging tracks now mostly overgrown. They were from another of the new vacation homes. He was mad at himself for hating them so, didn't enjoy being angry at anybody for anything but had been every time they appeared that summer: the worst ripoff he called it, of everybody's peace for miles around, the whole natural world must be shuddering with abhorrence and condemnation; it was after one of those vile intrusions a while ago that he had smashed his own rock records and finished off his roommate's tolerance.

They must have had a breakdown up there this time. There were a few minutes of quiet, in which he could hear the short whoosh and scramble in the woods across the road. An owl that would be, and some poor small creature on the way to being digested. The goat's pink vision split to a double rearview, blandly; really it was her bedtime, but she was aware of strange imminences in summer's end, the first of her life, and had no elders of her kind to learn from, so would try to stay awake. Above her in the doorway the pair of young human eyes flared in black intensity a moment, burning laserlike into the invisible spot across the road. In the boy's mind, as perhaps if more drowsily in the goat's, love and precariousness had it out, insolubly. Human cruelties, he had known for a long time, were far worse.

"Time for Mozart. Bedtime for you, my friend." She was ready now to be shut in her small shed. "Goodnight, sweet Lily. May flights of angels bear thee to thy rest, or however that goes. Sweet dreams; sleep well. When th'art old there's grief enough for thee. And for me too I suppose."

Yet to most in the Palz household it was a fireball of pure health and joy that came bounding over the high wild-yew hedge. Since he was big enough to clear it, his arrival that way, instead of by the gate a few yards farther on, had been by request—a common joke counted on and that would have left a dull spot by its forgoing. Hannah and Lem knew better, while agreeing privately that nothing in music was more fetching than that highjump and the face that went with it. They had nursed Chip through a bad siege of mumps all one summer in their house, when his mother had just died and his grandmother had to be on the road with one of her sadly overrated plays. Not that the mother would have been any more concerned if she'd been alive.

She sold the farm, the widow Banks did, was gay as a cricket the day of the signing, cooked Walt Hodge a final few dinners while every last thing was disposed of including the kitchen stove, and when that went she did too. It was horror beyond anything in his life to hear her turning the old iron key in the lock that last time. His own belongings fitted with space to spare in an old hunting bag of her deceased husband's, which after much inner debate she had decided to let him keep.

"Don't know which way to head," he said for the hundredth time, only this time he was crying. Just couldn't help it. Anything that bad has got to be a dream.

"Now come on, Walt, you're a strong, healthy man; with all the farm experience you've had, loads of people are going to want you to work for them. You just have to get out there and hustle a little bit for a day or two. You'll see."

Second wife she was, only been there seven years and hated every minute of it, except maybe between the sheets. A powerful handsome man Walt's cousin and lifelong boss had been, hair black as a crow to the end as he never let them forget, and as mean as he was vain but the not even hired man wasn't the one to say that or think it, however often he'd heard it joked and whispered about. The poor relation, taken in for charity as an orphan at fourteen, to sleep in the attic and do all the hard work with the thirty cows and the haying and sugaring, taking orders every inch of the way, that's all he'd ever been or thought of wanting to be, and now he was fifty. One winter when the Bankses went off for Cousin Ned to be in the state legislature in Montpelier, Walt slept in the barn with the cows. Big Ned wasn't going to waste fuel just for him. "I made out pretty good too," Walt would say of that time. "Didn't even catch a cold. I did get kinda hungry now an' then without the cookstove, but the Hortons 'n' some others down the road they'd give me a bite, an' old Sally, the one he butchered soon as he come back an' found her udders dry, she'd lay down in her stall an' let me snuggle up to her nights an' keep warm. Don't often see a cow lay down like that indoors an' I wouldn't be surprised if she done it just for me, with it twenty below 'n' more some o' them nights." That was one of the times in his life he was proud of.

"Now you've got enough money to get a nice room and eats for a week or two," said the widow Clara, "and you come see me and I'll cook you some nice pork chops any time you like." And off she went, and off he went too, in a few minutes, a little way, in the little old pickup truck that was the whole of his personal property outside the hunting bag. About the only decision he'd had to make, or been allowed to, since he was fourteen was what brand of whiskey and cigarettes to buy. Cousin Ned took care of the deciding side, down to how many sap buckets to set out and where and what timber to cut and whether to go for feed Monday or Tuesday. Once when Walt was fifteen and decided on his own to clear out the spring he got so put down for it he never took anything in his own hands again. Just did what he was told and knew pretty well ahead of time most times what he would be told.

"Oh glory!" he said to the empty dirt road. "Oh heavens to Betsey! Now what?" Ned only dead three months and never sick a day; just looking at himself in the kitchen mirror, one side and the other, chin up (for the legislature) and down (for saying which side of the manure pile to add to next), after the Saturday night hair-grooming he always made her do on him, proud like every Saturday not to be finding any grey hairs yet and getting in the usual dig at Walt for all of his, what he had left of any color, Ned being older by ten years so with a right to his weekly joke, keeled over right there in front of the mirror and that was that. She had his dog Suds gassed to death at the pound in town next day; said he was too old for a new master; damn lie; he wasn't but nine and always went with Walt when he had a choice between the two of them.

September first, noontime; hot; quiet as a cemetery, everything, everywhere, except the whine of a car once in a while a mile down on the blacktop, other side of the lower woodlot and the mowings acting so dead with the cows gone. Big barn back of him in bad shape, getting dangerous; he'd been waiting for Ned to say, "Fix it, get a move on! We'll fall that big pine over there, get enough four-by-eights for the job outa that, prop up the east wall there but you'll have to relay the footings first, get the rock from up there where I'm goin' to tell you . . ." He'd have come to it pretty soon, except for the pine, Walt had guessed wrong on that point; he made Walt fall that for cash at the sawmill and she never forgave him, said it was the one thing she really cared about looking at up there on that lonesome hill, beauty meant a lot to her and he never cared for her feelings. Never forgave him either for not building her a regular bathroom with plumbing, making her go out through all the sheds to the outhouse summer and winter. That was her way of talking; nothing wrong with it in summer that Walt could see except it smelled more then and Ned wouldn't let her spend the money for those air-sweetener things they have in the store.

He sat in the stopped pickup, no need to pull over to the side on that dead end, and had a long pull of whiskey before looking at the front mirror where the house showed, with part of the first sugarhouse beyond. "Why, come on in, Walt," they said. "What in blazes you been waitin' for? Plenty o' work waitin' for you. First you get busy with that chainsaw on them logs you left out there and then . . . " They didn't say a thing, not the house or the sugarhouse or the great big old barn he knew every last joint and peg and timber of a lot better than the palm of his hand which he'd never paid any mind to. They were locked and horrible with emptiness; they didn't even know who he was all of a sudden. His jaw went slack; his eyes felt unhinged.

Peasant on donkey, for some traveler say from Russia or Rio or New York to get a snapshot of only there weren't any on that high lonesome dirt road and he was more the donkey himself, though slumped in an eighteen-year-old pickup. Or say such travelers as those folks from New Jersey that paid the down money first and had big schemes for the place from what he'd overheard, maybe even going to tear down the little old farmhouse though Walt told them they'd never find a better cellar for keeping onions and preserves and all like that, even fifty degrees year round and timbers perfect still, no dry rot anywhere; and put up some kind of shallay or maybe a dozen of them, same as Jim Pace would now, who'd come along with a better offer and got her to screw the city folks some way.

The red-shouldered hawk didn't exactly speak to him either, planing slowly downwind. They knew each other very well; he knew its nest high up in one or another of the tallest beeches up above the north lot, and just when the young would show their open beaks every year. He always found a way to get up and see it no matter what chores got delayed, it tickled him so. Rabbit or fieldmouse—what'll it be this time? There he goes, better than you could throw a knife, and it's a young partridge. No babies waiting now, just him and the missus, so he beats it up to the dead top of a yellow poplar to pluck and guzzle right off, won't go home till he's full. He has a home! Think of that!

A week later, good and drunk but still in some manner walking and talking, and driving, he stopped in at the Brit Hortons'. Wouldn't take the coffee Louise tried to give him, couldn't make a grain of sense or get words out straight and they could tell he'd been drunk all week and probably sleeping in the truck. "Don't mind if I stink some, do ya? Some feller down there"—waving toward the valley he lost his balance and fell over a rockingchair—"some feller I never seen before slobbered all over me, right in my own car. Didn't even apologize, the bastard. Just wait till I find him again an' I'll show him some stink'll stink him up good . . . "

Jim Pace hadn't been around to his new property yet and Walt said he had to go get a shirt he'd left on a tree up back. Nope, thanks, couldn't stay, and sure he could drive, why shouldn't he, if Brit was trying to pick a fight suggesting he couldn't . . . Anyway Suds would be waiting for him, always did when he'd been away a while. "Suds is dead," Brit said, "and you know it, and so is Ned, and I don't believe you left any shirt on any tree, that shirt you got on's the only one I seen you in the last ten years. You better stay here or else get on back where you come from."

Around ten at night when the pickup hadn't come back by, Brit and Chip Holloway who'd come in to say goodbye, pretty cut up about having just parted with his goat, decided to go up and have a look. Out of habit the old man reached for his gun, but saw the boy looking surprised at that so put it back and took the flashlight instead. "I guess that's right. Couldn't fire sense into Walt, the shape he's in."

That was more accurate even than a few hours earlier. As feared, they found the lock of the kitchen door pried off. The emptiness inside was like an explosion; they both hated turning the flashlight to this side and that. "Boy, this is creepy," Chip said, making himself laugh and remembering some scary times in the woods with Brit when he was little, but this was worse. He'd never had a second's doubt in his life of Brit's knowing what to do about wildcats or bears or any wild thing. Here there was some terrible human power in the walls or somewhere, something needing darkness or just the one shaft of moonlight through the front window for its effective chemistry, outside even Brit's tremendous competence in the world. "Sure is," Brit said. They went through all the small downstairs rooms or what had been rooms and out through the connected, sagging sheds all the way to the outhouse, about to part company with the rest of the roofline altogether, its warped plank door hanging open on one hinge. The truck was on the grass in back. He had to be there. And was, in the attic, all the second story the house had, unheated and where he'd slept all his life since he was fourteen. The mattress on top of him was the only movable object in the house Clara Banks had had to recognize was not worth trying to sell. God only knew who'd sold him the pills, anyway the bottle was empty and the hospital people said later he'd stayed unconscious five days.

Brit phoned Chip at college to tell him they'd saved Walt after all, for whatever that might be worth.

Girls laughing and hi-fi rock somewhere near in the dorm came over very loud. "You there, Chip?"

"Yeah." He sounded strangely young and scared, like sometimes when he was about six and first going out trapping and fishing with this great friend, a new one then but already the man in all the world he most wanted the good opinion of. "I guess we had to do it, didn't we? Only . . ."

"I dunno. We had no choice is all I know." And for the first time felt he was failing the boy, who was about to go beyond him, somehow in that racket, because he had the secret strength and drive and will, would learn things Brit would have liked to, only he hadn't known that at eighteen, even if there'd been a way.

2

As Hannah Palz was to tell a close friend some weeks later, it was because she was already extremely upset that day that she happened to go on the walk. That is, seeing Brit out by his car she stopped to relay the horrid news; he was just setting out to run his dog on the old lumbering lot known as the Crump Job, as he often did before supper, and asked if she'd like to go along, and she thought it might relieve her bad feelings and said yes. Nothing unusual so far, except the upset. A large, girthy but muscular woman, of enduring strength and beauty of features and invincible untidiness of person—slacks bagging at seat and midriff, grey hair usually not all held up in a hasty bun, an overlooked chin whisker or two leaping to prominence in strong sunlight—she was a somewhat better than amateur botanist; had taught that subject several years at Waterville highschool, when the Palz children were small and income more so and state regulations didn't yet call for a Teacher's Certificate instead of knowledge of the material. She often hiked miles in the woods, on the lookout for a new patch of chanterelles or an unusual variety of fern or ladyslipper, and had been on many treks with Brit and his succession of dogs over the years. He suffered so every time a dog of his died, or was lost for good or stolen, he always swore he'd never have another, but he always did.

The bare fact of the news she told brought a typical growl of sardonic laughter. Just what he'd expected. The Boonton Collection, instead of appearing in print from the Harvard University or any other fool press, had been stolen. Of course he knew who'd gone off with it, everybody did, and he and Louise had said from the start that Thelma Nesbit was dotty to fall for that cock-and-bullshit. Lem and Hannah, however, having harbored the thief in their house for several weeks, had to take on themselves a good share of the blame. Thelma, on the verge of apoplexy, took the same view and wouldn't let Hannah in her door. "Go away!" she screamed from an upstairs window. "You commies, you hippie-lovers, now look what you've done!"

It came out through a series of bad checks passed by the charming young fellow in Waterville and other towns around. In fact the Palzes

had a few themselves, for repayment of cash loans, but were so careless and inept in money matters they had figured the mistake must
somehow be theirs. The couple had left abruptly in April, immediately
after taking possession of the picture history and without their knowing
about that. They'd been upset enough when Thelma in her pride and
joy told them a few days later; if she'd asked their advice before
parting with her treasure they could have told her things weren't done
that way, there had to be a fly in the ointment. Not that they'd had any
reason up to then to think too badly of the self-styled folklorist and
college instructor, of vague credentials but appealing personality and a
modest talent on the French horn. He and his wife had even been
better than some about doing their share of work around the place.

There'd been a number of other young people, not unlike that pair
in general bent of mind, around the Palz household the last two or
three years, since the last of their own four children married or otherwise moved away. The house had been a summer place in Hannah's
family for two generations before her, reached from Boston every
June, in her grandparents' time, by a series of train connections and a
long wagon ride. Her doctor father, more drawn to the sea, had given
it to her as a wedding present, and she and Lem had made their year-
round home there for almost thirty years, since the taxi accident that
stopped his career as a violinist of high repute, leaving him minus two
fingers of his left hand. She'd been a Trotskyite of sorts for a while in
her youth, before they met, enough to have hung around the house in
Mexico one summer and done some translating for the Old Man, as
they all called the embattled exile. But from that period she seemed to
have retained, along with a quickness to anger at social inequities,
above all a peculiarly fixed image of that leader's death, even though at
the time of the assassination she'd been neither in Mexico nor in touch
with the movement at all, except for a few lingering acquaintances and
a divorce she was getting. The hold on her imagination of that particular blow on the skull wasn't usually apparent, to herself either, only
tending to flare up in connection with other bigtime political murders;
after one such, of a Kennedy or Martin Luther King, the older Palz
son, now a beginning country doctor farther north, had gotten a little
rough with her about it, saying that for her Trotsky's death was like the
column they used to measure all distances from in ancient Rome. But

in general it didn't impinge or impose; she hadn't for many years needed to relate it to any other part of her soul's empire.

In Boonton she and Lem had been mainly sugar-farmers, with her rug-making business on the side. Now and then they somehow scrounged a few months in Europe or the Orient, and they had written some small books together, nothing very brilliant or ambitious: a manual of herb gardening, a memoir of Alban Berg of whom Lem had been a young devotee. They hadn't expected anything more from their last one, a modest potboiler on their way of life in Vermont ("We refused to say 'lifestyle,' they said we were cutting our throats") which to their great surprise had a fairly big sale and brought them an influx of disciples—pupils, boarders, spongers, depending: all of enough musical ability to take part in regular chamber music sessions in the evenings, always a custom among friends and the children in that house. There was plenty of room, several outbuildings having been winterized for various purposes long back, and the Palzes were the welcoming sort, willing enough to play back-country pedagogue as far as their capacities allowed. They allowed quite a lot, for the suburban and city-bred young, and Brit on the adjoining land could be generous too with his thousand jack-of-all-trades skills, even while dropping some wry remarks about the Palz "commune" or the "three peas in the pod"—for poets, painters and potters; who were actually fewer than in a number of other pods around, but it was true that some of the young musicians had rather grandiose notions of "synthesis," calling for engagement in several arts at once.

The two big P's, Lem and Hannah, did find themselves having to stipulate that the neophytes do a certain amount of manual work every day for their room and board, and it did surprise them to have to mention it. Their own regime for years had called for four hours a day of drudgery, which at least theoretically left four or five for music, books, etc., and they assumed in their innocence that anybody settling in for days or months would get the point without being told. But the real kooks and bad eggs, if through misjudgment they got in at all, tended to leave soon without having to be asked to; the others kept their sex and religious vagaries reasonably private; words like "relate" and "encounter" and "transmogrify" had a way of drying up in the atmosphere of the house, and on the whole their little Green Mt. Taliesin had been working out quite amicably.

Until now. The affair of the Boonton Collection was a real blow, as bad in its way as the talk of the new road about to come by their house.

So she told Brit yes, she could spare an hour from canning the last of the tomatoes, she needed the exercise, and got in his car with him and the dog. They'd be going by the nearly impassable back road, closed in winter, around the shoulder of the mountain, not the long way around through the village.

Then the other man, Mr. Johnson or Phil as he said to call him, who was renting a cabin of Brit's up the hill, turned up from the job Brit had helped him find at the sawmill and said he'd like to go too; hadn't had a chance to walk over where they were going; would like to get out and smell the air that lovely September afternoon. He'd walked and smelled plenty, the way Brit figured, before he and his wife or whatever she was, anyway a goodlooker about the age to be his daughter, turned up looking exhausted and half starved at the roadbreak in the Long Trail ten days before. No luggage to speak of, just a ratty knapsack apiece. He and Louise were pretty sure, after he'd given them a lift and then the rest of the help they needed since they seemed to have made up their minds right away to stay, that they'd walked all the way from Canada and on slim provisions. Something fishy there, Louise said, not that she cared particularly; they looked honest enough, and half the new people you saw were fishy one way or another; just so they minded their own business it didn't need to be any of hers.

For once Brit himself was a little bit more curious than she was, because of two things. One was the man's unnatural way of talking. He'd had plenty of education, you could tell, might have been a professor or lawyer or something, and most of the time would be trying to cover it up and make himself sound like a bum; then he'd slip and out would come the fancy professor again for a sentence or two. The other thing was his skill fixing up the trash car Brit told him about and he got for ten dollars, been lying in a yard in the village for two years, not worth fussing with. You'd have said the guy was trained to headwork, not a mechanic, but he found old parts somewhere and got the wreck running, maybe a little better than Brit could have done himself. Learned in the service he said in answer to the question, with the peculiar, fast, on-and-off smile he had, like a light-switch, and then, "No, not Vietnam. I wouldn't have any part of that. World War Two. Too young to know better then." So at least he wasn't trying to hide his age. Didn't need to, was Louise's view; she didn't exactly warm to him but did say he was so goldarned handsome, she could see how a young girl like that would go for him.

There was a further preliminary to the walk and it got to be quite important the next day, with the police and all. Brit had driven home just before, after some errands downriver, and passed the sawmill as the Johnson fellow was leaving; of course plenty of men had been after that job but old man Grout, the mill owner, had just fired the last of a series of loafers, and after one look at this newcomer, and learning he'd been foreman of a small mill in Canada, he hired him like a shot. The two men drove tandem to the store, where they both had to stop for something, and again the three miles home—except from the last turn where Johnson was delayed a few minutes by car trouble, and the young couple hadn't been dead more than half an hour when they found them. So that was one stranger in town who couldn't be under suspicion and not just on Brit's say-so. People still had some interest of a vague sort in new folks moving in even if they mostly moved out pretty quick, and there were several hanging around the store at the time, who got a good look at Brit's new tenant. He was the kind you'd turn to stare at anyway, in any store: over six feet, strong and straight, with a full head of lie-flat hair just barely greying and powerful nose and chin and the way of holding himself generally called "imposing"; the kind that goes over in politics and that you'd expect to have a speech ready in his pocket or head, not be traipsing penniless through the woods and glad to work his ass off in a village sawmill.

They left the car at the Crump Job, after a short delay for the Boonton road commissioner Dosie Willett, a slow but affable giant, to get his grader out of the middle of the road; he got his nickname from the do-si-do of square dances, for which he played quite a hot accordion when in the mood. On foot then they circled the old beaver swamp, where a blue heron heaved ponderously up from the tangled relics of the year's wild iris. A perfect afternoon, top of the mountain gleaming in sun and its shadow cutting down at their right, like carpentry work, black as the swamp water. Their only other human encounter was with the couple from the fire tower, who had just hiked down the steep five-mile trail from the summit. The pleasant-mannered young man, engaging in openness of glance and a certain pride of bearing, had a beard and ponytail cleaner than some, although it was a

long haul for water up there, and an amulet showing at the open collar
of his lumber jacket. He had had the job as lookout for several years,
with only snow months off. Going to thumb a ride, for provisions and to
return books to the Compton library, and maybe for a goodbye too;
the girl, not the same one as last year and pretty fragile-looking for that
kind of life, had evidently been crying. The books were *War and Peace*
and the I Ching.

"Did you enjoy them?" Johnson asked.

"Enjoy them! I adore them! I've read this"—the Tolstoy—"six
times, he's the greatest. And I do some I Ching every night, you know,
like about what kind of poem to write or something. Like it helps get
the kinks out." The wrong kinks, it seemed, from the girl's point of
view; she looked ready to slap him, or else weep again.

"The superior man," Johnson murmured as though to himself.
"Through clarity he brings deliverance."

"He controls his anger" the tower-keeper supplied in an easy tone.
"He forgives his enemies."

They sounded like two old acquaintances trading well-known road
directions. Brit said he guessed they'd all stay on the right path after
that, right now they'd better shake a leg and get after the dog; he'd
give the couple a ride on the way back if they were still there and the
young man said thanks, not much traffic there since Labor Day.

The little Tennessee hound, black like the mountain's shadow, with
a few brown spots, tore in and out of camouflage, this way and that, in
a delirium of temptations. Little Saint Anthony, Hannah remarked, and
she and Brit smiled. Not Mr. Johnson. Except for the curious exchange
with the fire-tower man it was hard to get any kind of reaction out of
him, they both reported later, until the surprising finale. Brit, old master of the yarn royal as Hannah called it, the kind with the punch line
infused all the way through, not stuck on like a maraschino cherry at
the end, in fact at its best there wouldn't be an end, he'd just stop
when it was time to—well, he was feeling loquacious. Talked about
some of the hundred and fifty kinds of jobs he'd had one time and
another when Louise thought a little cash might come in handy, and a
goddam supposed-to-be hunting dog he had one time who made
friends with a deer and a skunk and even a baby fox and wanted to
bring them all to dinner—he mimicked the "yap yap yap" and you'd

have sworn his tongue was hanging down ten inches; and the ornery backhoe he drove on roadwork a couple of winters that tipped over with him in the cab right in front of the schoolhouse and made him a laughingstock the rest of the winter; and the fellow from Philadelphia whirling up in front of the store in a big Buick just about that time of year and yelling where was the foliage.

"The what?" asked Mr. Johnson.

"Foliage, he called it. Fo-lidge. Autumn leaves; colors. Said he come all that way to see it, with his carful of city-dressed fellow beauty-lovers, come early to avoid the traffic and where the hell was it. He was early all right, about three weeks. Myrt Allen, she was still alive then, come out to investigate the racket, and we look at each other and she says, 'Ever hear of it, Brit? I never did. Must be one o' them new lodges over the mountain.' Of course I had to agree that's where it must be, and that was the maddest citizen of Pennsylvania I ever see. Whipped into such a U-turn he nearly wiped out a couple of hippies been waiting on the stoop there for a ride the way they do, doped to the eyeballs generally . . ."

Hannah was feeling quite cheered up by then, she knew the stories but they never came out quite the same way twice and anyway were apt to lead to something that just happened yesterday, but Mr. Johnson only managed a kind of polite little smile when he saw that was in order. Just didn't have any funny-bone at all was their conclusion. Or interest that they could detect, in anything they were seeing. When Brit used to go out like that with Chip or his own daughters or Hannah's children when they were little, or went now with the ones in the new young crowd he'd taken a liking to, they'd be just like the hound, into and after everything, all fired up with curiosity; Chip especially, more than any kid he'd ever known. Would come back with armfuls of what he called his "treasures" and his grandmother would mostly make him throw out so as not to clutter up the house. All kinds of leaves and rocks and scraps of metal that must have lain out about a hundred years and animal droppings to look up in a book even if Brit had already told him what they were and strange-shaped beaver logs. That's why soon as he was old enough he made her let him fix up the chicken-coop for his very own, to have his museum in. He was only about eleven then and Brit had to help him some with the carpentry, but he managed to be sly enough about it so the boy could be proud of his first big one-man job.

It really looked as if that handsome Mr. Johnson had never been a boy at all, even if he was so good at tinkering with a machine. When Hannah picked up and showed him a rare piece of beaver-work, hardwood less than a foot long and chewed to a sharp point at both ends—"That was either one self-defeating beaver or their most original architect"—he said, "Oh yes, very interesting," in a voice about as enthusiastic as his smile had been, off the canned-goods counter and been setting there too long, and dropped it. Then after a while Brit pointed up ahead and said that was where he'd come on the two of them with their knapsacks ten days before and he said again in the same way "Oh yes," but added quickly, getting the different, switch-smile on for a second, "We certainly appreciate your picking us up that day. And appreciate everything else you've done for us." Now what kind of a way to talk was that?

On just one point, besides the Chinese stuff, he did come to focus and get a pretty keen look about him, and for a minute then his eyes became quite blue, instead of a grey that could flicker almost to green. The Nelco Cessna had been out, after some more pictures probably, earlier in the afternoon, and now returned for one last swoop over that side of the mountain, so close to tree level Hannah thought it must be in trouble and about to crash.

"No such luck. That sonuvabitch when he gets on a scheme, ain't nuthin' gonna kill him. Plenty of folks would like to try if they didn't know he'd out-tough 'em one way or another. And to think I'm the one helped him buy his first piece of land, up in Quebec thirty years ago, the Lord forgive me! He had tears in his eyes, said he wanted something where his father'd come from and I think he meant it that way in the beginning. He had to sell out there in a few years, some business about Canadian citizenship, but he didn't come out with his pockets empty, that's for sure."

"I don't know anything about his business," Johnson said with an intense and expert eye on the plane's sudden rise, "but he sure is one nervous pilot. Won't be around long like that."

"He knows it too." Brit's jaw ground as over a sour taste in his mouth. "He'd ruther let most anybody else do it and just be along for the ride. He's told me so more'n once. Only he has to keep his image up with his employees, that's the kind of talk he gets off, and I guess with the general population too."

Johnson said his wife had gone to Waterville that afternoon, to see about getting a job in the new Nelco office somebody had told her about. He hoped there wouldn't be anything disreputable about that, if she got it—? Brit shrugged. "Ain't many jobs or money of any kind's lily-pure, in my experience. That's why I stayed poor and been my own boss most of the time."

The hound led them farther than he was supposed to, and Brit was cussing him by everything holy, which a certain religious revelation years before would have prevented his doing at one period of his life but didn't any more, when they came, short of breath, to where the dog lay flat on its belly making a sound between a whimper and a stifled howl, as though bitten by a snake. They'd seen an old blue Dodge in the widened-out space on the road below, hikers' parking space for that leg of the trail, and when they got back there it was gone, so probably if they hadn't been breathing so hard and also shouting for the dog they'd have heard the murderer; he'd have had to pass only two or three hundred yards from them. Anyhow he was caught over in New York State a couple of days later, some kind of psycho just let out of the hatch, to be held of course on mere presumption of guilt but the evidence was multiple and glaring; and the two young victims weren't known to anybody around, having hitch-hiked from New Jersey, according to the police and news people. At the time, the extra angle of interest was Johnson's behavior.

He went white as a ghost and before the two others had gotten over their own shock enough to move, had fallen with a groan stranger than the dog's on the matted balsam needles and was smearing, actually deliberately rubbing his own face with the blood still wet and warm around the girl's naked crotch. The young man's body was tied by a piece of fence wire to a nearby sapling, knifed several times in the chest, his bloody penis stuffed in his mouth. Not far away was a small trail shelter beside a spring they'd remarked on a few minutes earlier, the reason for the shelter's location. Johnson scrambled wildly to his feet, grabbed the amputated member from the male corpse's mouth, and with a sudden torrent of evangelical phrases, about the lamb and the father and the communion of saints, like a sermon delivered in a dream, rushed to plunge the now mingled bloods, together with as much of his own stained torso as possible, deep into the little rock-bordered spring.

"We damn near had to carry him all the way back to my car," Brit told the quickly gathered Horton clan that night, and spat, for him rather noncommittally. "And I tell you he weighs plenty. Younger than either of us and her a woman too, he was about as much help as a newborn baby. What he was blabbing there was Revelation Seven, verses fourteen and seventeen, with a snitch of the Creed thrown in."

The bloody knife the hound scratched out from under some leaves, a few yards from the bodies, was found by the police to have Brit's handprints on it, as he'd already told them it would. Naturally, he wasn't going to let Sam cut his tongue to ribbons and maybe destroy evidence too, so he cut himself instead, wrestling it away from him. For a few seconds then he thought of taking the weapon along with them to the sheriff, but agreed with Hannah they'd better leave everything as it was, except for what Johnson had dropped in the spring, so put the knife back where it had been.

The couple from the fire tower were still waiting. The only car to have passed hadn't stopped for them.

The For Sale sign on the store, put up after the owner's wife died, was as dilapidated as the paint on the building. The front porch sagged at several points, especially at the end by the locked gas pump. If there'd been any offers they'd been refused. Of course it would have to be sold eventually, and would probably be replaced by one of those fancied-up jobs called Village Store, with wares from Hong Kong etc., run by somebody from New York or New Jersey: a travelers' "mart," another tourist trap. People drive hundreds of miles for that sort of thing, along with the foliage and scenery of course.

But now its only concession to the times, aside from a few aerosols, detergents and such, was a rather antique freezer cabinet. It was a village store without any capital letters, Boonton's real center and neighborhood meeting-place, and the gang would have had trouble holding it up if they hadn't happened to pick one of the non-social hours. It was such a narrow little building, squeezed between the road and a nearly vertical hillside in back, you wouldn't have thought there'd be room for the two rockingchairs by the iron potbelly stove, plus all the stand-up sociability and customers, but somehow it didn't seem particularly crammed on occasions such as when the gang came by the first time, the week before.

That was when Mercy Grout, eighteen and dying to get enough money together to get to college and meet somebody new, who was tending store and being two-timed by her boyfriend, first got rather a yen for one of the motorcycle boys who came in, although she'd had a case of the hots in a very different direction a few minutes before. She was a tall big-fisted girl who looked small and looked made out of two different bodies in general; the top part had a pre-pubescent chest and little-girl wispy tight blond corkscrew curls above a pair of baby-blue eyes; the plump moist lips belonged with the bottom half, where paper-thin hand-me-down jeans bulged over luscious haunches. She got her strong character from her grandfather and was his pet hope in life, two of his sons being amiable drunks and the third, Mercy's father, paralyzed and speechless seven years now in a home for such cases far away. Her tiny bespectacled mother had been wearing herself out all that time running a tiny real estate business from their house next to Thelma Nesbit's, a good central location at least. Everybody had known for weeks that Mercy's boyfriend Granger had another girl in another town and it was that one's car he was taking Mercy around in, once all the way to New York City and back the same night. But she'd only heard it that day. One of her many cousins was shacked up with a swinger he'd acquired at the ski area, with a fatherless kid or two; one of several girls spelling Mercy at the store off and on and she was the one who told her. "Why honey, how innocent can you be, where did you *think* he'd get a car like that from"—that kind of girlfriendly talk.

So Mercy was upset, furious, disillusioned, and when that fine black leather jacket came in out of the sunset, with an unhealthy but not badlooking young male face on top, not gross like that two-timer's she never wanted to see again, more the kind you kind of want to take care of, it was just the ticket. But that was the final episode; the one who came in first about gas wasn't so appealing. Several people in the store so nothing to be afraid of just then, even if everybody in town had been nervous since the murders; the store had sold out all the padlocks and locks of any kind in stock and had to order more and her own mother had started making a fuss about locking the door at night, something never thought of before, and even in daytime if nobody was there but they hadn't gone that far. In general it wasn't quite time to be leery. Foliage and then hunting and then ski seasons were when you couldn't tell who was who or keep watch on the shelves; there'd be a few rough customers along with ordinary kinds nearly every day, especially city hunters boozed up by dark usually.

Just now Perce Allen the owner in his wheelchair was in the store-room counting fish-hooks and paper towels because those two deliveries had been short last time. He wouldn't have been much help anyway, but one of Mercy's aunts and another lady were there, and Brit Horton with his old hunting pal and a Connecticut couple from one of the camps up the hill, and then that new man who was renting one of Brit's cabins and had been with him when they discovered the murdered campers. He hadn't been to the store since then, couldn't stand all the questions probably; he and his wife must have been marketing someplace farther off where he wouldn't be recognized. He must have figured things had quieted down now, or was just in too much of a hurry that day to drive to another town.

He and Brit said hello, that was all, before going to pick out what they wanted here and there. The two women didn't speak to the new man, Mr. Johnson, except for a couple of Excuse me's when their purchases got mixed up on the counter. He was polite and apologetic too; elegant manners, she'd noticed that right away the first day; something almost unnatural about it but boy was he gorgeous, ought to be on TV and maybe had been some time. Wow. At least old enough to be her father and she could see how he'd get a wife that young. Mercy could imagine going for him herself if he'd been single, except her relatives would call it kooky and raise holy hell. It gave her a burning in the pit of her stomach to peek over the cash register to where he was deciding between cereals. As she rang up the others' charges she imagined exciting reasons why he had left his TV career and more reasons for that girl he was living with being all wrong for him; it couldn't last, would break up soon, and then . . .

He was real nice too when one of those hoods, not just black leather but emblems and all, came to the door wanting gas. There were four or five of them outside and they were probably all right only there'd been some bad stories from different towns around even before the Long Trail business, about out-of-state motorcycle clubs—a picnic group tied up and robbed over by Waterville Lake and a couple of sailboats sunk and a fire at a disco after some funny business, and it would be getting toward dark now by the time the store closed. She didn't know what she'd do if they refused to pay or went for the cash register but that hadn't ever happened yet.

She said she'd be right out, but Mr. Johnson offered to do it for her, so she said sure and gave him the key. From behind the counter you couldn't see the pump, but when she got through giving somebody their change she saw Mr. Johnson crossing the road to his car and then driving away. He must have left the key out there, and what was still more peculiar, he'd gone off without his groceries; they were still on the counter. "Why for heaven's sake . . ." Maybe it was because that no-good Granger pulled in just then to the parking spot that had been vacated, and a car from the other direction stopped too, that the gang decided not to make trouble, in case they'd meant to before; not that they'd given any sign of it really, it was just a general feeling they gave her.

Anyhow one of them, taller and skinnier than the first, came in right after her rotten lying sweetheart, to give her the key and pay. He was half gone, on his legs and in the eyes, but evidently not too much to ride, and there was something so longing and sweet in the way he looked at her, not tough and mean at all, even before he picked up the paper bag for her. She was just going to fill it for somebody and some-how knocked it off the counter on his side; he handed it to her with the cutest little smile, so you could tell that being deepdown polite and friendly was the way he really was. Granger had never picked up a thing for her, even her pocketbook from the street when she'd just been nearly run over by a truck that day in New York.

"That fella came out, he live here?"

"Well I guess he's figuring to, he's working at my grandfather's saw-mill down the road and his wife's got a job at the new Nelco setup in Waterville so it looks like it . . ." Stupid; she didn't need to tell him anything; must be just nerves made her gabble like that, from Granger standing right there and her wondering how she'd tell him she knew and being so cut up, if this other one had asked her to ride off with them then and there she might have considered it. "I don't know why he went off like that. Didn't even take his groceries."

The guy, maybe around twenty-two, twenty-three, it was hard to tell he was so blurry, said, "I just thought he might be somebody I used to know. But I guess not. I heard he was dead." He went out without any goodbye.

3

Travelers; all kinds, ages, income levels; wishing, hoping, expecting, regretting, wondering why. "Well, it was a change . . ." See new faces, that's true, as you could by staying in one place, everybody else traveling, watch them go by. Ah but no peasant on donkey, that's true too; not many left anywhere so hurry up, keep that camera clicking. But on the island of Kithnos there was one, a solitary old man at sunset wending toward a far village, had been out looking after his crop of stones. Finding a young peasant about like trying to catch a snow leopard; almost extinct; too hard and poor and lonesome, not exciting; he's gone to swell unemployment and housing crisis in the capital, whichever capital he speaks the language of, and sell junk to you and all the other tourists. He does not love you; you find him nagging and unpleasant; his sister may be a prostitute, that's more picturesque but hard to get a snapshot of after dark. Food best where only English heard. Get diarrhea, many coy travelers' names for that; get a cable about a relative falling dead or your favorite stocks ditto; deplore local airline strike and idiot provincial representative who keeps you misinformed; many such hardships and uncertainties; had wonderful time but glad to get home.

At Esna on the Nile, where a temple gives tourist boats the excuse to stop, a sick man of the village desperately exhibits a sick cobra, hopes for a few more small coins before one or the other of them croaks; a man on a—hey, yes, look!—donkey is carrying a small blind child too listless to brush the great flies from her pus-coated eyelids; at butcher-shop in bazaar, among shawls and trinkets crazy to open travelers' purses, the just now severed head of another donkey lies in the street and children with glad cries rush to their knees to drink the blood; the dust and heat are terrible; a shawl is bought; the temple is for some hawk-faced god, the guide knows the name. Way up north of there, a long river and half a sea away, young wanderers of many nations camp on beaches with guitars and marijuana or stronger stuff and one plays Mozart themes quite nicely on a flute.

39

That probably isn't Margo Philipson's son but could be; a good boy,
used to be a good student and will most likely come through all right
but she hasn't heard from him in quite a while; for the time being as it
happens that's just as well. For her daughter, married at eighteen, with
the baby and walked out on by that poor dear young husband although
they'd all been so sympathetic with his problems—that's what he had:
problems—wandering is more difficult even if she weren't too down-
hearted to try it, so she stays in job-rut and upstairs apartment in the
family house that now must be strangely reverberating, the ground
floor never having been totally vacated before. And without warning!
in a matter of minutes, that's how Margo left on her bus voyage, not
however without thinking up a lie to tell her daughter. Said she was
going for treatment to a doctor cousin in Minneapolis; told cousin, by
phone from bus station, she was going to look into a job prospect in
New England, didn't want to upset children till it was definite, would
he please cover for her and send on postcards. Cousin sounded suspicious, probably thinking she'd gone off her rocker, maybe even guess-
ing the truth but never mind.

Out in the swarm then, carried along on the great worldwide tide of
travelers, she thought of English cathedrals she had never seen, and
boats putting in at Singapore with Vietnam refugees who wouldn't be
allowed to land, and boats taking tourists up the Nile, and of some
hardly imaginable Aegean beach her son might perhaps be on that very
hour and she might as well be too for all the sense of destination she
had. Her son was probably not thinking God would provide, that was
one difference. In the last bus a friendly-mannered woman, after a few
questions, said there was a closed-down hotel in Waterville looking for
a caretaker; she'd worked there a while herself when it was open and
knew the agent. Practically everybody in Vermont just then looking for
something—truth, identity, ripoffs, drug deals, lost dogs, new mates,
carpentry jobs, socio-political this and that. And Mrs. Philipson was
perhaps not alone in looking for her own legal bona fide and presumably dead husband, a needle in a haystack if there ever was one, but
she couldn't know about the others if any and felt quite extraordinarily
alone as well as unique.

Furthermore, with no experience whatever in duplicity, she had to keep ultra-secret about it. A weaker or more modern woman would have said to hell with him. She wasn't even in good health; never had been; mean-spirited people had said all along that he had only married her for her kidney trouble, and there might be some truth in it.

This was five years after a cushion and other debris of his tiny rented single-engine plane, then missing over a month, was found by a river-bank south of James Bay, Ontario, and a year almost to the day since the lovely memorial service in the Fenwick church he had served so long and brilliantly. Of the holy father pilot, on one of his occasional errands of mercy or piety in the north, no trace had been found; the body was presumed carried off in the spring freshets. So after a succession of fill-ins there was a new pastor at last, nowhere near as imaginative or interested in the problems of young people; and the insurance company had finally paid. It wasn't much of a premium anyway, not worth any more expense of verification.

The payment was still intact in the bank. Even before the ex-neighbor woman's phone call, something had kept her from touching it, although the suspicions their son Robbie never could keep out of his voice and eyes had made her bitterly angry. The church paid a part-salary as long as it could. Then she kept alive by reading to a rich elderly scholar with glaucoma and selling bits of petitpoint. The children fended for themselves, Alice's marriage, shaky enough from the start when her father was still there, lasting till the baby was about to come. It was their pride as a family to have always been terribly close, with the grandparents too as long as they lived.

No, no, she said with her habitual brave, suffering smile, she was used to being alone in a big house; the empty hotel wouldn't make her nervous, it was right there on the main street after all; and the utilities being cut off would be quite all right, she'd make do very nicely with the space heater they proposed and kitchen hand-pump from earlier times that the various managers of the hotel hadn't got around to dismantling. The salary was close to nil, but she didn't expect to be there long, and with the two local ski areas bankrupt, one really and the other nearly—a little one off the Compton road that people said didn't amount to much—she knew she was lucky to have landed a roof over her head.

"She'll do," reported the agent of the holding company to his bosses in Rutland. "Looks around fifty, with glasses, sharp little nose, grey hair, never heard of make-up. Nobody'll want to rape her, that's a plus. Smart enough; has guts." Sounded perfect. Of course a couple would be better but try and find one; they had tried; were still trying when she wandered in with her middle-western speech and references and offered her services. You couldn't leave the place empty the way things were in Waterville the last couple of years and no telling when they'd unload if ever, with half the lodges around on the rocks. "At least if she gets murdered it'll be no great loss." The boss, though finding the remark crude, joined in the agent's slightly embarrassed little laugh.

It was a relief to laugh about that. Housebreaking was an old story and even chain-beatings and such hadn't been too uncommon the last few years, but murders close by, either in towns or the woods, were a recent development. A few suspicious hunting accidents had been about it, for as long as anybody could remember, and then whammo, this different kind of thing altogether. Of course the population had been changing fast, that would account for some of it; the state was crawling with creeps and crooks and phonies of every description. For that matter, neither the agent nor this particular one of his bosses was a native Vermonter, though they practiced the airs and speech of the real thing as far as possible and anyway were not to be confused with the last decade's younger immigrants. However, the Long Trail killings just now, as the crow flies only a few miles from Waterville, across Mt. Akatuck, hadn't been done by one of those and didn't have any robbery motive either; it was worse than that, but could have happened anywhere.

The new caretaker, poor old bag with her Bible and pop psychology magazines, would just have to take her chances. Remember, in letting her stay there they were doing her a favor and nothing illegal for once, barring certain little provisions of the sanitary code within town limits. Besides it would look good, having a matron like that on the premises instead of some bunch of hippies. She might even keep it clean, some of it; they hadn't suggested she sweep all twenty bedrooms.

She did take a broom to the one she would sleep in, before dusk. Then downstairs in the huge kitchen, left filthy after the last crisis and sudden closing two weeks earlier, ate her can of tuna-fish, took her pills, loosened her truss, and slowly removed from her large shabby black purse the photograph of her husband.

"Oh John. My poor Johnny. How you must be suffering!" In her solitude she had taken to whispering.

Only now, in the empty hotel, she imagined her own home, their home all those years together, empty, the phone ringing and nobody there to pick up the receiver and hear the click of the one put down at the other end. It had happened twice in the last year, not very likely from a Buddhist monastery but that was what she thought of both times.

She imagined it at an altitude of at least 18,000 feet. That was one of the two possibilities she had ever entertained, in the rare moments when Robbie's sulking or neighbor solicitude drove her to let a doubt snake in. The other was amnesia from the plane accident. She didn't want to be seen boning up on that in the public library but bought magazines at newsstands if they had an article on it. However, in her musings, really conversations with the departed by the tombstone she had finally managed to have erected in spite of the absence of a grave, the Wisdom of the East seemed both more probable and more comforting. His grandfather the Bishop had done a youthful hitch as a missionary in Bangkok and the family had always kept a strange, courageous respect for oriental mysticism, at some risk to their standing in Fenwick.

The thought filled her soul with love and a renewed sense of her own unworthiness and made her clasp the photograph to her chest, forgetting that the reason she was there was that that possibility was now slim. He was better than she; she had always known it; in the interest of his spiritual development it was only right that she should suffer. At that point a burble of laughter and obscenities came from under the kitchen window, well away from the street, and someone seemed to be trying the window frame, reminding her that the cross she must bear would take many forms; she called out harshly as though to a man in the house, as she had had to do fairly often at home lately since the neighborhood had gone downhill; it worked; the intruders left, with some more ugly words.

She put the candle out and in a streetlight gleam through the warped metal slats at the window gazed at the beautiful, noble features of her spouse, whose eyes she had come to see as a brighter blue than they usually were. The thrill of his proposal of marriage had never dimmed, and as always took the form of an immensity of gratitude. The hand-somest young man in Michigan!—so everybody said; a ranking tennis player till he got out at fourteen but still terrific; and grandson of a Bishop! Her own father, a smalltown Methodist preacher, was a truly good man with never a mean thought in his life, who left an excretion of failure like a snail's trail in any room he walked through. She grew up ailing, virtuous, plain, and knowing it terribly well. Furthermore John had been engaged the year before to the campus beauty, named Althea, no cheap hussy but a girl of character, always president of something, with sparkling humor and a lovely singing voice, whom everybody adored, even Margo from afar, and who was not only will-ing but delighted to become a minister's wife. A perfect match. She played tennis too, a fact that would appear in the sick woman's dreams later on, with such objects as bricks and pumpkins whizzing over house-high steel nets.

He was the one who broke it off, why she would never know though her guess as she came to know his family better was money—Althea wasn't big rich but a little too well off for his comfort; and next thing he was inviting *her* of all people, the ugly duckling waddling without hope between courses and library and cafeteria jobs, to the movies. It took her several years to suspect herself, just in a slight fit or inkling now and then, of somewhat playing up her kidneys, staying in bed a wee bit more than absolutely necessary, to keep him in place. One thing she had been canny about, anyhow, was his guilt.

It was partly a family tendency, making them all prefer bad taste in clothes, furniture and houses even at the same price as the handsomer article, but in his case related more painfully to his having been a flier in World War II. One of the youngest in the service so you'd think excusable, but it was clear that both his professor father and the old Bishop had more respect, in those years, for the ill-favored and less bright foster-son and grandson, up to then a worm in comparison, who went to the penitentiary as a C.O. John never forgave Carl that piece of one-upmanship in virtue. He tore through his theological studies like a shark near an unwarned bathing beach, leaving the Old and New

Testaments mangled in his wake and his average around B −; lacerated himself in good works, extra courses in counseling etc.; got himself wounded and jailed as a Freedom Rider in Atlanta—ah hah, Carl, how about you up there in your smug little unintegrated biology classroom; threw over the beautiful Althea . . . oh Lord, was that it? had she, Margo, been nothing but the hair shirt he required? There had been, yes there had, something evasive in his expressions of love. But love, the deepest kind of true, generous family love, surely it had been. "I never doubted it, John," she whispered. "Then or now." Actually they had never talked to each other in any such vein.

The call came from Mrs. Smith, their former nextdoor neighbor for some thirteen years and mother of the major thorn in their sides for the last five of them. A disreputable, well-off family, father running an inherited insurance company into the ground, both parents drinking more and more, grandmother ditto and usually in charge of otherwise neglected child, whose lavish presents graduated from toy Tonka trucks to real motorcycles. For several years in the beginning John Philipson was like a father to him, taught him to use tools and fly kites, told him the name of the baby in the Christmas crèche, invited him on their own family picnics. By age ten Jeff and his gang were stealing those same tools, also throwing cherry bombs over the fence at children and dogs; at twelve they were roaring out at night in the family's Cadillacs, and at fifteen had a business in drugs and girls going in a shed in the back yard.

Almost to the end the handsome minister struggled with that young tormented creature, one of God's after all, born in human shape; his readings in psychoanalysis and assumptions in counseling also encouraged the effort. "Hi Jeff, let's sit down and have a talk," he would say jovially when the boy, by that time glazed of eye and grey and sunken in the face, came over to borrow things as he continued to do—Reverend Philipson thought because he was secretly yearning for the contact with a better moral climate, really it turned out to case the joint for further loot. Jeff, through with his expensive remedial school by noon, with all the rest of the day to fill, would ignore the invitation to sit, so the minister had the awkward choice of looking up at him like a dog or getting to his own feet again. One scowled, the other beamed benevolence. "Let's have a talk about whatever's troubling you. I'm not going to repeat anything to anybody, you can tell me. What made you steal my typewriter?" or it might be "set my house on fire," or "run off the road here onto the sidewalk and deliberately kill our dog? You know how we loved that dog, you used to play with him yourself. Why? what made you want to do it?"

Of these patient questions only the ones relating to a chance of quick profit got any answer, as about the typewriter. "I wanted some money." Sub-human grunts, some apparently meant for laughs, were the only other response.

At last neighborhood disgust, fear and pressure drove the minister to take the lead in having the family forced out by the law. He was weeding pachysandra in front of his house that Sunday afternoon when Jeff came slowly over, not steady enough on his feet to look threatening but with rage enough in him to produce some recognizable syllables for once. "Two can play at this game." John Philipson started to make one of his speeches, of regret and higher reason, good of community and so forth, but nobody was there. The father died promptly of a heart attack, the mother disappeared, and so did Jeff when he got out of the correctional institution.

Mrs. Smith seemed to be calling from Fenwick, not long distance, but the other widow couldn't be sure.

"I heard your husband was lost in a plane accident about five years ago."

"Yes, that's so." Normally she added something about grief, or loss to world and family, but thought better of it in this case. The Smiths' moving day had been marked by quite a few rotten eggs and other missiles over the fence, not all thrown by the son of the family, they had suspected. Besides Mrs. Smith had also had her loss, such as it was.

"Of course it was in the papers and all. Well, I thought you might be interested. I guess you may remember Jeff, our son Jeff. He just called. He does when he needs money bad enough." Pause—for a drink?

"Yes? but I don't see what that, I mean why you . . ." She was already sweating.

"He saw your husband in Vermont last night. He was calling from Waterville. He saw him in some village near there, he didn't know the name."

"I'm sure there are lots of men who look . . . "

"One thing Jeff never forgets is a face. He wouldn't make a mistake about one he grew up next door to. He wasn't high either, I can tell, and he was absolutely sure." She hung up.

Margo lay upstairs in what was meant to be a hotel, rehearsing instances and theories of amnesia culled from her magazine reading, and woke at 5 A.M. with the worst pain of her life. She stuffed a corner of the sheet in her mouth to keep from screaming.

At eight as Fred the restaurateur drove whistling through the center on his way to market twenty miles away in Compton, a disheveled old woman fell to her knees in front of his car, just outside the closed Green Mountain House. He was all too used to human wrecks in town but they were usually younger. Brakes screeching, he made it up onto the curb; the state patrolman happened to have been waiting at Waterville's one traffic light, at the intersection two buildings beyond. "Hi, Dave." "Hi, Cheezit. More trouble, huh?" The restaurant, one of the more thriving businesses in the section, was called Chez Fred, really as a joke, in fact the owner and his wife, both marvelous cooks, had laughed themselves silly when they hit on it fifteen years ago, and didn't mind the name he was called by as a result.

To their great surprise the derelict woman, who was dreadfully pale and just able to mutter something about needing a doctor right away, seemed to be neither doped nor drunk but genuinely, as you might say, stricken. "I'll take her," Cheezit said. "It's on my way." She was so used to wearing a brave smile, she tried it even then between moans as they got her onto the back seat, and he sped the mile up the highway to the County Clinic. The head man, old Dr. Macklin, was always there by eight. The police car followed and its siren rather thwarted Cheezit's cheery conversation back over his shoulder to his unhappy passenger, but he managed pretty well anyway. He was both cheery and kind-hearted by nature, never at a loss for either anecdote or opinion, with many skills and activities aside from the restaurant so he had plenty to talk about; mainly he hoped to distract the poor thing, whoever she was, from her misery.

"Don't you worry, Doc Macklin's as great as they come, you're a lucky lady to be taken sick here and not in some big city; I can tell you.

That old mansion up there on the hill with the columns, I guess you can't see it just now, used to be the grandest house in this section. Been a motel the last couple of years, not very nice I hear. Owner's a strange one, young guy from New York or somewhere, won't talk to anybody. Got a riding stable over here across the road. Look at that now, every time I go by he's got two or three more of those nags in his corral, doesn't even fix up the barn or anything. Twice they've broken out and caused accidents here on the highway . . . " She was dimly aware of his good intention and of a certain cultivation in his speech, neither TV nor educated middle-western, which were all she had to compare it with.

"Never mind the forms, let's get to the patient." That too, from the doctor, was outside her experience; in her long medical history nothing like it had ever occurred; it scared her; he sounded like a doddering old incompetent who hadn't followed anything new in medicine for fifty years. He was indeed around seventy, and so was his only other patient at the moment, a man he called Brit, there to renew a prescription for some kind of heart medicine. They were old cronies by the sound of it and Brit lent a hand, along with the affable Cheezit, in hoisting her to the examining table. She yearned to shriek out a protest against all this rural amateurism, but couldn't and then he must have given her a shot for the pain, making her unable to explain that her medical insurance would never cover it all and she couldn't possibly agree to go to the hospital.

It was miles away, back through town and over a mountain from the feel of it. For a while in the beginning she knew that it was the second old man, named Brit, the heart patient, who was driving her; he had a friend to see in the hospital, so he said, and an errand to do over there anyhow. He was no steady talker like the other one but did speak to her now and then: "Take it easy," "Hold on now, we're getting there," "Doc Macklin'll have it all set up, he'll be over soon," in a hard country twang she'd never heard before. Or he'd be cussing out a truck on a hill, "Jesus Christ can't he move over, the goddam sonuvabitch . . . " They had put a foam rubber pad for her in the back of his beat-up old station wagon; couldn't risk waiting for the ambulance, she'd heard the doctor say. Horror stories, of rape and kidnappings, whipped in fragments through her brain, between flashes of wondering of a kind brand new to her, as to whether she was too old to learn to ski. But this was only September; whatever happened, she'd be gone long before snow. Nobody had asked even so much as her name.

Brit had really been meaning to pay Walt a visit one of those days, so when he'd handed over his unexpected passenger he went and found him in the sickeatrical wing as they called it—for mental cases not bad enough for Compton or unwilling to go there. It wasn't much of a visit. Walt goddamned him to hell for saving his life and landing him in a nut-house on top of it. The only time he could get to talk with reasonable people was when they let him push the magazine cart around the regular sick ward with no atrical to it, and some over there were too far gone to be much company. "Guess you thought you were a good Samartan. I'll outsmart you an' all these head-meddlers here too if I ever get my hands on a shotgun again. Never did own one o' my own an' that second-class widow went 'n' sold all o' *his*. You give me a house 'n' a woman 'n' a good herd o' cows, I might see the sense to it. An' what the bleedin' Jesus is a father fig-sation? you ever hear o' that? Cows I could understand, cold winter nights specially. But they ain't talkin' about *any*thing you or me could make sense of. Go on, git along, you're no friend o' mine. Looks like I ain't got one in the world, never did I guess." He wiped at some tears with the grey sleeve they had on him. "Didn't even sneak me in a bottle o' liquor, you old skinflint." At that he broke down and sobbed. Brit tried to rouse his interest with the big town news of the week: how the store had been held up, first time in its history, in broad daylight; Mercy Grout alone there and was too stunned, looked like, to phone the police when the gang left although they hadn't tied her up or anything, but her aunt and uncle at the P.O. got suspicious and came over and *they* called the state cops, so they set up a roadblock and the whole gang was caught, six and two of them girls. Walt had probably heard it all on local TV or the radio, anyway he just kept his face to the wall and wouldn't say another word.

Some morning, that was. Got home, that is as far as his brother's farm where they'd all grown up, half a mile before his own small place, and found work started on the fool road they'd all been trying to fight for two years: Jim Pace Avenue you might as well call it, all his doing and going to be all for his benefit, with the taxpayers paying for it. Oh sure, everybody on the Horton side of the controversy knew they were licked but not so as to have to see it that week or even that year and Louise had kept saying "You mark my words"—when she started with that he always knew it was going to be wrong—"it won't come in our lifetime." The machines had turned up, and not a local man on the crew, right after he'd left for Waterville just to get a prescription he'd thought, and when he got back, about twelve of the old family trees on both sides of the road were down. Spruce, maple, birch. Gasoline fires for burning the branches in the middle of the road, started with old rubber tires, and three heavy-duty chainsaws at work on the fallen trunks, getting them into eight-foot lengths. Never heard such a racket.

"Godamighty."

They and their sisters had all been born there, and their father and grandfather. Early in life Brit sold his share to Ellis, didn't want to be tied down but got to be anyway later on, with a wife and three daughters; he helped Ellis with the sugaring and took his percentage. Finest sugarbush in the area and most beautiful piece of land everybody'd always said. Not any more; not that day. "Looks like Veetnam." That war still hung in Brit's mind, as much as when the U.S.A. and two of his sons-in-law were still in it. They were both dazed by the new unnatural light let in where the trees had arched over the road, and couldn't stand to look back at the house where a parlor window was etched in rage and anguish, by their sister's face stuck there like a frost picture some winter mornings.

"We'll learn to live with it I guess," Ellis said, the way he spoke when his wife died and his two sons one after the other went off to take jobs in industries. "Right now we got to think how to get that wood piled some way or other before it starts disappearing."

It was Friday, the weekend cabin crowd would be arriving and they wouldn't be the only ones. Every scavenger and cheapskate for miles around would be turning up to load their trucks, jeeps, pickups, station wagons with the wood that was all the two Hortons could claim from this deal—their own rightful wood; and how two men aged sixty-eight and seventy were going to move such a quantity in time was beyond imagining.

Nevertheless they had a good laugh a few minutes later when the Palz pig got loose and came walloping hell for leather down the road with the whole bunch of long-hairs yelling after it even if they were all vegetarians. Scared the poor sow so she tore through the barn, fell six feet down into the manure pile, rampaged across the road to the shed where Ellis stored the syrup—the gallons were against the wall and held up pretty well but the pints and quarts went flying—and from there through the toolshed and entrance ell and kitchen straight on, oh Lord! into the parlor, Leona's holy of holies domestically speaking. She wouldn't even let her own brother in there in his outdoor boots and then there was only one chair he was allowed to sit in so he never did; Brit had said for years Ellis was a damn fool or else a saint, which might amount to the same, to go on living in the same house with her.

There the pig was at last captured but not before Leona had had her one crutch knocked away and been laid flat. On being helped to her feet and restored with applejack she gave a piece of her mind to all present, although by that time Hannah Palz herself had come on the scene, laughing with the rest in spite of her own grief and horror, not much less than Leona's, at what the chainsaws were doing. She'd always had a placating way with that member of the Horton family and had even cajoled her into making some hooked rugs, a good boost to pride and purse, Leona being a whizz at such work when her defenses were down. But nothing worked this time. Hannah came in for the general flaying—"Out of my house, you filthy bums, you and your dope and your loose women . . . " etc. Probably it was the awful screeching of the saws that got the pig in such a state to begin with, and probably it was the pig in the parlor that pushed Leona over the edge, into the condition they would see in full that night.

Brit went home for a bite and to tell Louise, luckily too busy with bakery work to take it in; from baking just for family and friends she'd gradually slipped into a regular business and soon had so many week-end orders, for bread, cakes, pies, cookies, he'd had to push out the kitchen wall six feet to make room for the huge ovens she needed—about the fifth extrusion on what he'd built as a bachelor cabin in the beginning, in his days of mainly bumming around the Far West with a gun and fishing tackle. When he got back to the farm with his own small chainsaw, a toddler's toy compared to those others and which wasn't acting right anyhow, the wood-stealers were at it and more on the way up the hill. Ellis had had some other things to attend to and if he was out of sight ten minutes a truck or jeep would be full and driving away. "Hello, Brit, howya doin', you look good. What? Why sure, we'll put it back if you say so, only this is town wood, ain't it? Cut for town road. That's what we heard, so naturally . . ." Sonsabitches, knew the law as well as he did. But all those others, like ants to sugar when the word's out—weekenders and the like, A-frame and condominium and every kind of camp owner from there to Akatuck and all the way to the trailer huddle outside Waterville apparently, plates from every other state around—some of them you had to deduce didn't know that law or any other law ever written, not enough to suppose it applied to them, and that's why he had to put the saw down and stand there with the shotgun he'd just happened to bring along too. Didn't raise his voice or use any bad language except under his breath, but things got confused with so many vehicles trying to turn around and the big machines blocking a lot of the space, aside from the deafening saw-screams and thundering crash when another big one went down—another coffin nail he'd be thinking, another artery in his body assailed—none of which let up at all until 4 P.M. when that devil-hired crew of unsmiling strangers knocked off for the day.

But even before that, help did begin to come and the looter cars began to turn back before they got up the hill. It was Chip Holloway first, come from college for the weekend, who started getting them headed away empty. Then he went up and set to work like a maniac on the big logs, heaving them behind the tractor on the sugaring sledge Ellis hauled out from the barn and unloading them by the nearer sugarhouse where they'd be needed next March. Brit told him he'd split a gut and for Chrissake to take it easy but the boy was grim, with his heartsickness at what was being done to the road, and hardly answered; just smiled a second and said he felt fine, he'd stop when he got ready. By then the others had come along and were pitching in, about half natives, half the new young kind, three or four of those from the Palz setup; Hannah and Lem must have suggested they leave off their chores up there for the rest of the day. Lem himself, with bursitis lately so not up to the heaving part, came with his own tractor for a few hours. And there was a Horton nephew, Ray Robinson, their other sister's son and married to Mercy Grout's big sister—a good worker when there was any work to get, foreman of the sugaring crew every year, while Brit and Ellis would have to stay in the two sugarhouses and see to the boiling and canning. But even he couldn't beat Chip's pace.

The peculiar thing was when the Johnson pair drove by on the way home from their jobs, hers in the enemy camp you might say, and just sort of nodded and went on to their cabin. Pretty unfriendly, considering they wouldn't have had work or a car or a place to stay or anything without Brit putting himself out for them. Maybe he was still in a fit of nerves over those dead bodies. But in about twenty minutes she came back, alone and on foot, and set to heaving logs almost like a man; apologized for her husband, said he'd been having some back trouble and had to lie down after his day at the sawmill.

It was eight o'clock and the half-moon was well up when they finished; the wood was all back away from the road where it wouldn't be stolen; tomorrow would have to look after itself. Nobody had stopped for supper but Louise drove down with sandwiches and coffee and beer so it turned into quite a party for a little while when they laid off, sitting on the ground or stumps out there in the moonlight; kind of chilly for a party but of course they couldn't be asked into the house after the day Leona'd had. Couldn't have been any day in the last twenty years for that matter; she'd never been one to appreciate having her floors tramped over.

They joked and chatted and asked the Robinson girl how Mercy was doing since the holdup—the word was she'd split with her boyfriend but nobody was going to ask that—and Brit told a couple of yarns, and several there were taking in really for the first time, in the quiet of the night, the awful devastation being perpetrated. "How come you work for those bastards?" someone asked Penny Johnson and she scowled, looking upset, and said she guessed that's what they were all right but the ski areas weren't hiring yet and she couldn't find any other work. She was so well-proportioned—had to give her that, though over-ripe in the chest area for Brit's taste—you didn't notice right away how tall she was; eye to eye with him standing, five ten that was now that he'd shrunk some. The dark unplucked eyebrows, extra long and thick as a man's, drew attention to an unusually deep and elongated pair of eye sockets—belonged in a TV Persian harem, that part of her, and the orbs set in those cavities too, dark, large, and pulsing like banked coal fires with some kind of deep, suggestive talk all their own, so strong you weren't apt to notice the little crow's-feet around or the other creases, the kind that can tell a tale of bad temper in women not old enough for them, on either side of a rather ugly and pouty mouth. She must be twenty-seven or eight, a little older than Brit had guessed at first, though for that rough work she had her long mahogany-colored tresses held by rubber bands in a perky spout on either side of her scalp, like a ten-year-old's.

Natty Robinson said she'd worked for Nelco in Compton one year before she had her baby and they weren't so bad. In fact she and Ray didn't exactly agree with his uncles on this road business. "Hortons and Grouts never did agree on much," Brit said but with a nice unclish laugh. He was fond of his nephew and had to admit Natty had been a good wife to him, against all expectations. Just like a Grout, though, to fall for anything called progress. "After all why shouldn't we be able to get to our own town's ski area when they get it built, without going all the way around the mountain, and there'll be jobs—look at Ray, what's he got now—and we might even get to a movie once in a while . . . " "And nightspots and trailer stink and honkytonk all the way, just like Waterville. That was a pretty town fifteen years ago." "Yeah and everybody starving or else drunk all day"—like her uncles she meant—"with no work to do. Of course it looks terrible right now but just wait . . . "

Same old talk, been going on for years. The last thing they'd heard her that enthusiastic about was some fool dishware party a bunch of her relatives put on, under persuasion from a plastic company sales-man, and made two or three hundred dollars out of. It was getting to be quite the rage, except by now everybody'd bought all the plastic dishes they could afford or had any use for or could think of anybody to unload them on for Christmas. Talking just at home to Louise, Brit had had some laughs at the disgust of the new young city-fleers, the

Palz gang and all the others you couldn't tell apart from them, for that sort of thing, and how plastic was their idea of a dirty word. Poor suckers, they'd actually thought they were going to find quilting and barnraising parties, what there used to be when he and Ellis were small; they'd shown him a handbook, a sort of encyclopedia only more like a Bible the way they took it, about that kind of thing. So it was oldtimers like the two of them they were after all the time, to learn how to do practically anything you ought to be born knowing even to planting a row of peas; not anybody their own age. He didn't mind, they were a decent bunch on the whole. For that matter Hannah and Lem hadn't known much about country life when they came to stay thirty years ago, her childhood summers not counting for much that way, and people didn't come any better than those two to his way of thinking even if they were kind of screwy to be running a free board-ing-house like that, and even if she'd been some kind of commie at one time. That didn't bother him, people have a right to their opinions and any he'd ever heard from her he agreed with pretty much anyway. What he cared about was good neighbors.

Well, there were some sitting right there, been breaking their backs for him and his brother for hours, only the reason for it, the new opening to the sky that had no business being there till the leaves were down and then nothing so big, with all the spruce and balsam there'd been, spoiled the good feeling. He'd never been in an earthquake but supposed it must be like that. Everything going; gone; his mother and father, their faces, their lives, crinkled up, worthless all of a sudden, something to throw in the trashcan; his own life too and his wife's. "It won't come in our lifetime." He should have said in the hospital that morning, "You're right, Walt, I'm sorry, I ought to have let you finish it up your own way."

And maybe that's what Chip was thinking, sitting there on the ground across from him, only he was much too young for that, even if he'd said something like it on the phone that time, and Brit hoped now he was just plumb worn out as he had every right to be. He looked it, and possibly the Johnson gal was too and that was why she was leaning against Chip more and more and finally had her head down on his shoulder. She'd asked Brit earlier who he was and where he came from and made some wild remark about his looks, "like a Greek god." As she made that too seem to require an answer Brit had to say Hummph, just looked like any other eighteen-year-old to him, which wasn't strictly true. Anyhow, Chip didn't seem to notice there was a female head on his shoulder and got up with no mind to what happened to it.

"It's a wonderful spot all right," he said with a sudden smile, and something in his voice, from some powerful complex of feelings, brought a hush on the company and caused all of them, even Natty, to turn as at a cry of "Look!" though he'd spoken casually and said nothing like that. What there was to look at was just the hills, unquiet to those like Brit who knew the wildlife in them, differently troubled for everyone under the reverberations of murder and holdup and land-sharking, but nevertheless, in the moonlight and crackling cleanliness of air, extending fold on fold in about a hundred and twenty degree vision of whatever peace, and whatever remembrance of those gone before, might yet prevail.

"Yup," Ellis said, a well of sorrow briefly showing, and was about to propose they go home and get to bed when the house door slammed. It was the front door, hardly ever used except for funerals, not the one to the shed and kitchen where the pig had gone in. Leona was on the stoop with her crutch, staring at the moon and screaming like a little lost child, "Momma! Poppa! Please! Please call the governor and make him give us back our trees! I said the magic word, Momma . . ."

Like spume far from any shipping lane the plea blew off into the woodland sea.

"Ay-men," growled Brit with a chuckle of despair. His feet ached all of a sudden; his dentures didn't fit.

"Oh yes, please! please!" cried one of the girls in the Palz group, the one who had lately been toying with the idea of becoming a witch. "Give us back our trees! Strike down the foulers of earth!"

"Beginning with snowmobiles and dirtbikes," muttered a bearded one.

"Well I don't know about that," Ray said amiably as they all crossed the lawn, not hurrying especially. As far as he could see, his aunt Leona wasn't much worse off than she'd always been. "We get a big kick out of our snowmobiles, and I just got a dirtbike the other day, a Dibson, and it's a beaut. Boy you can really go places on them things, I'm telling you."

Now where in blazes would he get the money for a thing like that? Must be the Grout influence; name any machine made short of a space rocket and they'd have it, on credit or some way; never saw a Grout yard wasn't strewn with derelict tractors, cars, motorbikes they'd taken apart and couldn't get together again.

Seeing he wasn't needed any more, Chip was getting in his little car when Penny Johnson ran over and asked if he'd give her a lift—his place was up past theirs, wasn't it? Yes and so were the Palz contingent up that way and they had two cars between them and had already offered to drop her off. Chip was looking past interest in anything but sleep, as well he might be, after whatever day he'd put in at college before the two-hour drive and the long log job. He said okay, neither too rudely nor with any enthusiasm, and she got in. By then she had taken the rubber bands off her head and her hair was the flimsiest kind of curtain swaying across those not-so-banked fires, just asking to go up in flames.

As waking moments lengthened she got hooked on a book somebody had left there, on the great pyramids; and watched the joggers on the hospital grounds, day in day out all the livelong day just like the park in Michigan the last year or two; and overheard travel talk among the other women in the four-bed room. One of them was a travel agent and kept the ward whirling with itineraries, new low fares, etc; couldn't stop trying to sell to all present even after Margo as they called her—only Dr. Macklin said Mrs. Philipson—told her she was a widow and not that well off. That only brought on the big spiel: oh but the group rates the advantages the plus in any kind of job application statistically beyond question people who've had initiative to get out and see the world stand better chance cheaper than staying home too . . . At night the agent lady sat bolt upright in her sleep, in the glimmer of light from the hall, shouting, "Cairo! Somambi Hilton! Galápagos!" until a nurse came and gave her a shot.

Mopeds apparently not allowed on hospital grounds, had them lately in Michigan too. Joggers all in same shoes, shorts, T-shirts, headbands; expensive all that, one of the ladies said, her son was doing it and she'd told him why didn't he call it running and wear what he did for basketball and oh my the look she got. Margo could remember when it was Tom Thumb golf and Shirley Temple dolls. What next?—what, to keep the weary traveler's weltanschauung going until the next tickets are bought? since even that impassioned businesswoman admitted that most people weren't candidates *all* the time, some had to make a living now and then unfortunately but also just talking to strangers and sleeping in strange beds could get tiresome eventually, you need to get home and show your pictures to somebody, she knew that, she didn't try to sell anybody three hundred and sixty-five days a year.

And what did the Tartars wear on their way to China?—something to look up some day. Meanwhile Margo adored the pyramids, which she had never thought about the least little bit before. Oh, fabulous astronomies, wonderful computations, inimitable pride of species and noble religiosity inspiring mathematics to be verified by the movements of stars and earth only generations hence, think of that! Tennis already overextended went the chatter in the room, johnny-come-lately entrepreneurs losing their shirts last season and all *that* equipment sitting unsold on the store shelves all of a sudden, they better get on the ball, think of something else, these fads come and go so fast. All right but don't use that word about travel business which continues to show as Christianity once did an impressive growth potential, for darn good reasons, for instance you wouldn't want to live in a country you weren't allowed to travel from when you felt like it, would you?

Two words from all that as she dozed—tennis, Christianity—turned Margo's thoughts, for no fathomable reason, to the girl named Penny Fried who had come into the Philipsons' lives the year before the plane accident. Margo herself had been extremely good to the girl, as health permitting she had always tried to be to people in trouble. Sick and destitute, after a rotten year of assorted sex and drugs in San Francisco, Penny had drifted into Reverend Philipson's church office for counseling, having once heard him address a large public gathering on the coast. He could be quite a spellbinder that way, as also in speaking words of comfort to the balled-up and the bereaved, and furthermore had a certain renown among the young for his stand on civil rights and other issues of the day, so when the trucker she didn't feel like being raped by stopped for coffee outside Fenwick, Michigan, and she happened to see the name in the local paper left on the counter, she was ready to go and seek what most of her peers called "help."

A good deal of the help soon came from Margo, who enjoyed her company, thought that in her struggle for "clarity" (the big word in *their* set and family) she'd be a good influence on their volatile and often dispirited daughter married to all those problems, and was glad to have her stay in the house for two or three weeks in exchange for minimal housework. It was actually she, not her husband, who later found the girl respectable living quarters downtown and a job clerking for the blood bank. "Such a sweet, pretty little thing," she said of her to John, forgetting that the little thing towered over her by more than half a head, "now she's washing her hair and beginning to get some flesh on her bones. And she's not completely uneducated. She told me she'd been to college one year somewhere in California, and I caught her looking into Teilhard de Chardin—what do you think of that! I think you've done a good deed there, Johnny—as you always do when it's humanly possible," and she gave him the usual bedtime pat on the arm. It was some years since they had kissed except on the cheek, though they slept in the same old double spool-bed, a wedding present from her family out of their attic, unless her pains were too bad and he moved to the couch across the room. However, another and very strange picture had come to intrude since her operation. At some point in delirium she had seen, and could have sworn she did see, that same girl helping John to fold something like a parachute, on a frozen lake at night, in the dead of winter, while she, Margo, tried to run toward them over the ice to prevent whatever terrible thing was about to happen, but the wind kept knocking her back and onto her knees, again and again, until the two figures and the big white cloth were gone. Her husband's eyes in that vision were the near-green of rather murky ice, as when he was interrupted in his work.

But now she is in the hospital in Vermont, sitting up at the end of the hall for the first time, and a man who reminds her of pictures of gnomes in children's books though taller and not particularly hairy, in fact cleanshaven and with two pinkish fjords above craggy temples, where before his personal ice-age the blond or greying hair must have extended—all this in her bewildering new alertness she took in—is standing beside her with a cart full of paperbacks and pop periodicals. He is staring at her, with a little smile that seems the very counterpart of her own newborn astonishment. She smiles back, feeling she knows him too well for a mere Hello but does say that word, recalling from some depth of past stupor his having stared at her in the same way two or three times before, when she was lying scarcely conscious in the room he wouldn't be allowed to enter so it must have been from the door.

He said, "You're the prettiest thing I ever seen."

Saw, not seen, her mind corrected him, before letting itself be boggled by the remark. Nobody had ever said that or anything like it to her in her life. She was close to giggling but suppressed it, it would be unbecoming at her age. But she couldn't help blushing. "Oh shoo! you run along, what kind of silly talk is that . . . But wait, yes, I'll take one of your magazines, let's see what you've got there." Out of the habit of recent years her hand went to Mental Health: Strange Stories of Ups and Downs, but withdrew without touching it. "Oh my goodness"— she was that surprised at her hand's insight. "Well, what would *you* recommend?"

He laughed. "Me! I dunno one from t'other o' them things, all look the same to me. TV's all I got time for, some pretty good programs if you can stay awake but I generally don't." Seeing there were no nurses around he sat down in the chair next to hers. "What you in here for anyhow? Gallbladder? hernia? You don't look so sick, not today you don't. I could show you a lot o' pretty things over the other side o' that mountain where I live"—his face darkened—"where I used to live all my life since I was fourteen. Goddam widow Clara went and sold it, just to go live on a goddam street and see cars go by. I *told* her I coulda gone on doin' the sugarin' for her, been doin' it all my life, there ain't a tree or a bush on all them hundred 'n' fifty acres I don't know. Course he always had to give the orders but I'd know ahead without him sayin' 'em. She wa'ant *my* woman after he dropped dead or any time. Lord no, a lot too swell for me. Why, I never felt right even pissin' out the back door at night if she was anywhere near, that's the kind she was. I never had a woman all my own. Just nights down in Greenborough once in a while, two bits a shot it used to be 'n' if you got enough good rotgut under your belt that's all right. None of 'em near as pretty as you. Clara Banks either, not by a long shot, even if she does get herself up so careful. Sumthin' real sweet about you.

"I see you got the Bible in by your bed there. You read much o' that? I ain't seen or heard much of it since I was a boy. Jennie Banks, that's his first wife, died eight years ago, her 'n' me used to take turns readin' it some, course I didn't understand a whole lot only she had an agreeable kind o' voice, like the brook I used to think, down at the bottom of our big mowin' . . . The cowbarn's up at the top by the road, see"—he made the map with his enormous hands—"an' the brook is down here where the woodlot starts. But *he* didn't like it, he'd say if we was awake enough for that she could be makin' jelly 'n' me mendin' the stall or a tractor or sumthin', so we got out o' the way of it. What *he* liked best after sundown was for both of us to be fixin' his hair while he watched in the mirror, tough as our old mare's mane it was so I'd be snippin' around back while she used the curlin' iron up here"—he touched his own bald bays—"to get it just the way he liked. Ran a good farm though, the best around along with maybe Ellis Horton's. But I guess you wouldn't know who that is. You're a stranger here, I can tell from your way o' talkin'."

The next day when he came to keep her company again he told her a marvelous thing, or it might have been his thinking it worth telling at all that pleased her so, and made her hardly notice his grammar. She told him a marvelous thing too, since he asked again what she was there for. She was still scared of believing it, it threw her into such a new, strange world, such a new way of looking at everything. When her daughter, her first baby, was three weeks old, she'd carried her to the door to see the full moon, saying, "Look, Baby, look! That's the moon! This is the first time you've seen the moon in your life!" John was reading just inside, trying to find a good quote for a sermon, and looked cross when she came in and told him their daughter had just seen the first moon of her life; he didn't like being interrupted at his reading.

Now she was the wide-eyed one, seeing more than moons; voices surprised, wonders abounded, and Walt Hodge was right, delight and a loss of weight had given her an appearance almost of beauty, like drooping grass after rain. It had become an anomaly for hair to be grey over such a glistening of eyes and skin, her complexion having always been delicate and young for her years.

The miracle she reported, or rather her having had to wait until then for it, sounded to him like just what you'd expect from them city doctors; never trust 'em; they're what did for poor Jennie Banks. Margo's dropped kidney could have been moved up when she was a child and she needn't ever have been an invalid and had to be grateful for crumbs of kindness all those years. It had been a bad operation all right, coming so late, but half the badly infected kidney had been saved and now she was well, or would be when she got her strength back. Meanwhile, circumnavigating the pyramids, she had had whales and astronauts and magicians for her traveling companions, such were the deeps traversed.

He nodded, not surprised. She knew better than to ask what *he* was there for, over in that other wing. He'd tell when he got feeling like it, if he was able to.

"There's a place over there I could show you—I *will* show you, if you don't mind a kind of a rough walk some day. If they ain't gone 'n' wrecked it with their goddam plans 'n' progress"—this brought the stormcloud over for a second—"but I guess they can't 'a' gone far yet, the time there's been. Brit Horton, you'd like him, I might even get around to forgivin' him myself what he done to me a while ago . . ." She said why that might be the one who drove her to the hospital that day, his name was Brit, and Walt agreed it could be, it would be like him, even if acts of kindness weren't always such a favor. "He knows this place I'm talkin' about. He's the only other man knows the woods around there 's' well 's' I do, huntin' and trappin' there all his life. An' I took Chip Holloway up one time—real spry young feller, goin' to college now an' I hope it don't ruin him. He's the kind o' boy when you show him sump'n he'll set his mind to seein' every last thing about it. None o' that nose in the air an' don't waste my time look you get from Mr. Jim Pace 'n' his Nelco buddies. He's the one bought our place just now, the Banks place that's to say. I'm not denyin' it was rightfully

Ned's and he wa'ant under no obligation to take me in when I got left orphaned—from a fire that was, two sisters gone too. Only it was my great-grandparents' too, we was related that way, who come down from Plymouth Kingdom, that's where Cal Coolidge come from, an' made a real farm of it. If they'd stayed where they was one o' *us* might 'a' been President an' probably done just as good a job, but that's water over the dam." He grinned, and the lady from Michigan noticed his two missing teeth, and also that the gnomish effect, as well as from merriment and a somewhat splayed, turned-up nose, came from his being just a trifle hunchbacked.

"Well, that boy Chip, I knew he'd go for that place 'n' he's the only one I ever did take up there; except when Clara Banks made me walk the whole land with that fat-assed prospective purchaser, that Mr. Jim Pace, an' he didn't have eyes for nuthin' but his bankroll. I'd a good mind that day to get him lost 'n' leave him there. Coulda done it easy, dunno why I didn't.

"Here's the way it is. You go way up back o' the house, see, 'n' go by the spring—that's a great spring, moss growin' all around an' never seen it dried up, even the driest summers when everybody else's did. Then there's underbrush 'n' it gets steep for a piece . . . Jesus God," he interrupted himself, "I ain't never been so long in my life without a slug o' whiskey. This goddam reformatory. You ain't got some tucked away in your satchel by any chance? What? You come in without even a satchel? Fish out o' water, I know how they feel now," and he made a face like one, making her laugh. "So then after a while you come to this place where the boulders are. Near as big as this whole building here, a couple of 'em, an' some others near as big. Gneiss they are, I mean with a g, not nice like you. Erratic boulders, got picked up 'n' carried there, right on top of a granite outcropping. I ain't much for books as a general rule but I sure was curious about them rocks an' Lem Palz, he lives down over the hill there an' they got all kinds o' books, geology an' all—so he helped me study up on 'em, 'n' even him had some trouble with it. I know where I'm at with schist an' feldspar an' like that, 'n' even Ply-sto-cene, that time when the glaciers come pokin' down, thousands o' years apiece roundtrip. But them fellers, they use words you could wrap round that parkin' lot an' still have the tail stickin' out. Anyhow, them boulders sure seen a story o' this poor

world. An' now been settin' there so quiet about maybe thirty thousand years! I bet you ain't seen nuthin' to beat that where you come
from."

She allowed as how she hadn't and she surely would like to see that
place and the spring too.

"But that ain't all. There's a ledge there, a good steep one, drops
away about twenty feet with a good steep slope beyond, mostly balsam
on that part an' ain't been timbered in I dunno how long. *He* never got
around to it, too much work gettin' the logs down an' no sign of any old
loggin' road left. Well, the time that boy Chip went up with me, we
come on a big doe snufflin' around right up top o' that ledge. She
stayed stock still an' looked at us a couple o' seconds the way they
do"—he made the frozen doe-face and she laughed again at the way
his pale blue eyes could look dark as a startled deer's—"an' then you
know what she done? I seen plenty o' deer an' this is sumthin' I never
seen before or since. See, to her way o' thinkin' we had the way out
blocked, so she just turned, didn't even bunch up or else it was too
quick to notice, an' sailed off over that ledge. But wait, I forgot to tell
you. About eight feet out an' two or three feet under the top, a great
big dead balsam got caught when it fell a long time back, with a lot o'
branches stickin' toward the cliff, so she had to clear that too, couldn't
just jump straight down. Well, she done it! Just went flyin' like a hawk,
right out over that dead balsam an' on down an' landed runnin', didn't
break a leg or nuthin'. Prettiest sight I ever seen—speakin' o' woods 'n'
animals, I mean." A fit of shyness quickly put out the twinkle over that
and he lurched to his feet.

"Course I couldn't promise you to find a doe there every time, but
there's the rocks, an' ferns, Godamighty I never seen the ocean, never
been near it, but I bet if you was to say an ocean o' ferns that wouldn't
be far off."

In one of the voyages of the days just past the sky had been not
exactly ocean but sea, of Ionian blue, and in the other sky below were
pleasant little clouds like islands to walk on. To explore was everything, hardship unthinkable. She didn't think to ask her new friend how
long he expected to be in the hospital.

The agents let her go back to the empty inn, not having found any substitute caretaker, and on her third or fourth night there, as she was deciding she was strong enough to head home to Michigan, since her object in leaving it seemed somehow to have dissipated, Walt Hodge arrived dead drunk at the door, smelling dreadfully. She managed to haul him in off the porch and get the door shut before he passed out altogether. Having no experience with drunks, she supposed he'd be fit in the morning to go off to wherever he lived. The photo of her dead or missing spouse was by then no longer in her wallet, but face down under the one spare blouse she'd brought from home, in a bureau drawer.

4

Of the three who had happened on the Long Trail murder scene, the one most showing the strain a month later was Hannah Palz. By the time she had somebody to confide in, one day in October, her gestures had become jerky, there were bags under her eyes, her fine features had a slightly bloated cast and her usually unkempt grey hair was positively dirty. A rumor had begun to spread that she was drinking, which old friends like the Hortons called calumny.

The friend she talked to was a painter, Claire Nolan, a summer and occasional weekend resident in a cottage several miles from Horton Hill. They were friends from way back in New York, and it was through the Palzes that Claire with her then husband had acquired the place in Vermont. Short, rotund, white-haired though a catapult of energy, she was Hannah's age and at least until that day had for a long time looked ten years older; she had had some bad disappointments in life, in her aspirations as a painter among others and most recently in two of her three children. She had a reputation as an excellent teacher of drawing at Yale, had already left for that job at the time of the murders, and was back now on the first possible weekend.

Until chill drove them indoors, the two women sat bundled up on Claire's sundeck, one of several Nolan additions to what had been a hunters' camp originally. This was the wilder side of Boonton, in character and vegetation very unlike the Horton Hill part. Here too at one time there had been farms and fields, in local parlance mowings; many remains of cellar-holes, miles of stone walls in the woods and little twisted apple trees far older than the cottage told of a history that only old Thelma Nesbit had had the passion and patience to try to record. But there seemed never to have been maples that side of town, and for some years even the lumbermen's loading stations nearby had been decaying, unused. Nowhere else was the mountain's profile such a presence, or so elongated, its two unequal humps aligned as in no other view across the lower third of the western sky. Close by, indeed a menace in floodtimes, a first-class brook, Boonton's longest, played its

loud or muted continuos, as diverse according to spot and vagaries of
the moment as were qualities of light on and from the mountain's
silhouette: another instrument, for weather and diurnal time to play.

The painter was able to keep hearing these accompaniments along
with Hannah's unnaturally strained and at times hesitant voice. In
youth, no dumpling then but a dark little beauty of remarkable intensity of glance and voluble silences, Claire had become known in a
certain circle as The Listener. Narratives of her own, any discourse
initiated by her, were rare and apt to be elliptical. Yet her voice was
clear and strong, without self-effacement, and her few questions and
interjections were so much to the point, they could seem to consist of
many more words than they did. Though she would never say this, she
had come back to Vermont that weekend for no other purpose than to
play the old role of listener in her friend's need, and she had guessed
rightly that what had been in the news would have blasted a way into
quite a different story.

"It keeps happening, over and over—those two ordinary, decent
young people, as far as you can tell; they haven't turned up anything
against them. You'd think we'd have heard screams, or something, even
talking all the way. He must have been fiendishly strong and fast—and
motivated, as they say in school; all fiends must be that. Then over and
over it slides into that other scene, absurdly—how could murders be
more different, in meaning, in every way?—as if all these years in
Vermont hadn't been our real life at all; as if we'd been travelers in a
motel stop, and hadn't been what we thought to each other either. All
those hours with the police, that's part of it, of course. I'm surprised
some philosopher-shrink hasn't written a big treatise on ambivalence
toward cops; maybe they have. It's original sin, I suppose, with whatever frills you pick up from your life.

"It's in that long stucco room in Coyoacán, near Mexico City.
Friendly, conversational voices; the visitor's chair drawn up beside the
principal one, at that enormous desk. I know it wasn't really that room,
the whole bristling, impoverished, haunted menage had moved to an-

other house the year before, but that's where I see it, and it may have been the same desk. Had to be one like it anyway, he was so methodi- cal about his papers, those endless stacks; needed a huge work surface. The visitor gets to his feet on some pretext, the short pointed axe hung over a shoulder under his coat flies out, and comes down. Blood gushes over the papers. The enormous top-heavy skull is split. And now the more incredible event. The victim, the reason we're all there watching, refuses extinction—think of it!—long enough to cry out and even grap- ple with the killer, who had planned to be far away before anything was known and instead is caught there, or was it just outside the door, running? detained too long by the dying Titan's last superhuman act.

"Don't think I forget the political assassinations here at home and in some ways at least as dramatic, since then. Not to mention Julius Cae- sar and Caligula and Alexander II and Lincoln and all the rest, good and bad; it's scarcely a new story. To Lem, for one, it's just boring. And about the cops, I just can't tell him that, he thinks it's so silly of me. He went through so much worse, being hunted by the Nazis in France all that time, hiding and running and his friends caught before he was. You remember that time years ago, before your divorce, you two were having dinner with us; we'd turned on the radio for something and got that Da-da-da-DA from the 'Eroica,' and Lem went green and vom- ited. He was smoking a cigarette at the time, he put it out and has never smoked since. He and two others, listening to the BBC in a fisherman's attic in Normandy: Da-da-da-DA and then the door break- ing in; he made it out the window, got under some thatch somehow; the other two didn't. It's only in that general connection that I think he holds it against me a little, or a lot maybe, that I'm not a Jew too. At least it's true I never spent more than a night or two in jail and there was no danger at all those times, it was more fun than anything and we laughed a lot and knew we'd get out.

"Then it slipped over into something else. That's what Lem can't understand, and I can't blame him. For one thing he never went through any political phase at all, he just isn't made that way. I'm not either but it took me a while to know it. After all we were depression children, with that much suffering around you were bound to try to see the causes, read Marx, get drawn in one way or another. Yes, you were too, you understand very well, and how our children thought it was the same when they blew up, over Kent State and Cambodia, or Water-gate and Vietnam—funny how these trigger-labels come in pairs. Well, you know as well as I do, it wasn't the same, by a very long shot and a huge chunk of history. It may well have been the words 'New Left' that stopped *me* smoking; they still turn my stomach. Oh yes, some were just as committed—another word I can't take, it covers such brainlessness—and a few got killed. But the difference . . . Well, one name for it is Trotsky, isn't it?—his being alive then, somewhere in the world, Turkey or Norway or Mexico.

"Most people would howl at that. Yet would agree that the big difference between the 30's and the 60's—aside from what some of the trade unions have become; oh how we loved them, remember? any strike noble, unless run by Stalinists of course (you came in a little late on that part); those grand Trotskyite teamsters, yes, imagine, in Minne-apolis; the killers and gangsters all on the other side and it was partly true; all those millions of natural friends and allies, the 'proletariat' (and just where and what is that now, by the way?), the beautiful future in embryo, only waiting for the light we would help bring them; quite a scenario . . . But the real difference was that the Russian Revolution had been finally liquidated as we used to say—the whole body of ideas that had gone into it.

"As long as Trotsky was alive that wasn't so—reason enough for killing him. Find fault with him any way you like, I can't say I really liked him very much myself, you can't deny him that. He was the finger in the dike. Had the stature to make what was happening in Russia look, to some of us anyway, like an aberration by one hateful tyrant (Stalin! I never get over the horrible reverberations of that name, any more than of Hitler) and hold off that tremendous collapse: of an ideology that had taken a hundred years to build up—Marx, Engels, Lenin, plenty of others, contributing by disagreement some-times—in smithereens. I suppose it's anybody's guess how long he could have done it if they hadn't gotten him, but that's something else.

"I gather Marx is back in in some quarters. I bet I know which and how big. You must see one or two around Yale. But I suppose Marx wouldn't be much in your Art Department, not in this decade. He certainly isn't for the welfare rolls, or that dream 'proletariat' with their color TV's and vacation homes around these woods. Or for the European and other terrorists, except maybe as a name to stop clocks with, like Jesus Christ and Buddha around here. If they actually read him, or any of the Fathers, they'd have to shoot themselves and not just in the legs. As I remember from my youthful studies—tell me if I'm wrong—if there's anything old Karl, and Lenin too, were more scathing about than the capitalist system, it was exactly that kind of nihilism.

"Your children and ours are pretty bright and we know they weren't reading *Das Kapital* in '68, not more than a few pages anyway. God knows the angers were justified, and might be more so now that they're gone, but for political thought, well, it sounds like too much of a compliment to call it a vacuum; suggests the presence of surrounding oxygen. Fascinating, really. A new kind of blank—from TV, do you suppose? killing off thought cells, something like leukemia? Nothing there at all, nothing that took two cents' worth of thought or study or knowing history; just a ready-mix; just attitude—punch and burn and bang bang—so of course it had to fizzle out that fast, and help leave all these crazies. By the way, maybe you've heard, that bomber girl who's been on the lam several years, looks very like one who wanted to stay with us last year, she got picked up the other day, in Compton, working at the record shop, the one where they sell all the handicraft stuff too. Helped kill four or five people. Has turned quite sweet-natured and alcoholic, they say. Of all ways of going down the drain that's always struck me as the most disgusting and least comprehensible, alcohol I mean; it's so sick-making.

"Forgive me, I know you have a lot to do; will this be your last time up before Christmas? I was just so relieved when you called and said you'd be here this weekend. You'd only been gone a couple of days when it happened, out there; yes, I remember, you heard it on the news. If only I could have talked to you then, there's nobody else I can say all this to, perhaps it wouldn't have . . . As you see, I'm smoking again, and drinking a little whiskey before dinner too, for the first time in my life. The doctor in Boston—we went for Lem's bursitis and I thought I might as well see about my nerves—he said I should stop being so stiff-necked about that and take a little, it would help me sleep. I'd hardly slept for days after that horrible walk; I'd doze and then wake up trying to scream, and half the time I'd be thinking I was in Mexico. That's stopped, but food becomes more and more repulsive—after all those years of priding myself on my cuisine, and I really did love doing it. I haven't cooked a decent meal since that day.

"Lem, you know, hated the Stalinists at least as much as we did—in France, during the Spanish Civil War. One of his cousins was murdered in Spain; not by Franco people; by the CP; he'd gotten friendly with the anarchists, the POUM, in Barcelona. Besides, Lem still had relatives in Russia, and reacted violently to the big purges in '36—I guess he'd reacted to plenty else before that—and couldn't stand the whole hypocrisy of the party blather around Paris. He was way up in the concert world there and of course they were after him. But he just rejected all the lies and deaths and mind-twisting on human grounds, as repulsive, didn't try to think it out politically. And I guess he doesn't think I ever did either, and he's not far wrong.

"But this business about the police. Any police. They were awfully nice, the ones who were asking us everything about that afternoon, they mostly are around here. And of course they know Brit well enough, everybody does. We obviously wanted to help them, except maybe that Johnson man who sounded rather peculiar, even if he was telling the same story we did—naturally, there wasn't any other to tell. But I'm still scared to death of them. How can you explain that? We had a good deal more reason to be afraid of the Stalinists with their assassins operating all over, and plenty of respectable sympathizers to help in the cover-ups. Of the deaths of all of Trotsky's own four children, three can probably be called Stalinist murders, if you include persecution leading to suicide in one case. In Europe two of his secretaries were murdered around then, and in New York a woman ex-agent of theirs whom I'd known slightly vanished. People would just disappear, never to be heard of again, gangland style, with a high percentage of the world's writers and artists applauding, but that part you know all too well. Of course inside Russia his adherents were being massacred in great batches, by the hundreds. And in Mexico at least three different plots to kill the Old Man were going on when I was there. I heard about one in a café—I looked so bourgeoise and innocent and was so young, people would say things like that in my hearing. Silly little playboys and girls, that particular bunch, like Patty Hearst or the bomber girl here, poor ignorant fools looking for kicks. But others were well-trained and serious, plus some ground-down Mexican peasants in the party, happy to go along with them, with axes, guns, whatever they had. Must have been disappointing for them that the actual killer was somebody the Old Man had let in himself, on the flimsiest kind of introduction; out of the craving for new company, I'm pretty sure, feeling caged. He used to walk for exercise around three sides of the little courtyard the house was built around—the fourth side had a high exterior wall up from the ground, no raised walk; there must have been cactuses and bougainvillaea and such but what I always see is a single orange tree in the middle; back and forth, back and forth, like a lion in the zoo.

"So, yes, it was sinister, under the surface. Can't use that word any more, with TV and all. It was real enough then, and the man I married in my high-hearted confusion—I really was swept away, the Old Man was an overwhelming force to be exposed to—he may well have been up for assassination. He wasn't one of the secretaries. It's gotten quite fashionable for people to say they were Trotsky's secretary, it's like that overcrowded Mayflower, but the key ones I knew were Europeans, not Americans, except for one later; still it's true the functions were mixed and anybody might be part bodyguard, part typist or whatever. Ginko, as I called him, had a special kind of job; he called me by a foolish nickname too, part of the sentimental fraudulence between us. He was a kind of roving personal emissary for the Old Man, to the Fourth International, on dangerous missions to various countries. American, yes; Columbia graduate, son of a dentist, ex-Zionist; brilliant, witty, neurotic as hell. I was to be a cover—so respectable; he needed that.

"We lied to ourselves. Pretended it was a paper marriage, but were having an affair anyway, that's how I happened to go down there, and fell into a regular bourgeois state of matrimony for a year. A lovely, tender-hearted man really, when he wasn't chewing himself up; we were just miserable together.

"We were lying to ourselves in another way too. Couldn't admit he was on his way out of the movement. Aside from ideological points, and there were some, it was killing him to live under that fabulous personal domination. He was thirty, almost twelve years older than I, and all of a sudden—maybe partly through my fault, I'm not sure—he was like a drowning man grabbing for a life raft. Of course neither of us ever said anything like that. We kept up our semblances and self-delusions for a time, and real fondness too—it's awful being that unhappy with somebody you like so much. Anyhow, as I said, he was very likely on the list to be wiped out, and it was a two-level life we had on West Fourth Street, creepy underneath. I had a part-time job at a music publisher's and we lived on that, while he tried to get his bearings. A tall order—finding work that satisfies you and making at least a minimal living in a society you profess to want to overthrow. I knew a number of people with the same dilemma but for him it was the most acute.

"I'll bum a cigarette if you can spare it, I've run out. How I love hearing your brook down there, I've never stopped envying you that, ours is so small and far away. And your view of the mountain is so different from ours—how beautiful, in this light! We drove almost by here that ghastly day, came over by the back road . . . You're not sleeping alone here tonight, are you? Wasn't that your nephew I saw getting the woodpile covered? Is he staying?

"The Old Man never forgave Ginko for getting out. Or me, but that was less than nothing, he scarcely knew my name, though I sat beside him a good many hours at that big desk, thrashing out translations. I don't know Russian, had to do them from French, and often one of the secretaries would have had to do that in a terrific hurry—it always seemed that a revolution in some country or other would go astray, get in the hands of a wrong faction or something, if his analysis or rebuke didn't go off at once. But he was passionately precise in language, couldn't bear any slurring of meaning, any careless ambiguity—you understand: lives, the fate of societies could be at stake in an imprecise verb, that was the feeling—and though his spoken English was terrible he knew enough to probe and question unmercifully. A word like 'impervious' for instance, or the exact time-span suggested in one language as against another by 'imminent.' I almost think his only true comrade was James Joyce.

"The comedy is that there I was thinking I was performing a fine revolutionary act, something worthy of the Great Presence—and which my bourgeois family would have heart attacks over, a good criterion for Marxist dedication—going that day to the drab little office with a couple of pickup witnesses and saying 'I do' in Spanish, as if it were nothing more than getting a driver's license, though we did go out to a restaurant and drink wine with the witnesses afterwards, the first of many inconsistencies. And the Master, the Fountain of Revolutionary Purity itself, took it quite the other way. What he saw, correctly I must say, was that I was stealing one of his most trusted and valuable aides and was about to cause him great inconvenience. And of course any inconvenience to him was a setback for the world. I don't say that sarcastically; we truly believed it.

"It didn't help either that I'd been introduced as a musician, a pianist. I wasn't much of one, as I was discovering, but that had been my training, my life you could say, after I gave up the viola. Suspect. Not serious. Though one evening after dinner—and my goodness he was courtly at those dinners, the old-world Jewish-aristocratic host and patriarch, made you feel terrible if you refused a second helping of cake so you'd end up having it whether you had any room or not . . . What was I saying? Oh yes, he consented to having the radio on a little while since it was the symphony—culture, you know; occupied a strange place in his thinking, always does in big world-swayers, people of action, I suppose; they have to pay lip-service to it generally. They played the 'Bolero' and he asked me very politely about Ravel, was he a really good composer, what should one think of him and so on. He didn't know a thing about music; I don't believe he'd given a minute's serious attention to any art since he was in school. That's understandable, there hadn't been time. However, the one time I ever dared to express a disagreement with him—and I still wonder at the nerve, I must have been out of my mind—it had to do with that.

"I asked him—imagine!—how he thought people would spend their time after the revolution, when the working day would be a few hours and everybody would be getting the just fruits of their labors, no more exploitation of anybody and so forth. He said, as if it were the most obvious and elementary thing or else he'd never really thought about it, 'In art; of course. People will have time for art.' Like a fool I went on another minute, asked did he honestly think many people would spend the time that way, said I wasn't so sure myself that it followed from their having the time that that was how they would use it. He got a little look of impatience, like Jove with a fly on his nose, and we went

on to the next ornery word. Such questions were too remote and hypo-
thetical, not interesting, didn't bear on the great task to be done. And
that's natural—I guess nobody's great in any line who's trying to be all
kinds of people. I'm just reporting how young and foolish I was, to ask
such a thing. But boy, I wish he could see some of the art around here
the last few years!

"On a day like this, and about this time of year—the leaves had
turned and color and light seemed to be pouring from them—we were
driving somewhere in Connecticut, I and my, what can I call him? I
never could say husband, never fell for the comrade stuff either. He
was by nature quite a sensitive man and he was dazzled by the light
and the leaves that day and delighting in it all as much as I was. He
sighed, and said, 'Oh, after the Revolution how beautiful all this will
be!' I swear it's true, he said that. And how many others must have, in
history, no less intelligent than he. It's just the eternal gulf, isn't it? Not
Rosa Luxemburg, though; she kept her heart whole, could see as Lenin
and Trotsky never could what their fine principles would lead to, so
had to break away. 'The old sow is dead at last!' somebody crowed
when her bloated body was found in the canal. It's always stuck with
me as one of the horrider remarks in history. Perhaps it spared her
worse decisions, more impossible choices later on. Well, I'm no
scholar. And as Lem says, there can be an awful fallacy in only sympa-
thizing with suffering, never with happiness; still, compared to people
who don't want to see or hear of any suffering . . . Actually, revolution
isn't fit work for decent people, they ought to figure on that beforehand. I mean social, not national revolutions though they can get mixed
up, overlap. I'm not saying the social ones at their worst haven't sometimes been necessary, or say inevitable; plenty of cases you can think
of. Only it's a pity we can't hire our natural-born criminals to make
them.

"Like that, what word is there for it—by the trail, over there—I
guess we have to say 'person'; our *semblable*, our *frère*. Yes, thanks; not
too strong, I don't want you to have to drive me home. It wasn't done
by anything with claws and fur. That would be more of a story. This is
so commonplace, in every way. Run of the mill college students apparently, from what we've heard. She was a cheerleader in highschool,
that kind; no drugs, no nothing; plenty of friends, nice to their families,

as far as that may have been possible. Quite a string of divorces and remarriages on both sides and they'd both lived in about twenty states—the junior executive mobile set, mobile upward or just in circles, I don't know. The sex maniac who butchered them is their perfect counterpart, whatever he may turn out to be. Society, they talk about! give it to the computers, they're in charge anyway. We tend to forget it, or try to, living here. Like man this is some trip, into the big asshole one 'n' all, last one in's a rotten egg. It does make Marx and Company look adorably quaint, you can't help loving them for it— figuring on, and addressing, a world of more or less rational human beings. How sweet.

"But to finish the memoir of olden times, when you and I and the rest of the human race were young, before frozen orange juice and the paper diaper—

"I went to the Mexican Symphony one night with Ginko and one of the secretaries, because the Old Man had taken it into his head late in the afternoon to go. What a scramble. The Mexican guards alerted— there was a little guardhouse across the road from that enormous double door, I forget the word for it in Spanish, and it was always a question whether this one or that might be open to bribes; and police escort to be arranged and made to look as if it weren't that, concealed weapons, secret route, somebody waiting at the hall to hustle him up back stairs to a seat at the far back of a box. Hardly for the music; just for a change, not to go cabin-crazy. He'd get a yen to go butterfly-hunting the same way sometimes—machine guns at the four corners of a field somewhere and the poor secretaries, with their steely visions of the final conflict, having to scamper around after him with their little nets and jars of formaldehyde. Another time he was suddenly hellbent on going horseback riding. I'd always loved riding and was doing it there every day, on a rather crazy horse I rented mornings from a second-string movie company. When he heard about it, that was it. I was to rent another horse or two, and go along myself, at six in the morning—the usual cars fore and aft, with guns etc. I don't know that he'd ever ridden except at the head of the Red Army but the pictures show him doing all right there and Mexican saddles do have a pommel. Luckily there was rumor of a leak and the plan was dropped. I was giddy with relief.

"So we went to the concert in case there should be trouble, got last-minute seats in the orchestra, and nothing happened until the intermission. Then as the applause was starting—for Respighi's 'Pines of Rome' of all things, I haven't heard of anybody playing that in years now—a great shout came from the balcony, 'Abajo Trotsky!'—one man alone first but it was taken up immediately and turned to a roar; people jumping up, craning, jabbering, some rushing for exits. I don't think he had leaned forward at all but somebody caught sight of him when the lights went on. My friend had a pistol in his pocket and had his hand on it, but of course it was all very impromptu and the Old Man got whisked out and away fast before anybody could spot the cars. It was the role of the police, strange to think of, to be his friends—protectors anyway; he was a guest of the government, to be tolerated if not loved. I've never quite understood why Cárdenas invited him to come; a gesture of independence toward Stalin obviously; I don't know the ins and outs of it.

"But here, in this country, the cops were not our friends, and to us they were strikebreakers, lackeys of capitalism—you'll remember the phrases. Probably our dread of them was rooted more in theory, plus a lot of nasty facts and episodes that hadn't involved us personally, than in any particular illegality on our part. I suppose my . . . companion, Ginko, had left out a few salient facts in his passport applications; didn't say it was his intention to overthrow every government in the world, and that what he held against the U.S.S.R. wasn't their trying to foment world revolution but on the contrary, their failure to do so, via the switch to the principle of communism-in-one-country. And I vaguely remember co-signing a joint bank account application that involved some false statements of a mild sort and made me very nervous; I think it was for funds he would transfer in some roundabout way to the household in Mexico. The sums must have been tiny, and when you think of the oil companies or any big multi-national now with their immense thefts and deceits, it's too laughable. As far as acts and general trend of life went, we were pathetically respectable. It was our thoughts that put us outside the pale, and as I've said, they weren't, in either party to the non-marriage, as pure as we went on trying to pretend. The serious question, for many besides us, was who was really believing what on any given day. Erosions, evasions, those deep changes of mind and spirit have their own mysterious pace and logic. Who can ever say later if a certain conviction was lost or arrived at in a matter of minutes or of months, or years?

"In any case there was the double dread. If the doorbell rang unexpectedly—which it hardly ever did, we were being so careful—it might be either the police or the Stalinists: agents, strongarm men. Actually one time it was my mother bringing us a bunch of flowers; she was quite fond of Ginko, hadn't had any heart attack over it, thought he was a fine man and would 'find his way'; and once an alcoholic ex-professor I'd met on a transatlantic ship, wanting a handout. Of course I'd had to stop seeing Stalinist friends, fellow-travelers—yes, don't smile—like you. I'd gone on having a few in spite of the big disagreement, a big area of hatred really; musicians mostly, and a few painters besides you, and writers. Political imbeciles all of you—at least you shook loose before September '39 and that left-wing force of all time, to the tune of massacres in Poland. But we know what friendship there could be, strained but even so, on other grounds. Not any more. You were to be avoided and feared, and properly; as you've often said, those high-minded simpletons, your fellow-believers, caused or aided in some hideous acts on occasion. But even other friends, Trotskyist sympathizers—and for that matter that's all I was myself, I was never in the party—were suspect; not politically oriented; might easily betray without meaning to, through bourgeois habits of chitchat. The creed posted over the bed should have been, as I presume it is for terrorists now, the Nechayev nightmare. It wasn't. Only you never get over that feeling about the police, and the rest of the apparatus—another of those words.

"About twelve or fifteen years ago it must have been—two of the children and I were all in bed with German measles—an FBI man appeared at the house without notice. To see me. That's the only other time it's all come over me like this. I had a high fever, he had to sit on a chair in our bedroom and I felt as if I wouldn't be able to speak or breathe . . . Why? could anything be more ridiculous? Lem said afterwards I was a baby, he was disgusted with me. You know how unshakable he is in his serenities; he gets upset enough about flats and sharps and lousy behavior, he's been in a state over the theft of that Boonton history of Thelma's, but not about imaginary things; he has no patience with that.

"The agent was inquiring about that brief ex-intimate of mine, whether I knew where he was and all that. Well, I hadn't heard a word from or about him in years, neither had any of the few people we knew in common. He'd married, way back, I hope more wisely than the first time, and that was the last anybody knew. He might be dead, or a successful businessman almost anywhere, or perhaps idling away the rest of his life on some Greek island. I've no idea why they wanted to know. Dead or alive, I could have assured them he was no present threat to any government, I'm positive of that. Probably just one of J. Edgar Hoover's boys on a little witch hunt, wasting taxpayers' money; they'd been rifling the party's files for some time and must have gone after some jokers—several of the Old Guard I'd known had gone over to something to the right of right-wing Republicans years before. Anyway the agent was very nice, thanked me, never mentioned Mexico or any of that, was sorry I was sick, and that was that.

"Until last month . . . All right, with a lot of water, then I must get home, he'll be worrying. And now look at me, seeing that ice-axe in Coyoacán along with the butchery I did see, I think—oh but I can't have made it up, they went for the bodies, it was on the news! and with that sight in my eyes probably forever, I don't know how you'd erase it—the one here, I mean—I can tremble at a bunch of decent hardworking cops only doing what we would denounce them for not doing. So who's crazy now . . . We're told the unexamined life is not worth living. I agree. But if the life has been a fraud, a dream, a willful illusion, is examining going to make it real?

"Look—about Lem. Until that day, that cursed walk to the Crump Job, I'd have said the watershed in our lives had been the taxi accident. Thank God we'd been together a year then, I'd heard him play, every day, gone with him to his concerts, all over. He was a wonder, as you know. That day when he came to and knew the fingers were gone, I thought he'd want to kill himself, or would at least say he'd never listen to music again. And you know what he said? not with any tears or rage at fate for the piddling way it picked to do him in, after he'd survived the tempest and the volcano and the gates of hell—no, just with that deep, gentle, funny smile he has, he said, 'So—I will be a music-lover.' Then I thought he might smash the violin. He walked out with it one day, without saying anything, and came back after a while with a big bag of groceries instead. It was a Strad, a rich patron lady in Paris had bought it for him when he was eighteen. We lived on it for three years. Various friends tried to push him into conducting but he said he didn't have the temperament for it.

"I thought I had tried to understand his life—his mother and aunt dead in Dachau, and the rest of it. But this last month I've felt I never understood anything of what lay behind that remark, after the accident, or why Sophocles and Homer mean what they do to him either. If what's happened here could throw me back into that really rather insignificant—no, beneficent, murder in Mexico—

"Yes, I do think that. Trotsky had played for those stakes after all; had to; couldn't play ball with the stinking, tottering Czarist league at that point, and Russia doesn't go for our kind of pulling and hauling, as Kerensky discovered but wouldn't admit. But to rule, as an everyday killer? no, he wasn't fit for that. Some people say he too if he'd had the chance would have killed off all the old Bolsheviks. I don't believe it. He was always being called to account for the shooting down of the Kronstadt sailors and never made much sense about it that I could see; how could he?—wrong man for the job; hyper-civilized, super-intellectual, good for a hateful act in the pursuit or consolidation of power, which he couldn't or wouldn't apologize for, but that doesn't make an abiding principle of government. If he'd been up to that he needn't have been booted into exile. So his death was appropriate, and timely. He gained by it, as historical figure and political analyst—he's unbeatable at that—and I've always thought the war years would have diminished him more than they did, if he'd been alive to show up his blind spots as a program director—even without the later fossil aspect; that's postwar. When the blow fell I dare say he was thinking the opposite: that the war was going to vindicate him, bring on revolutions all over including Russia, under his guidance, D.V.; if so he was underestimating that mustached Satan, our century's contribution to devil-lore, and his power to call up from the deeps the world's last outrage.

"Come to think of it, I rose from the deeps myself. Worked three years in the government, as you did, in the 'war effort'—we weren't hearing that locution about Vietnam! I was quite a valuable citizen, I was told. I could have mentioned that to the cops; I keep forgetting about it for some reason. By the way, I understand the murder instrument, one of those mountaineer's axes, is in the police museum in Mexico City.

"Well, what are the scenes that Lem must live with that way, or a lot more and more often? and that he's scarcely hinted at to his healthy American children. Vermont children, I should say; they're that first, even our oceanographer. Yes, she was still snooping around the floor of the Indian Ocean the last we heard.

"It seems we've been two ghosts in a ghostly marriage of convenience. He reads Simenon quite often, but only the ancient Greeks really speak to him, and I realize now it's only in certain moods he can stand to be hit that way. And in music, almost never. You remarked once on our not having any recordings of the Bach Passions, Matthew and John. There's one Vivaldi he won't have either—the 'Gloria.' And a certain few of the great works he grew up on, Mahler's Ninth and Debussy's 'La Mer,' they're almost as taboo. We had such a fine flutist around last spring, he couldn't resist doing one of his little arrangements of 'L'Après-midi d'un Faune,' the Prelude, but that's rare, though as you know we play lots of other Debussy, straight or in one of those little rampages you've heard; just the two of us, grabbing from various pieces, in what he calls a devotional spoof. Of course it's not that—'spoof' is just one of the words he took a shine to, learning English as late as he did, and that he loves to use even when he knows he's not doing it quite accurately. Mozart is the only other composer we both know well enough to have that kind of fun with. And now it seems we weren't, we can't have been, playing the same music, he and I. Perhaps we should go back to speaking French together, neither his native language nor mine, as we did before the children were born.

"We've been shot off into two worlds completely separate and unknowable to one another, by this horror in the woods that had nothing to do with us. Except everything—everything to do with us. As if we didn't read and hear such news nearly every day; elephant hides, all of us. But when we do get hit between the eyes, the dislocation, the shock of unreality in ourselves, what can I call it? That lovely mountain there that I've known so well, that's been part of my soul all my life—I've tramped over every part of it; there are old hunters like Brit who know the animals better but I probably know the flora as well as anybody, and I've slept out on it so often, like a baby, feeling it under my bones as the great sheltering presence, and protection and peace. It's become strange, hostile, and as if it always had been.

"What kind of mirage is this Vermont to us? Where have the two of us been really living all this time?

"I'm sorry. I haven't cried like this in ages, not since Lem was so sick that time. And I did shed some tears over your bust-up before that, as monstrous and incomprehensible to me as . . . I couldn't bear it for you, and now it would look so dull: nice faithful husband after twenty years walks out as nice respectable gay, happens every day. Oh, I know what I've been spared all right, and why you're smiling like that. Tell me I've been raving, that I'm the luckiest woman in this putrid world, I'll believe you. We have a lovely life together, we love and are true to one another as the saying goes, I don't doubt any of that; if only . . . For God's sake, I mean it reverently, in the sight of God if there were one, who are we? Who and what is anybody, for that matter.

"As for why the sight of murder, the most atrocious but of and by absolutely unknown people, should have opened up this irrelevant hell, perhaps you can tell me some day. Come to think of it though, why shouldn't it? To be unflappable would be the real hell, and the tree falls to the side of the old crack; I'm sure Brit is pondering some strange questions these days too.

"Just one more picture from Coyoacán that sticks with me. It's Trotsky's wife, Natalia, talking about the rain. Second wife, mother of his two sons, both about to be wiped out, as far as can be known, within a few months, the older under very suspicious circumstances in a clinic in Paris. The younger, who was completely unpolitical, was apparently shot without trial in Russia, where he was accused of poisoning wells and so murdering millions of workers. The two daughters of the first marriage had died earlier, one of TB after being deported. That one's husband and three children and mother, Trotsky's first wife, all vanished in the usual fashion. One grandchild, son of the suicide daughter, would survive; whether any other lived through the gulag may never be known.

"The House of Atreus? Well, perhaps that story does lie coiled in all historic upheavals, or did as long as conscience was up to it. The Furies seem to be tired of their job now; no penance, no doom; it's all like what happened over there by the trail. Hardly even a story. But Coyoacán could still be one, isn't that strange? And that was real, not theater, unless everything we do is just theater, or the other way around, nothing we do has reality until it becomes that. But Agamemnon had been a real person too, a very flawed one, before he rose to the stage . . .

"I'm getting befuddled, you've given me too much whiskey, that insane killer here has gotten me too, he's chopped my feet off; see? there they go, merrily down the stream; bye bye . . . All right, I hadn't realized it was so cold; what a nice fire; that's better, and we don't have to see that nasty mountain . . . I suppose what I was groping for is that the era of drama, of anything that could hold the imagination, at least in public affairs, for our western consciousness runs from Agamemnon to Leon Trotsky and then stops, in one second, in August 1940. Natalia lived on, more and more unpolitically as far as I know, for twenty-two years. But I'm speaking of 1937.

"It was summer, the rainy season but usually it only came for a while in the afternoon. She and I were sitting at the big empty diningroom table; it was afternoon, not mealtime. She was being very courteous, almost formal. If she had any friends there I wasn't one of them, but just one of the many transient faces of all nationalities she had to accommodate to. I never heard her speak of deaths and dangers. She began talking about the rain, in a most ordinary tone of voice, that somehow began to convey every strangeness and terror of that long life—it seemed long to me then; she was about the age we are now. She said they were quite comfortable, everything would be all right, except for the rain. It got on your nerves, you kept waiting for it, and thinking if only it would miss a day or two but it never did. Some days it would be longer and harder than others, or it would stop and start again when you'd thought it was over, or would be just a long drizzle like that day. In some form or other it came every day; it was inexorable. She was sitting opposite me, facing the big window that gave on the patio as all the windows of the house did; if any were to the outside originally they must have been bricked up. She went on smiling politely, and the drops kept drooling down the pane. She said it must be good for the orange tree; she had grown quite fond of that. Her husband was more taken by the white-bearded cactus, and even spoke of digging some up in fields outside to transplant there, but that would be difficult in the rain. He was just over a severe cold; it would be bad for him to catch another.

"By the way, Claire dear, forgive my saying so but you're getting too fat. I wish you'd start dieting. You really mustn't let yourself go like that."

5

It's hard to hush up much in a place the size of Boonton, speaking of regular residents, accounting by then for less than twenty percent of the town's assessed property but close to a hundred percent of its non-assessable treasure of human interchange and speculation, once known as gossip. The motorcycle gang were let out in a few days, with orders to get out of the state, and it was generally whispered that Mercy Grout had gone off with them. Her family said she was visiting an aunt upstate, to get over her nervous condition after the holdup, but eventually she phoned her sister Natty, who told her husband Ray, who let drop something when he was stacking wood again one day with his uncles, who wondered when the state cop appeared if that was what he had come about. Wouldn't make much sense but they were used to being asked all sorts of queer things, just because they were known as two citizens with nothing to hide or lie about. Brit had had plenty of enemies in his many years as First Selectman but even they had never dared suggest any venality or other improper interest on his part.

Or the visitor might be nosing around about the latest drug scandal in Waterville highschool which also served for a number of villages around, or the series of mysterious fires in the town dump, or the recent break-ins at various weekend houses and town clerks' offices including Boonton's in the loft over the fire engine; in most towns the culprits found cash in the safes, from hunting licenses and other fees, but the local clerk didn't leave money there overnight and they were so mad they strewed the town records all over, even in the swamp out back.

The officer had not come about any of those matters. Mercy had gone off of her own accord, and from her phone call her mother and other relatives had reason to think she'd come back the same way, and soon, so better not stir up any more scandal than necessary by going to the police about it. The cop, a new one but Brit knew him from the talks after the murders, was just doing some snooping about the stolen picture history, the Boonton Collection. It seemed the thief in that case had tried to sell it to a publisher of such stuff in a town near Boston, and the publisher must have smelled a rat, anyway for one reason or another the Massachusetts cops were making inquiries with the Vermont equivalent about where the couple had been living when the precious package was purloined, which had already been thoroughly hashed over.

"You know Hannah Palz. You had her and Johnson and me over there all day after that time on the trail."

Yes, the tall, decent-looking young fellow in uniform nodded, in the usual friendly fashion of the force around there when dealing with conspicuously law-abiding native citizens like the Horton brothers; he remembered all that very well and thanks a lot. As an afterthought he threw out, "Mrs. Palz—she seemed to be a friend of yours. Did she ever tell you about being a communist or anything like that?"

Brit laughed. "Oh sure. I don't rightly know what kind, seemed to be dead set against the Rooskie system anyhow. That was maybe thirty-five, forty years ago. She tried to explain it all to me one time but I couldn't follow it and wa'ant much interested. I can only vouch for her character the last thirty years."

"Yes, I'm sure they're fine people, everybody says so. They just seem to have some funny ones living on their place."

"This one you're talking about, took Thelma's history thing, he's the only bad one I ever heard of and I guess I've known 'em all. They're after my brother and me all the time, making us their Professors of Country Life." He and Ellis smiled, over their private backlog of jokes in this connection. "Foxfire University, one of 'em calls it; that's that Bible they can't sleep without having under their pillows. My wife too, she gives 'em the home bakery course, postgraduate you might say. Anyway, there wa'ant nobody felt as bad as Hannah and Lem Palz when that fool nut run off with that fool book."

"Well now Brit, hold your horses," Ellis said in his mollifying way. He'd been the peace-maker in the family from birth and in Boonton too though he hadn't ever wanted to run for office. But about the various crosses Brit had had to bear in his long public life, and his tendency to get rather steamed up over them, his brother had been as soothing an influence as anything could be, considering the saps and stinkers you have to deal with in any local politics, even without the extra headaches of the last few years.

An impressive pair, the young man was recognizing, these two broth-

ers who didn't look much alike except in the canny squint they'd give
you over whatever you weren't quite saying aloud, and the big long
lawyerish nose that struck you as sickle-shaped from the front but in
profile showed up as quite majestically straight. Ellis, older and taller,
was a trifle stooped, more as though from ducking low doorways all his
life than from age, and the even, deliberate pace of his words and
motions too seemed congenital, not elderly. Brit's more excitable nature had grooved his face more heavily, and his belly sagged since the
heart trouble. Neither of them seemed to have lost a single hair of their
grey heads, an upspringing bush in Brit's case, the other silkily flat, as
though that too had come under the general pacifying control of Ellis's
nature.

The officer felt oddly reassured about life, society and his job, just
standing in the road with them beside the tractorful of logs they'd been
working on, and would have believed anything they told him, no matter how improbable, as everyone else always had.

Brit could see that, and therefore felt a slight twinge of duplicity
concerning one thing he wasn't telling. Hannah had gone on to him
more recently than he'd implied about her old Bolshevik connection or
whatever you'd call it. It was when they were driving home together
from the police quarters after all the questions, the day after the murders. Either delayed shock from the afternoon before, or something
about the questioning itself, had gotten her unstrung in a way he'd
never seen before; sounded almost as loony as Johnson, babbling on
about that fellow what's-his-name in Mexico and how he got killed
with a hatchet or something thirty-forty years ago; as if that had anything to do with what they'd never have had the bad luck to have to
see if it hadn't been for that fool hound Sam. So for once he'd had to
be the pacifying influence or try to be. But he didn't see any call to
repeat that silly conversation to anybody but his wife.

"Why it's them, Lem and Hannah, 's been paying that Compton
lawyer to try to track it down, the one that took Thelma to see you
people about it. Why'nt you ask her? She hit the ceiling the first day,
but she'll tell you herself ain't nobody doing what they are to hunt the
bastard down. Ain't worth it either except for her feelings. Excuse me,
Ellis," they smiled again, "I mean I expect it'll turn up."

Another thing pretty generally known was that Ellis had been sweet on Thelma in highschool, when she turned him down though he was considered the handsomest young man in the county, and things had lit up again after their respective spouses died, and now that sister Leona was away in the Compton Retreat, Thelma had taken over his housekeeping and didn't seem to be spending much time in her own house. They could even be seen late afternoons sitting in his porch swing, holding hands and looking at the sunset with such an expression on both faces, Brit didn't honestly think she cared much any more if her lifework was ever retrieved.

The cop turned his car around, didn't bother going on to the Palz house, didn't mention Mercy Grout or the vandalism at the Town Clerk's office, and the brothers went back to their wood job, the last of that kind; the road-widening had gone beyond Ellis's land and nearly to the Palz front door when the operation suddenly halted. The word now was that the crew were working over from the other side of the mountain, but the Hortons hadn't taken time to verify that.

"Or they might," Brit had an edge of savagery to his grin, "be studying how to engineer them ledges they got to get across instead of my woodlot." Ellis asked, as he had before, if Brit was sure he could withhold a right of way over those twenty-seven acres he was so crazy about because they were what he had kept of the original family land and where he shot his first deer, and Brit said he sure was, hadn't looked at the deed in years but it wasn't one he was likely to forget. The access they wanted wasn't for the new road itself but one off it, to a planned development on Pace's land; he wasn't going to want it coming out in court that he'd sold the town on a route costing nearly double what it needed to, assuming any such road was needed at all, just to put that extra little fortune in his pocket. "I'd have to give it to him if there wa'ant another way in to his land." They both made a face, the kind with a wisecrack embedded in it; it was a family expression they shared, with Leona too. The other way in was so tough, it could delay Pace's grand schemes a year or two; he had offered Brit five hundred dollars for that right of way, "And I'll croak before I'll give it to him, you can count on that." He didn't have to tell Ellis it was his oldest daughter and her family, his only offspring still nearby, he wanted to keep that woodlot peaceful for; they were crazy about it too and meant to build there as soon as they could afford to.

A few hours later, as he and Louise had the sound cut off between news and sports as usual, long after dark, they heard an unfamiliar vehicle turning in there. He turned on the outside spotlight, went out to investigate, and there was Mercy Grout, alone on an old motorbike of her brother's, not making it up the grade to the Johnson cabin, where he could tell she'd been aiming to get without being seen.

"Hi, Mercy. Glad to see you back. I better give you a hand there."

He knew, and something told him she knew, that the Johnson girl, the wife, wasn't home just then. She liked music, she'd told them, and was spending most evenings at the Palzes' where there'd be some kind of little concert several times a week; they said Lem was still a wonderful teacher even if he wouldn't touch a fiddle any more with that ruined hand, just piano, he managed marvelously with three left fingers on that; which was why the young seekers had been drawn there instead of just going in for country life on their own. Phil Johnson never went, didn't seem to be wanting much society in general, so he'd be alone up in the cabin.

Mercy looked so sick and wild and exhausted, he thought he should drive her home and let them come for the motorbike later. But she said she was all right and had a message for the Johnsons from an old friend of theirs, and please not to phone her mother, she'd be getting right on home. So there was nothing he or Louise could do except wait for her to come back down, which she did pretty soon, just as Penny Johnson turned into the lane on foot with her flashlight. Leaving the TV a minute to go to the window, the Hortons had a glimpse of the two girls passing close, Penny stopping as though to speak and the other just tearing on away. Then Louise did call Mercy's mother, who said she'd drive part way up Horton Hill and meet her. What Louise had said was that Mercy didn't look safe to be riding anything, Brit had seen her close up and she looked awful.

The particular kind of awful she looked was so familiar to the older girl, she was close to laughing as she went on up to the cabin. She'd had her nights and days in the motorcycle set, only the holdup she remembered best was a gas station, not a store, and she hadn't been on the side of the cash register; hadn't fallen in love in the process either, was falling out if anything. And that rapturous torment on Mercy's haggard, swollen face—that really made her laugh, all by herself

among the autumn leaves, under such bright stars. The wise handsome
fatherly presence, the kind and ever so knowing voice, the blissful
safety, the comforting embrace, the aura of the still vigorous man old
enough to have seen and understood everything, yet who could do no
wrong . . . She wondered what excuse Mercy would have cooked up
for the visit; there would certainly have been one.

"What? no lipstick?" She twinkled at him, more intimately than for
several weeks past, sniffing at his beard and T-shirt.

He didn't smile or lift a hand to touch her. He looked about ninety,
she thought, not for the first time. There had been a message after all.
And she was bringing another. She'd seen Margo checking out at the
Grand Union in Waterville that afternoon.

"Margo! Around here?"

She had to giggle, at the mixture of relief—or hope?—in his conster-
nation. She knew he knew that her long absences in non-working hours
hadn't all been for music's sake; for the two Saturdays she'd stayed
away all night she hadn't bothered to offer any explanation. They had
quarreled about little things and refrained from discussing big ones all
the way down from Canada, and the last few days of that trek had
gone hours at a time without speaking, except to the occasional north-
bound hikers they passed. The nights were cold. The sweatered, sleep-
ing-bag sex that came about the two times they weren't too tired was
also in silence and left them less connected than before.

Yet they stayed together, after a fashion. He would have to be a
witness when the murder trial came up, or at least if he went away
would have to leave an address, inconvenient if not insuperable; that
was one professed if feeble reason for staying as they were and anyway
the only one that bore speaking of. She'd made friends in the Palz
group and with some of the other young refugees from the ratrace, and
he'd started playing tennis weekends over by the ski area. Somehow
the subject had come up one day with a customer at the sawmill, who
quickly recognized in Phil Johnson a likely partner and fellow-addict,
and the ex-minister couldn't resist. Of course he hadn't touched a

racket in five years, but after a little warming up found that his cross-court backhand could still be spectacular; his wicked serve took a little longer but came back too; he was still very good indeed, so in that one context took whatever risk there might be in a certain amount of public exposure. The nerve-wracking talks with the police hadn't resulted in that, leaving him mercifully, or miraculously it seemed, incognito; he had plainly been an innocent passer-by in that horrid affair; no need to probe further.

Or was exposure what he was wanting? She thought so at times, had been convinced of it when they left Canada so suddenly, after the clipping arrived anonymously in the mail and she heard him out by the lake afterwards preaching a sermon to the loons. The next morning they'd put what they could in their knapsacks and made for the trail, knowing perfectly well that in Vermont or anywhere in the U.S. he'd be recognized sooner or later. There was one overnight stop before the start of the trail, they splurged on a cheap motel room, their last bed for quite a while, and that was where she caught him making the strange phone call; a dirty one you'd have thought from his face, like a nasty little boy's, when it was answered and he guiltily shut off the connection with one finger.

"Who on earth have you got to phone to?" she asked, rather harshly though she'd betrayed him twice by that time, with a couple of American army deserters her age who were staying on there, rather unprosperously but not liking the amnesty terms much better than the Vietnam mess they'd walked out on. Phil, as everyone outside his family had always called him, had been a door-to-door peddler of kitchen gadgets the first year, before the initial sawmill job opened up; the small Ontario town they were near, except for the draft-evaders and a few oldtimers, was a dreary place humanly; it was also ugly. He could hardly have any pressing business calls to make; or social. "Oh nothing," he said, then flushed and mumbled a correction. "I just had an impulse to see if my daughter was still there—Alice," as if she didn't know. They burned the clipping in an ashtray that night, and perhaps even he knew that a lot more than newspaper was going up in smoke. However, for some months she'd been aware that his capacity for not seeing in front of his nose was very deep.

The news story, from one of the larger Michigan papers, was on the stirring memorial service that had finally been held for him in his old church in Fenwick. She couldn't tell if it was all the old names mentioned, of friends and family including his adored octogenarian mother, or the inspiring picture of himself in clerical garb that made it such a wrench for him to burn it. He turned away from the little pyre biting his lip, eyes full of tears. "Oh Lord . . ." She never knew exactly how he meant that, as prayer or expletive. She hadn't seen him actually praying on his knees since they'd been together, and when she tried to draw him out on his honest-to-God religious beliefs, she herself never having had any, he would go off in such a relativistic maze, of hedgings and qualifyings, she had trouble following him.

"But the Trinity," she'd insisted once in their first year, "do you literally believe in that? The Father, the Son and the Holy Ghost I seem to remember is the way it goes. Are you telling me you do or you don't honestly believe there are three such personages, or two personages and one entity or something, that you're actually visualizing and think is a definite creation or maybe representation of something called God?"

He said well, that was quite a sentence she'd gotten off there—this with a whimsical smile, one of his most attractive expressions—and of course it all depended what you meant by literally; the literal and the figurative after all weren't such precise concepts as was sometimes thought.

"For instance, an uncle of mine who was a fine archer, made his own bows and all that . . ."

"Yes, you've told me about him." He had in fact, through the long winter evenings, told her about practically everybody he had the slightest recollection of, which wasn't a great many; his memory didn't seem to run to much precise personal observation.

"He was giving me a little archery lesson one afternoon. And he'd just pulled the bowstring when he noticed the moon, a little white one of course, in daytime, up above the target. And before he let the arrow go, anyway I think he was still holding the string stretched . . ."

"Must have been or the arrow would have fallen out."

"Well maybe. Anyhow he said, about the moon this was, 'Sometimes, just every once in a while, I manage to see that for what it really is.' "

"He wasn't talking about the target?"

"No. Not at all. The moon."

"Oh."

"And that's always seemed to me a very helpful way to think about such matters as the Trinity . . ."

"Now you see them now you don't." They were snuggled up on a bed together, though not undressed. He would never discuss theology naked.

"Not exactly. Or rather yes and no. As Yeats said—W. B. Yeats, the Irish poet, you know . . ."

"Sure I know. I recited 'Innisfree' to you the second time we met. You'd never heard of it."

"So you did." He smiled and patted her cheek but didn't react to the nudge of her knee. "Yes, I missed a lot in those busy years. It was one of our parishioners who gave me the quote about the fairies; about whether they existed or not. He thought it might be useful for a sermon. Yeats's answer to that question was, 'It depends on the configuration of light.' Now I think . . ."

She shrieked with laughter. "Oh darling, you're the funniest man I ever met. And I suppose you did use it in a sermon?"

He was rather hurt, momentarily. "I certainly did, and you might say it brought the house down."

"I should think so."

"I mean it brought an unusual amount of thoughtful, affirmative response. I don't want to boast, the credit goes to Yeats, the Irish poet—oh yes, I forgot, you do know that. But quite a number of the younger people told me afterwards that that was just the way they'd been feeling, about the more difficult lessons of Christianity, only they hadn't found such a good way of expressing it. To be sure, that's only a first step, toward the true vision you might say, though I prefer to call it faith. We can't always trust the light, at any given moment. However, given the will to believe . . ."

"You do occasionally see real fairies."

"Or find yourself in the real triple presence of God—the Father, the Son and the Holy Ghost."

He sighed heavily, as from longings too deep for tears, but soon they were making love quite satisfactorily. His initial impotence had lasted only two sessions, and she had soon managed to teach him her special requirements.

They couldn't imagine who had sent the clipping or could have known where to send it; perhaps a repatriate from the AWOL colony had happened to be in Michigan just then and recognized the picture. It was terribly upsetting, especially as it came months after its printing date, which meant somebody had been hoarding and exhibiting it. His oratory by the lake that night had a ring of passionate appeal, nothing like their earlier fireside or mattress chats about the true nature of holiness. It was more reminiscent of the eloquent public address on the coast, where she had first seen and heard him from afar, or some later ones she had accompanied him to, with his sick wife's blessing, at midwestern colleges and universities, where he had an enthusiastic not to say rabid following. She wondered this time if he was deliberately getting back in practice—for what, for heaven's sake, after what he had done?—or if he really thought the loons' screams and cackles were the accustomed prelude to the cheers of applause he could usually expect.

"Yes, my friends, let's face it"—that colloquial touch, well short of vulgarity though, always got them. But so far it was only a murmur she could barely make out from the door, like a last run-through of the script memorized. She had run out thinking he must be speaking to some stranger, though it was a dead-end track, scarcely a road, and far from any other dwelling. "We have to be what we are—what God made us, and let's not quarrel with our Maker, as our granddaddies used to call Him, if He gave Tom, Dick or Harry a better figure"— giggle there and a whir of wings along the dark water's edge—"or a smarter eye to their investments. But let's not forget this. One choice we do have, every single one of us, is between the best that we are and the next best, on down to the worst. The worst takes many forms, they're all easy to see, we don't need to go on about that. It's the best that takes some thinking about . . ." Screech screech; his fine baritone was beginning to sound forth, so that even a moose far up the lake gave out a snort, of approbation no doubt though the speaker did draw hecklers in some conservative communities. ". . . and the one point I'm here to make tonight is that the best we think we can ask of ourselves one week or year may be way below par a little later. God had a reason for making us different from a bullfrog in a pond, with one glummph! for all time. As the great Spanish philosopher Ortega y Gasset said—a friend of mine reminded me of this the other day and I'm passing it on to you—he said, or wrote, that the difference between man and the chimpanzee is that the chimpanzee wakes up every morning as if no other chimp had ever existed before him. Wouldn't that be awful? Just think of it!" The loons missed that. Penny, in the doorway, knew the signaling little smile on the handsome face, the uptilted chin, the invitation to share in relish; the crackdown would follow immediately, and did.

"We've been spared that fate," the preacher intoned, with an edge of warning and prophetic wrath. "We can see, we can learn, we can remember. And because others have taken the trouble to learn before us, we ourselves can do better than we thought was our best yesterday." Here a single piercing scream did break out, a long descending glissando echoing far in the night, and stirring at the end a few responsive clucks and growls from the winged and somewhat dispersed company. "That's right. We understand each other. The Vietnam War may be over, officially, but the horrors and miseries of it aren't. Neither are hunger and misery and racial intolerance right here at home. Don't ever say there's nothing we can do about it. There's plenty we can do, every single one of us. We don't all have to go march and get arrested in Washington"—smile again, self-effacing, in semi-profile: the audience would know and admire his own record in that line. "That's not for everyone, and not always very effective anyway." Ha ha; big splash; must have got a fish jumping. "But we can vote, can't we? and we can vote for a congressman and a senator and eventually a president who *will* do something. If they don't we can kick 'em out."

Here he must have decided to cut it short, or else was a little too out of touch with the news. "I just want to wind up with one little homely anecdote. Seeing the full moon up there—or I guess it's nearly full— made me think of it. I have two children, so don't think I'm just talking to the kids among you. You who are parents here, I know very well what you must suffer sometimes, seeing your children go off on paths that wouldn't have been yours, and more so now than ever before in history. 'The center does not hold,' some poet said, and that was never truer than now. We have to make our own centers, together, and *be* together in them." Little cough from platform, slight further splash out front. "But what I wanted to tell you was this. When our first baby was born, a little boy—no, it was a girl that time—her mother took her out to the porch one night to show her the moon, because she'd never seen it before. I was busy and didn't pay much attention, but somehow it stuck in my mind, and now I just hope they've both forgiven me for not putting my work aside and going out to *share* that experience. We all need to take a fresh look at the moon, at life, once in a while. That's number one. And number two is *sharing*, with someone, with everyone.

"Thank you and goodnight." He turned away from the faintly lapping black water, wiping his mouth, more from habit than spittle. "Oh for goodness' sake, I thought you'd gone to bed."

She laughed, they both did, as he put his arm around her. "I could hardly have slept through a performance like that. Anyway if we're leaving at daybreak we've got to pack. So you haven't gone crazy? You had me wondering for a minute."

Packing reminded him of the fright, the clipping. "Me too. But it was fun stretching my lungs again. And I got quite a few laughs, didn't I?" Smiling, entwined and nervous, they went into that Canadian cabin for the last time. "Don't worry, sweetheart. Everything's going to be all right."

"Except that you do miss your public so horribly." She began to cry, for the first time since she'd watched the parachute drifting down like a dead moth in starlight and strained to go on hearing the empty plane whirring north to its death, as if all her hopes had been in that instead of the parachute. He had flown up there, and to the Barren Lands, a number of times, though usually not alone, on missions to the Indians and once to drop off a zoologist friend interested in wolves; and on one such trip, the month before, she had gone with him, to stay and work out last details: flares and snowmobile, exact location of drop on the frozen lake, itinerary and destination thereafter. High-risk but not too hard to arrange. Report wrong position, then icing trouble, then that he was bailing out, rather far from where he did. He wasn't the jump-happy type, had been transferred from the paratroops when he was found to be second-rate at that but ideal pilot material; happy or not, in later life he had gone on doing a few jumps a year with a parachute club, as a safety measure he had told the family but really because of the ecstasy of his terror in the seconds of free-fall. Penny had been too smitten at the time to argue long for the much simpler, humdrum alternative of his getting a divorce. The very thought of that broke him to pieces, it was abhorrent, unthinkable, she could see why; besides this other way was more exciting. To be exposed, to his wife and the rest of the world—in his position, with his reputation—as a dime-a-dozen adulterer and cradle-snatcher too? Never. He would not inflict such pain, on his old mother above all. Let them mourn and cherish him with his noble image intact.

The relations of the two who were fleeing were of course at that time terribly romantic. Even so, as they tried to get the parachute gathered up that terrible night, preparatory to weighting and burying it for disappearance in the imminent spring thaw, he was already suffering certain pangs of conscience, since conscience had always been his much loved pride and guide and he hadn't foreseen being stripped of it. Also in his roll on landing he had misjudged the depth and wetness of snow over the ice, had a dislocated shoulder and sprained ankle, had had a bad fright over real icing trouble, knew the plane would crash much sooner than planned, and was hardly in a mood for a long snow-mobile ride past a sparse sprinkling of closed-up summer camps, even though the temperature was by then a little above zero F. instead of far below as at the rehearsal. A third and stranger embarrassment in that first hour of their new life was his impression that the wraithlike figure of his aging and ailing wife was trying to come toward them from the wild lake shore. It was so vivid he was on the point of shouting her name, "Margo!" in a tone of annoyance and reprimand, when Penny, in alarm, asked what on earth he was seeing: a polar bear? a moose? a person?

However, news of the search, off by a good fifty miles, and pictures of him in Canadian papers, were short-lived; the shoulder mended, in spite of the nightlong train journey before they dared see a doctor; they were lucky in their encounters.

She refrained from remarking, after his speech to the loons five years later, that he seemed to be missing his old home as well as his public.

Now in their new cabin, in Vermont, in a new life that was so mean a parody of that other one, they had to wonder when Jeff would turn

up. Phil hadn't really needed Mercy's warning about that. He'd had a
pretty good premonition of trouble after their encounter by the gas
pump, though in mentioning it to Penny, which he had to do to explain
why his hands were shaking and he'd left the groceries behind, he'd
said he was sure the boy was too doped up to try anything even if he'd
wanted to. Actually, Phil had had the trembles off and on for ten days
before that, since the day of the murders, and had had a couple of
scares from it at the sawmill. One of the old regular employees, now on
such jobs as fixing the sawdust conveyor when it acted up and straight-
ening lumber piles, had had an arm cut off there years before, from
coming to work drunk they said. The only times now when the minister
felt at least half way like his old real self, minus the doing-good part,
was playing tennis. At those times, especially when giving the two little
ritual bounces to the ball before a serve, he felt so clean and masterful
and beyond reproach, he vaguely fancied he'd be acclaimed again as
an outstanding asset to the human race after all, the details thereof to
become clear in due course.

But now . . . Mercy Grout's report, as the poor little thing lay
sobbing in his arms, was that Jeff Smith, that once sweet-faced little
neighbor boy to whom he'd been such a father, was absolutely carried
away, obsessed, by vengefulness toward him; blamed him for his hitch
in the reformatory and his family's eviction from wherever that was
and his father's death of heart failure, and had sold the gang on a
blackmail scheme, to what end she hadn't heard. From the sublimities
of the tennis court, the details to become clear had shot down to that.
Anyway she, Mercy, would never tell on him. She'd known from the
first time she laid eyes on him that there was something mysterious in
his past, and he was unhappy, and the finest, noblest man she'd ever
seen.

The next time Penny saw Margo she'd have had to jump off a cliff to
avoid speaking to her, and although panic did suggest that in the first
instant, reason told her it would be extreme, because unnecessary.
She'd left Michigan a month before Phil, saying her family needed her
in California, which was true. They'd been ultra-discreet. There was
no reason for his wife or anyone to connect the two departures, or to
have connected them over the last five years. It did occur to her that
Margo must have acted on a tip to have gone so far from home, and

precisely there, and that she just might at this juncture put two and two together. However, Penny happened to be with another and much younger man when the meeting occurred and with her clothes off. Leaving out certain inconveniences, that was one piece of luck. Another was that she didn't give a damn who knew what, hadn't since the second night before they left Canada, listening to that speech; the moment of panic was just a throwback to earlier times, way back. *He*'d be getting in trouble one of these days, and she felt sorry for him, but it also amused her to think that that silly little ignorant Mercy Grout would like to share the experience with him.

And perhaps she would have, but she was shortly having to marry her no-good boyfriend instead. She probably wouldn't have been invited to anyway, never having heard of Teilhard de Chardin or for that matter having read any whole book in her life, or given much thought to the race question either. Besides, her family wouldn't have approved.

At the spacious old Retreat in Compton, Leona Horton had not only found a new interest in life but had also decided she was Harriet Beecher Stowe, who might or might not have been one of the more famous early patients there. She was known to have "taken the cure" in that little metropolis, gateway to the Green Mountains and site in her day of some kind of appropriate water long since flushed into the general city supply; for Leona that was enough. Brit, who for his sins went to visit her every week or so with offerings of cookies and jelly and home news, only balked when she introduced the friend she had made there by the same name.

"Harriet, this is my brother, I'm sorry to say. He's a ne'er-do-well, always was. Brit, this is my friend Mrs. Stowe, author of *Uncle Tom's Cabin*. Of course you haven't read it and wouldn't understand it if you did."

"Yeah, I read it, 'bout the same time you did. And if I remember correctly I'm the one told you what it's about. But I thought *you* was Harriet."

Leona drew herself up tall, with a grand little condescending smile. She'd become rather grand in general since she got there, had her white hair tidied up on top instead of straggling all over and was much better dressed than she'd ever bothered to be at home, though still in an ankle-length skirt to hide her bum leg. The place clearly suited her, and indeed was sociable and attractive, with broad lawns speckled with brightly painted iron chairs that it was too chilly to sit long in now but there was a pleasant suggestion about them, and its huge many-gabled frame building of the last century kept in good repair, two rivers in confluence giving a gracious view out back, and a cheerful hum of traffic in front beyond the lawns. It also had a reputation as one of the finest as well as earliest mental institutions in the country but that aspect was better left out of conversation. The maples and oaks were majestic and nobody was cutting them down.

"I *am* Mrs. Stowe. We both are, silly. A case of double identity." Must have been some fool doctor filled her up with that kind of language; he'd never heard anything so fancy from her before.

"Your name's Leona Horton and you darn well know it."

"Oh yes, it was, for a time. And my friend here was Mrs. Sims too, from Parson's Landing." The other Harriet, a robust, bespectacled lady about Leona's age, continually rolling up and unrolling a ball of red yarn, nodded vigorously. "So it's really a case of quadruple identity; two of us, two people each, two times two. You don't think we're born with just one little life apiece to live, do you? That would be too ridiculous."

He allowed as how it might be; he'd have to think it over.

Her new interest, in which her friend seemed to act as a kind of assistant or secretary, had to do with Missing Persons and the Most Wanted, one or two of whom she was fairly sure were masquerading as doctors or attendants right there at the Retreat. The walls of her bed-room cubicle were half pasted over with newspaper photos and stories bearing on such matters, and flyers she must have gotten somebody to request or snitch from the P.O. These last with their convict numbers and crime records she took special relish in. "Did you ever see such an ugly mug? And look at this one! I can't even bring myself to tell you what *he*'s wanted for, you'll have to read for yourself. How would you like to meet a face like *that* in the dark?" She salivated loudly. Among other things she was convinced that she alone had exposed the girl bomber who'd been apprehended at the Compton record store after a search of several years. "They weren't on the right track at all, weren't even warm, but when I told them . . ."

Brit cussed himself for losing patience again but just couldn't help it. "Goddam it, Leona, that was weeks ago and you ain't never been near that store, or Compton either in about ten years. When I used to offer you to come shopping in town here you'd tell me to do it myself."

She gleamed; you'd have thought she was wearing diamonds all of a sudden. "Hah! That's where I fooled you! You and Ellis thought you had me shut away up on that hill all those years . . ."

The other Harriet went into another fit of corroboration, lips pursed in sympathetic outrage. "Same story all over. Same as they did to me. Doing it to us right here too. That sneaky daughter of mine, got her hair colored like a wore-out delphinium, now she's got herself married to that truckdriver it's nothing but lies I hear and she only got to know him a few weeks ago, over her CB radio zipping down the interstate, that's how they met . . ."

"But I had my ways of getting places and seeing things, never fear. And still do, and my lawyer tells me . . ."

"Hush!" put in Harriet Two in alarm.

Leona went conspiratorial. "But you'll get that surprise when you get it. Right now I just want you to know that I have letters here from the FBI thanking me for all I've done for them, all the help I've given . . ."

"Yes, Leona, yes, that's right. Take care." At least she never asked how many more of their trees were gone.

Brit came away from these visits done in and once or twice with a sick headache, so the next time he got Louise to go in his place after she finished at the beauty parlor while he did the bakery shopping for her and took Sam to the vet's. Ellis she refused to see at all, blaming him for her incarceration as well as stealing her share of the family silver.

"Well, how did it go? Any new cases solved?"

"Oh yes." Louise laughed, rather wearily; it upset her too to go there. "And one right close to home"—which cast a shadow briefly, reminding them both of the Long Trail affair and the scare over Brit's "damn pump" later that night. But it had nothing to do with that. The Harriet team were sure they had seen Phil Johnson, under another name, on a morning TV program the day before. Like most people around Boonton, the Hortons were TV regulars from 7 to 10 P.M. but didn't have time for it in the morning, so weren't in a position to say if there'd been any such program—one of those back-look, summing-up things called "Ten Years of Dissent" according to the Harriets. And there right in front of their eyes was that man Leona said she'd suspected from the start, first making a speech (there were just a few seconds of that) on the steps of the Capitol—in Washington, mind you!—and then being hauled off by a whole bunch of cops. The announcer said he was the Reverend John Philipson of Michigan, the well-known activist who'd been killed later in a private plane accident. Leona said she'd soon be getting another letter of thanks from the FBI because she'd written them at once, saying killed my eye, he was living right there in Boonton in a cabin owned by her own brother so she ought to know and had recognized the voice besides and the face too even if he'd had more hair on top and none on his chin at that time.

Brit and Louise laughed, though it was all rather saddening. They actually missed Leona at times for all her quirks and were pretty sure she'd have hung on all right if it hadn't been for that damn road. Still, Ellis was getting some happiness out of the way things were; they had to be glad of that.

"I guess it's good she's got something to occupy her mind. Can't do any harm."

"And a friend, that's nice, one as whacky as the other so that's all right. Why, I can't even remember when Leona ever had a friend she'd be willing to pass the time of day with, except a little bit with Hannah Palz when she got her making those rugs for a while."

This was on their way home. They went on to comment, as they had before, on Hannah's not looking like herself, since that hateful walk in September, or the day after. That was when she'd started cracking up, and now they had to admit the rumor was true, she was drinking; never had before in all the years they'd known her. They could smell it and tell from her eyes and her driving. But this they hated to speak of, even to each other.

"That Johnson, he's a queer one. My God, you'd have thought he wanted to be accused himself . . ."

"I don't know who wouldn't be shook up by that. The whole town is, seems to me, and they didn't have to see it the way you three did." She didn't feel like saying that Brit himself hadn't been quite the same since that day. She'd noticed a new streak, something gloomy and apprehensive in his face and voice now and then, that he wouldn't bark off with one of his old pessimistic jokes. "Anyway they got the real crazy one, right off, that's something. We've just got to remember it had nothing to do with us or Boonton or anybody we'll ever know. If we let every crime in the country get to us we'd all be in there with Leona."

"Yeah. I guess so." He didn't sound convinced, and hadn't the other times they'd had more or less the same conversation. They were both sick to death of the subject and longing to forget it but somehow it came back and back. "*Reverend*, though, by gosh that's a funny coincidence, I mean the way he was yammering scripture that time."

"Well, you told me you weren't far from it yourself. We all took in plenty of Bible talk one time or another, you get a shock like that and it comes back to you. We haven't got much else to fall back on, I guess. Except the family, of course. My, I do hope Joe and Wendy are getting settled all right, maybe there'll be a letter from them when we get back."

Brit hadn't ever quite managed to tell his wife how he valued this kind of talk with her and how much good it did him, the way Ellis did sometimes or getting out alone with his dog. There wasn't really any reason to think Leona's trouble ran in the family, except for maybe their maternal grandmother and she wasn't much more than ordinary ornery, never had to be put away. But he did let himself get fussed up now and then when there was no sense to it, or anyway nothing to be done about whatever it was, like Nelco and their goddam road or all those years as selectman, scrapping and heaving and hauling all the time, always some s.o.b. you had to be fighting about something, until Doc Macklin said get out or be dead, with that pump he had. Now, since that afternoon they'd been talking about and that he'd worked hard to put out of his mind, he'd started listening in a new way to sounds outside at night, not animal noises the way he always had; human ones—footsteps, a cough, somebody hiding out there. Never had been nervous about such things in his life before. And he'd gotten to stewing about Chip Holloway up there alone in that coop of his when he came weekends. If he saw him arrive with a friend or two from college he'd forget about it. Otherwise it would get to be on his mind so, he'd usually go up and check in with him; they'd always visited back and forth a lot so he didn't need to cook up any excuse or say anything to get the boy nervous, such as that his grandmother was stinking rich and everybody knew it and he'd be a good prospect for a kidnapping, just for instance. Of course he knew it was a heap of TV stuff and not just news that had put that in his mind, but he figured it could put it in some less reliable kinds of minds too.

He'd even mentioned that to Louise one time and she'd proposed they get his head examined. He could see the logic of that. Not that she didn't understand that Chip was as good as a son in his feeling, maybe as close to one as he'd ever have even though they had two grandsons who'd be big enough to be company for him before long. Her remark came light and easy, in the middle of a bran muffin recipe, and he'd gone back to figuring for the new cabin he was going to build, for rent or sale, up the hill. He'd made some mistakes when he pushed their kitchen wall out to make room for her new stove, it worked all right but looked tacked on and ugly outside. The new cabin would probably be his last big job and he wanted it to be just right, all over.

That day when they got home from Compton, early in the afternoon, there was quite a pleasant surprise for once. Walt Hodge had stopped by for a chat and had with him, of all people, the woman Brit had driven half dead to the hospital back in September. Couldn't hardly recognize either of them. Walt had on clean clothes and was sober, on the water wagon he quickly announced, and going to Bible meetings! and had a job driving cats at Akatuck—yes, it had been bought up by some kind of west coast grain and aeronautics and newspaper combine and would be running that winter after all; and the widow lady from Michigan wasn't the sick, grey, miserable creature he'd had in the back of his car but spry and pretty in a nice middle-aged way and bubbling with pleasure over the autumn leaves and this and that. She and Louise hit it off so well you'd have thought they were old friends inside of five minutes.

Walt was going to show her something up in what had been the Banks woods, Pace or maybe really Nelco now, and Brit had to warn him he'd find some changes. Louise said to stop by again on their way back down and have a doughnut, they'd be fresh off the stove. Being herself fresh out from the hairdresser's, with the extra-inviting smile that that always produced, it would have taken a stone to say no or maybe. Brit thought it might be just those fluffy white curls that had made him appreciate her so on the way home, and wouldn't that be silly, but it always did affect him and then he always forgot till next time. She'd gotten rather large around the middle, just a comfortable size for her age, and didn't care much about clothes, but wasn't above knowing what she had in that fine-gauge, naturally curly white hair that she'd have to tell him to keep his dirty hands out of, it felt and smelled so nice just under his nostril level, after she'd been to the beauty parlor.

6

There were changes all right. In spite of all the wonders in his new life, Walt had to fight back tears for a minute, but she took his hand and said it was better that way, it had all been a prison and a dream and it was good that it was broken to pieces, and he knew that was true. It seemed Mr. Pace, rumored to have just gotten another divorce and who mainly lived in Massachusetts, was using what was left of the Banks house as an overnight camp, for when he was seeing to company business thereabouts. The big barn across the road had been torn down, so had the sheds with the outhouse at the end that used to make Clara Banks so mad to have to go to especially in winter; so had all the partitions inside, making one single big funny-looking room out of what used to be five, six if you counted the pantry. Another new road, not the same one as by Ellis Horton's, had been started up back and the idiots had dumped a couple of tons of dirt and trash smack on top of the spring so there wasn't even a trickle coming out below and nobody in the world but Walt could have told where it was or ever had been. But that was as far as they'd gone; the place he'd promised to show Margo wouldn't be touched yet.

Although her face didn't show it, she was still a little weak from the operation. He had to help her over deadfall and up some steep places, and he held small branches and brush back for her more than necessary until she objected, laughing. He felt a terrific urge to burst into song at the top of his lungs—"Glory, glory, glory!" was all he could think of, since "Way down upon the Swanee River" and "Red River Valley" didn't seem to suit—but he wanted to keep the woods quiet for her, so choked it down and explained things almost in a whisper: about the moraine and why the ferns grew where they did and where the main entrance to the foxden would be in relation to the one they saw first, and why, and how it happened that the different varieties of fungus would grow on this tree and not that. One benefit from the horrid new clearing below was that at a certain fold of the hill where the growth was thin they could see out much farther than he ever had

115

before, way off over the lake below Waterville and to the range beyond, nearly the western border of the state.

"Well now will you look at that!"

"Yes, I will. I am looking at it."

"You makin' fun o' me again?"

"No, no! I never liked anything more in my life! And why again?
when did I ever?"

He went sheepish, as often with her. "I just thought you might, you
bein' so goldarned advantageous compared to me."

She had learned to understand his language most of the time. "I wish
I'd had some of your advantages, dear heart. Look at all you're showing and teaching me up here. And the stars last night. Why, I'd never
even known which was Arcturus before, that's how underprivileged
I've been."

He passed a finger, marveling, across her cheek, in a touch as light as
with two ferns a few minutes before to show her their different tex-
tures; then turned and led the way on. Strange man; strange wonderful
god-baby, born at fifty, as she was, out of a so different womb and
world. When he had first come to her bed, the third night after his
disgusting arrival at the inn, she would have shrieked in horror but for
fear of being heard in the street. She stifled it down to a gasp, and then,
halted several feet away, in a ragged pair of underpants, he was very
timidly begging her to pray with him. "See, it's so long since I done it,
Margo"—he'd begun calling her that in the hospital—"I just can't
remember how a single one of 'em goes. If you'd get me started . . ."

It was like a sickness suddenly flooding her bones. She turned her
face from him and pressed a wad of sheet to her mouth, holding back
that time a cry against all the years of her life and its misuse of prayer
and mockery of the sacred. At last with great effort she murmered,
"Our Father who art in heaven," feeling the words foul in her mouth.

"Yeah, that's it! and something be thy name. Go on, I'll start gettin'
it, it'll come back to me . . ."

"You'll be drunk again before the week's out. You better stop this
foolishness, and find yourself a place to live too."

"Oh, I ain't denyin' I might get a thirst, and if you was to offer me a
slug right now . . ." He grinned. "But if you and the good Lord between you'll just keep yankin' at my shirttails I might—just *might*,
mind you, get to be satisfied with singin' hymns instead. Hallowed,

that's it! Hallowed be thy name. Used to think it was harrowed when I was a little squirt, it perplexed me for years how you'd do that to a name."

Outside, close by under the window, one of the local Hindu-flavored groups, called Boo-Boo-something, passed on their way home from a meeting, wherever home might be. Walt went over to peek behind the curtains at their robes and scalps glistening in the streetlight. "Bunch o' kids, don't look more'n twenty, any of 'em. Oh well, live 'n' let live, they ain't carryin' guns or cuttin' people up anyway. Hey, there's one been livin' up at the Palz place; I bet Lem and Hannah don't think much o' that, never heard 'em have much patience with screwballs. Now Margo, listen, you lyin' there so quiet 'n' pretty, sweetest thing I ever seen, I know what you're thinkin', 'bout why I come in here. You think all you want 'n' you'll be half right but only half. I ain't a *bad* feller, just never seen the light enough to steer by very long at a time. But I'm speakin' truth now. If you'll help me learn to pray and mean it, not just rattle the words off an' be thinkin' about somethin' else, it might be some good to both of us. If you ask me, you ain't so almighty sure o' yourself either. So what comes after the harrowin'?"

She bent slowly to blow the candle out. "We could start tomorrow, Walt." Her voice was thin and shaky, like a very young girl's of some bygone generation. "Right now you're shivering. Maybe you'd better get in here and keep warm."

She couldn't tell if the little gurgle of response in the dark was meant for a laugh, and if so what degree of pleasure, incredulity or menace it might express. From her readings in pop psych the last few years, as well as in more ponderous works in that field left in the house by her husband, she was aware that the man in her room was the classic type of the sex criminal and she was probably about to be strangled; he'd gotten very down in the mouth and wouldn't answer the one time she'd asked him why he was in the psychiatric ward.

Her eyes adjusting to the light from outside, she saw with vast relief that he hadn't taken a step toward her.

"Free?" Again that hoarse gurgle that must have been, yes, a kind of laugh. "Not even two bits?" In answer she had a vague sense of letting out a little laugh too, or perhaps a censuring "oh!" of the "how could you" school, and then he did take a short step toward her, just one, which left him still at more than arm's length although his arms were abnormally long for the short stocky body. In a different, gentler voice, as in a fit of boyish wonder, he said, "I ain't never done it with my pants off. But I seen in the movies how that's the way they do. Some o' them magazines too, show you pretty near everything; course they cut off at the prick but growin' up on a farm like I did that ain't much to see. Or gettin' it in either. I'll tell you the truth, I felt good and foolish comin' in here like this"—he seemed to be pointing to his underpants. "I ain't never showed myself this near stripped to a lady before. I just didn't want you thinkin' I don't know how folks behave in real society, judgin' by them TV shows anyway." There was such sweet drollery in his voice, he might have been playing up his Vermont twang on pur- pose to amuse her, and this time she really did laugh. "Well, you asked for it. On your mark, get set, go!"

It was the first true love-making of her life, and a goodbye to her handsome, admired husband dead or alive, who had never touched her body with anything but regret and repugnance, often perhaps thinking of the beautiful Althea he had so quixotically thrown over, while she tried never to doubt his high-minded aversion to the needs of the flesh. She'd heard about this business of the body taking flight, going off like a rocket; heard it first from her older married sister who'd been frowned on as the emancipated one in the family and was considered to have died young as the wages of it. Margo had read Masters and Johnson and other such treatises, in the line of research and secretarial assistance to her husband, and one reason she'd been thrilled by the pyramids was that the book didn't once refer to the orgasm; from other literary exposures she knew that the bowel movement would be less trite, as term and as subject. But as those huge, loving hands played in bemusement over her slowly unstiffening body, the current verbiage in the matter slipped from consciousness, along with all other objections. He had heated water on the stove downstairs and had scrubbed him- self hard all over, standing in an old wash-boiler, before coming up; she'd heard that. The rest was astronomy, requiring several hundred years to be verified, and she was amazed at the ease of her translation into it.

As it happened it was just two days later, driving Walt's truck to leave him off early in the morning at his new job at the ski area, and passing a fancy motel's tennis courts, that she knew for certain how wise she'd been not to spend the insurance money. She pulled off to the side of the road to stare a minute, then in answer to Walt's question said, as though rid of a last dull weight on the heart, "I just thought I saw an old friend but I was wrong," and they went on.

Of course she'd heard about New England autumns all her life and seen the pictures, but the reality, up there in the semi-clearing looking over a hundred miles of color, knocked her silly. "Oh, look at that one, look! look!" she kept crying out, as if her operation had been of a very different kind, giving sight after a lifetime of blindness. From their base everywhere in evergreen the golds and reds leaped in cataracts and pinwheels across the dazzling air, to be grabbed at in their flight and won for keeps, never to fade—no, no, dangerous, don't touch! but you laugh as they and you whirl in the wind and you try again, for a single flaming maple, a lone gold leaf knocked from the treasure mountain to dance round your shoe. An old sneaker to be exact, and above that was a pair of very faded jeans found on a closet floor at the inn and which happened to fit more or less; the blouse was her own, the ancient, enormous brown sweater one of Walt's, worn many winters at logging and manure-heaving and all, and for sleeping too, up in the attic they were looking over, where the mattress might still be.

She was so pretty in her delight, with her little sharp nose, so different from his splayed pug one, not sticking out like a dead twig the way it had but just touching up the new rosy fullness of cheeks, and the grey hair blowing up wild and free from a forehead she'd always thought she had to keep covered, with a rat's nest it used to look like, having been told it wasn't high enough for such a thin, pointed face. It was her body that had thinned down now, not so as to be artificial and girlish like pantyhose ads, he wouldn't have liked that at their age, but just right for a nice silky stroke over the hips, by a second party that is, and for the party herself to feel easy without that nasty girdle that had given her a lifesaver of pudge around the top for thirty-odd years. And just right for blowing, more than dancing, among many-colored crystal toys and mountain-tops. Her eyes, rather small and narrow-set, were a dove grey, with a curious faculty of seeming to grow physically wider as they deepened in luminosity. He had remarked on that, as his own pale blue ones did nothing of the sort as far as he knew, and besides he had never had reason to examine anybody's pupils that closely before.

Nor had he ever taken a child to an amusement park, nor been a child in one himself but that was less pertinent just now, he for his equivalent delight being in the role of guide and grown-up. What a jump that was!—as giddy as hers the other way. He, Walt Hodge, eternal boy, underling, taker of orders, Walt do this Walt do that and mind you do A before B or you'll get a piece of my mind, so trained to it he'd get in a blue funk and fall into the absolute necessity of getting drunk if he had to figure out A and B for himself—well, you know what he'd done a couple of days before? so that's aside from taking the sole and whole responsibility for her safety and happiness up in these woods where she didn't have a trace of any alphabet in her noggin whatsoever and it was all the palm of his hand to him. He'd paid for their groceries, for the two of them, that's what. Yes sir, out of his first paycheck since it all happened. So you see, he hadn't got drunk and been fired after two days the way he'd been from two town roadgang jobs before that time under the mattress, at least to the best of his recollection; must have gone something like that. No, stayed sober all week and got the check and what's more bought the biggest juiciest sirloin steak in the market, after a week of beans and pancakes on what she got from the fool agent for looking after the inn; lucky he'd still had a few gallons of Banks syrup in the back of his truck, the widow Clara's whole parting beneficence to him, so it was time to get something over their ribs and some celebration too. Scared her to death, the cost of that steak did, she was so churchmouse parsimonious, even if her insurance did cover most of the hospital business. He'd noticed that in people before; they get used to pinching pennies, you can't blast it out of them, no matter what they come into. She'd loosened up in bed a lot sooner than that way. So he just jumped into manhood, as you might say, over a hunk of meat; said he was getting it and paying for it and she could like it or lump it, he beaming like a nut from the extraordinary sensation of not only having made such a decision entirely on his own but having imposed it on somebody else besides, and in the end she didn't lump it, not a bit. She smacked her lips and loved every bite; said she hadn't had steak of any kind since she couldn't remember when and never one as good as that; and she'd cooked up some fine greens and cheese biscuits to go with it. He hadn't had the nerve to say so but it felt like a wedding feast, with just the two of them. To hell with her dead husband; good riddance was all he was going to bother to think about him, never mind what he'd been or done or looked like; he hadn't been any good for her, that was plain and enough for him.

She'd never seen a deer before outside a zoo—this was a little before the boulders they were heading for; what in God's name *had* she ever seen? so as often as she yelled "Look! look!" at what you'd have thought from her expression were auks or at least elephants, he was asking that, though it certainly was a treat and he knew it to be in such a position of superiority. "Godamighty, where you been livin' all your life?" Catching sight once more of the roof now tiny, far below, over that attic, it occurred to him that a person might die of happiness, it felt like such an explosion, as easily as the opposite way, but then he put his arm around her, walking on an easy stretch, through the fern garden as he'd named it long ago, and thought he was probably going to bear up under it. At five seven he had three inches up on her so his powerful hand, used to gripping such hard heavy things, could comfortably cup her little shoulderbone, treating it like a fresh egg. He did have a hankering to pray, then and a couple of other times that afternoon, but something told him she wasn't in the mood for that. He figured it was the air, her not being used to it, and she said so herself, that the way it went from your lungs to your head must be like getting drunk. He said, "I wouldn't know about nuthin' as lowdown as that."

So amid sky-high balloons crimson, saffron and burgundy, and painted horses galloping every which way in a tinkle of sunlight, to rejoin their proper rhythm and round eventually if they felt like it, and clashing musics and glad barks of invitation from all sides, they came to the first boulder, and very suddenly sobering it was.

"See what I told you? You ever seen anything like that in your born days?"

Of course she hadn't, nothing anywhere near like it, and her upturned widening eyes took on a deeper grey, as though absorbing the very substance of the rock with all its immense, quiet history, along with a story far from quiet—when? oh, when? she must get Walt to tell it again—of unimaginable grind, crack, splinter and terrible transformation. If it had been a giant it would have been the tip of his boot she touched, with the highest reach of her hands, and she'd have done it as gingerly, the great shape being apparently balanced on a pinhead, held up on their side for the moment by a decaying little chunk of fallen birch. Walt whacked it with all his might, grinning at her trepidation. "It's been teeterin' like that for about five thousand years. I guess it ain't gonna pick today to come down just to spite *us*. It don't even know we're here, that's what always gets me. If it did and had good sense it sure would have picked Jim Pace to come down on, that time I had to show him around up here."

He had kept his voice very low, anxious not to scare off any wildlife there might be, but it caused a scramble of some kind over the other side of a second boulder, the one nearest to the ledge he had told her about, and this time it was no doe. Didn't sound quite right for a bear either, but it could be, so he kept her behind him as they moved cautiously through the tangle of underbrush, giving the young couple there time to get up and pull their pants part way on.

Walt coughed theatrically and acted nearsighted till the zippers were up.

"Hiya, Chip, I see you found your way back," and as the boy seemed unable to speak: "Nice weather we're havin', ain't it? How's college treatin' you, all right? Oh yes, I forgot, this here's Mrs. Philipson, from Michigan, wanted to see the fo-lidge so I said I'd show her some. Ever see so many cars as down on that road this weekend? Godamighty!" He waved toward where the hum would be, a mile below the old farmhouse that hadn't even been visible the last twenty minutes. "Couple o' million nuts gettin' out movin' around just to be movin', whether they see anythin' when they get there or not . . ."

By this time a certain composure had been attained, though Chip was biting his lower lip and still looked rather sick to his stomach.

"Margo! what on earth . . . But how wonderful to see you again!" Penny stepped forward holding out both hands but stopped short of a kiss. "I was so terribly sorry to hear about your husband's death. And then I don't know when, somebody sent me a clipping about that lovely service for him . . ." Her voice trailed away. Walt had a hunch that Chip was thinking about the doe they'd seen together, standing exactly where he was by the cliff before her grand leap out over the dead balsam that was still there.

"I've often thought about you too, Penny," Margo was saying, while noting that the boy was a good nine or ten years younger than she and not looking very pleased about any aspect of the situation; he had sidled dangerously close to the drop, his gaze moving intently, as

though following the progress of a wounded ant and sharing its hope-
lessness, up the forbidding rock face. No, even allowing for youthful
embarrassment, this was a young man hooked, not enraptured. "Yes, of
course it was a bad time. But that's over and past now. Well, I'm glad
to see you looking so well. You're living here now, are you?"

"I always said college'd be the ruin o' you," Walt grumbled at Chip,
not caring who heard.

"Not really," Penny shrieked, with a smile off its hinges and eyes
going wildly from one side of Margo's head to the other, the strain only
then fully catching up with her, because it had only then dawned on
her that what she wanted more than anything, even more than the
adoration of her young Greek god just then, was to have a heart to
heart with this good, kind, motherly woman whom she had so bitterly
wronged but that part of it scarcely figured in the girl's sudden yearning: for such generous female counsel as only Margo, in all her acquaintance, had ever unsparingly given her. "I'm just visiting for a few
days, you know I went back to California and that's where I mostly
live. But if you're going to be around I'd so love to come and see you.
Could I? Where are you staying? Could I phone you tomorrow?"

"She ain't got a phone," Walt said. "And she ain't got time for
tramps either." He knew she was the Johnson fellow's wife or passing
for that; he'd seen them go by when he stopped over there the day he
left the hospital, and Brit and Louise told him. "Come on, Margo. Now
our day's gone and got spoiled on us we might as well git on down and
join the folidge traffic."

Instead of retracing their way up, he led her down a more precipi-
tous grade that brought them around under the ledge. The two
women, one still up above where they'd left her, screamed at the same
instant, and even Walt hollered, "Stop, you damn fool!" but the figure
was already in the air, soaring out over the dead branches exactly as
the doe had that other time. "No, no," Margo was gasping as he landed
by them, not running like the deer, not on his feet except possibly for
a split second before whirling into a triple somersault, pressing a scar
across the underbrush.

They couldn't believe it. He wasn't hurt at all that they could see,
except for some scratches, but just got up as if it had been the sensible
way to catch up with them, to say what he felt the need to. He was
smiling piteously, and looked so handsome in his wretchedness, with

his bronze-tinged curls tumbling around features that had kept some
enchanted boyhood in confluence with manliness, Margo was sadly
reminded of her own son. He too, taking after his father in stature and
extraordinary good looks, had retained some such angelic infusion in
his growing-up, until the year of that father's disappearance.

"You're still my friend, aren't you, Walt?" the boy was pleading. "I'd
feel awful if you weren't. You can't still be mad at Brit and me for, for,
you know . . ." Tongue-tied, looking closer to eight than eighteen years
old, he made a little gesture that seemed to take in Margo and Walt's
obvious present health and happiness and the fact that it was, after all,
a perfectly beautiful October day that nothing should be allowed to
mar.

"Just a runty little cunt-hunter you are. You make me sick. Couldn't
you at least find a decent one your own age?" Walt turned and pulled
Margo brusquely away.

"You didn't need to be quite so hard on him. He's so young, and
after all . . ."

But he went on grumbling most of the way back down to the road.
He'd never had the time to spend with Chip that Brit Horton had,
going back about fifteen years, so it wasn't that close. Still, in Walt's
limited circle of attachments, including a few specific dogs and cows, it
was close enough, and it really did hurt him to see the boy throwing
himself away like that: on a pile of dirt was the way he put it.

However, he cheered up at the doughnut stop, back in the Horton
kitchen as per invitation; that last, the invitation, was in itself enough of
a rarity to snap anybody around. Being invited wasn't the way you
went to a house, in his experience or the Bankses' or anybody else's he
knew about; the rule was just to get out and leave people in peace for
their dinner at noon and supper at five. So of course he wasn't going to
spoil the party and Margo's having such a nice chatty womanish time
with Louise—he could see she'd been missing that—or Brit's load of
new stories such as he never seemed to go a day without picking up
somehow: about the goddam new road and also a crowd of developers
from all over who never even heard of the Green Mountains before

probably, a batch of Connecticut dentists and psychiatrists for one bunch, trying to muscle in on Jim Pace's act so he might be getting some of his own medicine if he didn't watch out—Walt wasn't going to upset all that cheerful sociability, even if he'd had a chance to, by telling them about Chip and that hussy. He wouldn't have felt right describing a scene like that in front of Louise anyhow. So what with all the stories and him feeling shy at the same time as he was close to busting with pride to be showing off Margo and letting it be understood that she favored him—him! Walt Nobody, Ned Banks's poor relation!—and one thing and another, he didn't think of it again until they were all four outside saying goodbye and making bets on tomorrow's weather from the look of the sunset.

In the middle of that they had to move over to make room for the Johnson man, beard and all and a tennis racket on the front seat beside him, to turn his car in there on his way up to the cabin. Then Walt really wanted to give a horse whistle, but didn't.

Margo, speaking to Louise by the door, had her back to the road when Johnson stopped; he had some little plumbing problem to ask Brit about, and had just begun on it when she turned around. The plumbing problem broke off there and never did get any farther.

"I guess you people ain't met," Brit said. "This is Mr. Johnson, living in our cabin up the hill here. And this is Walt's friend Margo, what was it?"

"Philipson," Louise quickly put in, with a laugh at his bad manners and memory.

"Mrs. Philipson. From Michigan. I remember that part all right. I'm the one had to check her in at the hospital last month, so far gone she couldn't hardly whisper, had to tell it in my ear, name and address and all, so I could tell that fool clerk. Nearly let her die then and there, just to get the damn sheet of paper filled out. And now look at her."

"Fit as a fiddle," Louise said, as pleased as if she'd helped get her to the hospital too and it was a star and a very nice one in both their crowns.

"Well . . ." Walt started for the truck.

"You hang in on that job, Walt. Ain't many going begging right now."

"Don't worry. And I'll get you to a meetin' one o' these Sundays, you see if I don't."

"Like hell you will. I been in and out o' that stuff before you were born."

Margo and her husband meanwhile, standing a few feet apart, were locked in silent and ghastly communication, which none of the others seemed to notice. It broke off with her saying, as in sudden distress at seeing the sun was down, that they'd better hurry, she had to be in a rehearsal. Yes, she was going to act in a play, an awful one so please nobody come; the man everybody called Cheezit, the restaurant man, had gotten up a group in Waterville and found out she used to like amateur theatricals and he'd been good to her one time so it was hard to refuse.

Only well on the way home, home in a manner of speaking, Walt said, "That's the feller you stopped to look at at the tennis place that day and said you thought it was somebody you knew but it wasn't. Looked tonight like it was, the way you was starin' at each other. The poor cluck, with that wife half his age two-timin' him up there with a kid ain't hardly dry behind the ears. That's who she was—your old friend; the little dirty dealer. She's that Johnson's wife, legal or not. So it looks like you knew the both of them some time or other." He sounded about to burst into tears—at her lying to him; he just didn't see how she could, it was horrible, made him want to whip around and get right back up there under that mattress. But when she put her hand on his knee and smiled at him he knew it was all right, just absolutely wonderfully all right. The stormcloud raced away; it had been a grand afternoon. She'd had some reason to lie and he didn't even want to bother to know what the reason was or was about because it didn't amount to a row of pins. If you laid a row of pins from there to Canada it wouldn't amount to the way she smiled at him.

"Walt, tell me something, honestly. Do you think I could learn to ski, at my age?"

Dimpling, he said she'd better go to prayer meeting, not make an excuse to stay away like last time, and ask the good Lord's advice about a serious question like that.

And Louise at supper was exclaiming, "Michigan! That's funny, I didn't think of it before. Her being from there and then just now Leona's story about Johnson. She said Michigan too. Okay, I'll get my head examined. Let's just get sports tonight, news is nothing but bad anyway, all those murders and earthquakes and everything, I'm sick of it. But didn't you notice how they were looking at each other? Oh, you men, you never notice anything. You can't tell *me* they never met before."

As a football huddle came on, Brit said, "How 'bout that. Walt no more'n back from the dead and latches onto a nice dame like that. Wonders never cease."

"You can say that again."

Foliage traffic moves along and along, a million cars, campers, trailers, whatever. Can't just sit on your ass all the time, got to go somewhere, do something, see something, Disneyland's too far. Motels jampacked, the one open disco blazing and roaring half the night, that's nice. Also plenty of longtime senior citizens with somebody to drive them, the one thing to look forward to, some crabby with toothache or bellyache or mislaid their teeth and had belly surgically removed, or just naturally crabby, it's a way of making your presence felt, isn't it? Others okay, pack up their troubles, really do enjoy those autumn leaves, also have reservations maybe made a year ahead and that's nice too. The couple from Philadelphia or Baltimore or wherever shriek, "Foliage! where's the goddam foliage, came all this way . . ." Same every year. Too late, mister. Too late or too early, something always wrong, this dumb state, lousy food, terrible beds. No, lovely eats, delightful accommodations and did you hear what they call the proprietor? Cheezit! Ha ha ha. Bang bang on Green Mountain House door. Let us in, no place to stay, yeah it says closed but we got our rights too, get all these people up here for your fucking foliage and won't give 'em a bed. You get offa that porch or I'll blow your bloomin' head off; a man's voice that time and by God he means it, that's a gun he's got sticking out of that upstairs window. Find a farmhouse. Sleep in the car.

Blow along, travelers, keep blowing, and now it's the wind and the rain blowing and the foliage is washing down the street gutters, and on all the quiet miles of wooded hills around makes the annual luscious brown wet muck for living roots and animals to revel in, and here and there an extra-stubborn leaf, already brown, nothing to drive from anywhere for, tugs and blows and at last falls like an unpaid bill, disreputably, in the dark.

Also unseen, unhonored and insentient or nearly, though statistically in the prime of life, the four in the stolen car from wherever out of state their chicks and ponies are parked, cruise in angry torpor, supplies and patience about out, no bread even for a hick disco and who wants it anyway. If they could get their hands on that bigmouth fossil Mercy Grout they could find their way around and get on to something. Three are fed up with Jeff and the big deal that's been riding him since he saw that phoney churchrat he's got it in for, big stuff, sure thing, oh sure so let's see it. His authority is slipping, leadership is passing over to the one who talks bigger, when in condition to talk, about banks and kidnappings, or hijackings—they give him a hard-on; something worth the trouble, and then buzz the hell back to L.A. or Tiajuana where the action is, on civilized six-lane highways and wheels that understand you, out of this four-door coffin and these ghoststory woods. But Jeff swears he knows what he's doing and it can't miss, just one more try, he's got the goods on old sloplip and his phoney plane crash, it would just be easier if that funkcunt Mercy hadn't skidded out on them, you can get lost on these back roads. That piece, never left home before looked like, the squawk she made when the rest of them got their crack at her, had to give her the needle first, thought she was getting just Jeff who as a matter of fact was too strung out to even want it that week. That was funny. Nothing much else to laugh at except that judge being so kind-hearted. Better give up for tonight, in this rain, get over the New Hampshire line and try again. Only one more time though, Jeff better pull it off or he's through. He'll pull it off if it kills him and doesn't care if it does, he's got this one ambition burning him so; they got to stick together on each other's enemies don't they? That's the pledge, and this one's bugged him in his dreams for years, it was like a bag of horse falling out of the sky running into him like that when he was supposed to be dead.

But just a minute, some kind of barn dance going on, might as well look in, you never can tell. Square dance, all bouncing and twisting like a bunch of frogs with their brains cut out; must be forty cars out there. No, hold it, fuzz inside with a gun; that's right, Mercy said they always came to the dances just in case, and this just happens to be their old friend from after the store job that would have been worth about two jars of pickles anyway, another of Jeff's bright ideas, probably thought he'd find the shmuck there again. Well, look in the window a minute while somebody cases the cars, see if Mercy's there, or even old choke-collar himself. The guy up front is yelling into his loudspeaker, "All join hands and circle south, with a little bit of moonshine in your mouth . . ." Side-splitting; tell me another like that and I'll crack up.

Another car that nearly went off the road on a curve on the wet leaves is a maroon Caddy convertible with just the driver in it, on his way to a certain joint in Atlantic City. He can make it if he steps on it, once you hit the interstate you're all right and he can't face a weekend in this wilderness even if he as good as owns most of it. Just keep going is his motto; age forty-six, third divorce, third goldmine; he'll keep going, that night and the rest of his life because he knows his own mind and how to get what he wants, two basic principles you've got to be born with and he was. If obstacles choose to get out of his way pleas-antly that's fine, he can be very amiable and prefers it that way, but if not there are other ways. He has that night just put the finishing touch on one such procedure, concerning a small piece of forest land block-ing progress on the new road over the mountain; question of right of way; he's dealt with plenty like that; he got it.

Now feels a quirkish desire to see some admiring faces turned his way, so drops in at the square dance, just to greet old friends and neighbors before hitting the road. The little Banks house suits him all right when he has late business and just goes there to turn in and roll out again in the morning, or if he has a curvaceous companion; not alone on a Saturday night. And then in one of the squares he sees the new girl in his Waterville office, Penny Johnson, whom he's tried to make a little time with once or twice. Would succeed eventually if he kept at it; mightn't be worth it but those bumpers she's got out front are quite inspiring, in the office and a lot more so jiggling around with no bra in that dance. Hair dark brown, long and loose, he likes that; good and tall, 5'10", waist about 28"; nose a little too big, teeth not so good; eyes (brown) and smile quite flashy just now, hadn't seen her that lit up before. Everybody knows him; nice sensation; pays his seventy-five cents admission, with a lot of smiles and hellos and a joke or two about a country boy like him of course knowing the figures. He hap-pens to own the barn and a hundred acres around it so could have saved the six bits and feels warm and rosy about paying it; that kind of thing makes for good public relations. "Swing her high, and swing her low, swing the gal in calico . . ." Always liked that one, it's catchy, brings back sweet memories, he's not sure of what.

Waves at the caller, shakes hands with the cop. Some dancers make significant faces, "Look who's come in!" He's a regular barometer for all that, never misses an eyebrow. That's part of the secret of his success, along with imposing height and stride and air of authority. He's kept his waistline in shape too, with all the tramping he prefers not to delegate. Altogether such a fine figure of a man and with such readiness to please and be pleased, even his opponents tend to forget how a camera would make him look; beetle eyes, prizefighter's nose almost though he was never in that kind of ring—cash is his gloves he'll say in private—and sledgehammer jaw. Charming, practically everybody says so, he can charm the pants off you.

Even Brit Horton says so and has for years, with his own special intonation, which figures now in answer to Pace's hearty greeting just inside the door. He had to accept the handshake but didn't linger over it, although it rather touched him at times to see in this swollen entrepreneur traces of the poor, bright-witted and then desperately hardworking boy, with a job at minimal pay in a mill he had to bike twelve miles to and a sick mother and younger sisters to help support, who'd been so proud of the fourteen dollars he'd worked extra to save up so he could go on that fishing trip to Canada and get to know where his father came from. You can't stop a man getting rich if he's smart enough to do it, that's his right, Brit used to argue with his wife; it's just the methods sometimes you have to quarrel with.

"I didn't know you danced, Brit."

"I don't. That's why I'm standing here. Louise likes it. Had to bring her and the grandchildren."

"Quite a night out there, isn't it?"

"Yup. Making quite a mess o' your road too, that's one thing to say for it. Might turn into just a logging road after all if this keeps up, like you was claiming before you thought of a better idea. How many other logging roads you got started lately?"

Pace laughed good-humoredly and gave him a clap on the back, as the round ended and several of his cohorts and hirelings gathered around, amazed and delighted at his coming to such a local affair. Mercy Grout was far away but her sister Natty and husband Ray were there and came over to join the well-wishers, while their aunt-in-law Louise Horton, the best square dancer in town and having a wonderful time until then, huffed and scowled and bristled at the far end of the floor. "Look at them all! Wait till they get their tax bills next year and start paying for *his* road, to *his* developments! He's got this town so in debt already they had to cut out half the school buses, my daughter had to buy a second car to get the children to school . . ." Outrage so filled her, her little grandson had to pull her out to be his partner in "Buffalo Gals," the one they always had the best time in. Except when Dosie Willett felt like working the accordion it was all from records but the caller, an old hand, was as much with it as if he'd had a real live fiddler up there beside him.

Penny was in their set, learning fast, after having to laugh at her wrong turns, wrong hand out, wrong everything earlier when she didn't know what allemande or do-si-do or even grand right and left meant. But a couple of the retired-rich kind of new inhabitants, the man actually a selectman that year, were messing up the adjacent eight even worse. Johnson hadn't come, as was noted through the streaming window. Chip Holloway had pulled out this round and gone over to the refreshment table for a coke and a chat with Brit. Louise danced now with a heavy heart and the little boy objected, "Come on, Gramma, you're supposed to smile, you swung me a lot harder last time."

The sight of that man Jim Pace set off such rotten feelings, at home she and Brit couldn't even speak of them any more, or if he did she would brush it away, saying, "Oh, they'll run out of money, you'll see," the way she used to say "It won't come in our lifetime." All day for three weeks they'd heard the trees fall, the machines coming closer. They loved their quiet land, it was their life, they were too old to start over. They wouldn't know how to live in a Nelco kind of countryside. Why, it was going to put them on easy street, he'd told them a while ago; look what their land would be worth! He was doing everybody in town a big favor the way he saw it, beginning with himself but that was only natural. "Sure, I'm a capitalist and proud of it, I'm in it for number one, that's me and the rest of the company, but look here . . ." What she saw when the looking was forced on her, as now by the sight of him spoiling their dance—he could at least stay away from that!— was a black hole. It was the beginning of the end of life, for Brit too who'd been so moody lately and just yesterday said something not like him at all. When she asked what he'd been staring at out the window instead of sitting down to dinner, he said, "A man's got to try and make sense of things before he dies." She said she'd never known anybody who made that kind of sense all on their own, and probably that's why they went to church and let somebody else take care of it. Then they'd started wondering if they should move, themselves, to the woodlot, change the plans for the new cabin a little, build it there and sell the old place; it would be hard, after so long, but it was beautiful land, with the finest daisies you ever saw around the old cellar-hole, and there'd be room for both them and their daughter's family to live the way they wanted to and not have to keep a dog tied up all the time for fear of traffic.

Right now she just felt—well, she wasn't going to think any such word as murderous, not ever again, and she couldn't help laughing with everybody else at the face Rollie Grout made, one of Mercy's drinking uncles, when he stumbled; it was in the song with the moon-shine line that he was apt to play for the big guffaws if sufficiently upright, or compost mantis as the summer-resident professor would say. They were all still half smiling at the end of the promenade—"you know where, and I don't care, take your honey to a soft armchair," not that there were any such in the barn—as Jim Pace approached, to say hello to her of course, something he would never neglect, but mainly to have a word with Penny Johnson, perhaps on business though it didn't look it. It had just occurred to him that she might be married or otherwise tied up, he had no idea, but it wouldn't matter, or might rather add spice to the procedure; he'd handled that sort of thing plenty of times before too. However, she wasn't about to drive off to Atlantic City with him then and there, in spite of that glimmering smile, and he hadn't really expected or even much wanted it. Give her time, give her time; meanwhile he had other fish to fry.

At the door he had a strong impulse to tell Brit about his latest stroke of good fortune on the business front, one the old man wasn't going to like but it would sweeten it to be aboveboard and humorous, with a nice friendly "Sorry, old feller, but that's the way it is." But Brit was deep in talk with the Holloway boy, they'd have their friendly scene some other time, and then as he reached for his coat he found himself yanked instead into the nearest set, where they were short a man because Dosie Willett had been persuaded to go up beside the caller and do a rowdy number of his own, called "Backhoe Bash," on the accordion.

It was a good fast one, always a hit, and he really could make that squeeze-box rattle the rafters so the caller, who knew all Dosie's words and maybe had helped with some, the composer not being too bright that way, had to yell over it into his mike. Jim Pace's partner was an old schoolmate of his, the plumber's wife, two hundred pounds of vivacity and as dainty on her feet almost as Louise Horton. He demurred, felt asinine, said he hadn't done it since he was about fourteen, but he was caught and in a minute was throwing himself into it with both grace and unaccustomed glee. He'd forgotten how good he used to be and how he'd loved it long ago. "Well will you look at that, pretty neat too, never thought we'd see *him* out there."

The song had been inspired by a backhoe ride the road commissioner and his wife and some friends and relatives had taken one time when they were all half soused after a party and didn't know anybody with a sleigh or horses any more.

"Pile on the backhoe, one an' all, goin' ridin', bump bump bump"— rapid hip grind there and Jim Pace got it, wasn't missing a beat— "honor twice and smile so sweet. Take your corner"—lady on his left, he remembered that much—"round that curve, back to your own and help her swerve"—here he bent his voluminous honey over backwards nearly double but they were in on the whickety-whack right on time, which the other six in their square were too busy to admire but it made a hit on the sidelines. "Now circle all in the backhoe bash. Bump noses"—mighty screech from the accordion—"bump knees, bash your fannies all you please. All in a bunch now, bad grade ahead, hug your sweeties or you'll both be dead. Right hand out, now in, left hand out and go in a spin . . ." But at the promenade instead of hitting top pitch the accordion went strangely dim, and Dosie then clipped it shut and came back down, not to dance any more either; usually there were two more verses and a repeat. One rumor was that he and his wife were splitting up; another, that he hadn't been feeling so good lately and she wanted him to see the doctor; a third, that he'd been out of sorts since he learned it was the runaway crazy murderer he'd had a tiff with that day on the Crump Job when his grader was blocking the road, and he kept a gun now in his cab; he'd meant to get that word "dead" out of the song but couldn't think of another rhyme.

But most people were still glad-eyed, including Jim Pace who really wasn't that eager to drive all the way to Atlantic City any more but would anyway and better get a move on; hadn't had such a good time in a coon's age; it gave him a funny feeling, like mislaying an important document and then finding it didn't matter except you might be wrong and it did. Jelly he felt like, apple jelly, sweet and soft, perfumed with a hodgepodge of memories of life on the tree and destinations unknown.

The watchers from outside were among those who took it all in. That was Pace all right, no mistake about that, and Jeff made a good guess about the girl he'd given the come-on to and another about the kid with the rich grandmother that Mercy had gone on about, saying how goodlooking he was but too kind of off in his own thoughts for her: stayed up in that lonesome shack all by himself for days at a time, she said, and she didn't go for that; Jeff was dreamy too but look how sociable he was, never by himself for a minute, and oh that bike! That was her first day with them, before the rough stuff. The best-looking man there was the great big one who played the whadda you call it, but he seemed to have a wife with him and was too old to have a grandma. Probably wasn't there; or maybe it was that one with the coke, over by the table. Never mind, they wouldn't need to know. Get going now; fuzz looking at the window; somebody must have noticed.

Somebody had. Dosie's wife and Brit had remarked at the same moment on the not very jolly-looking faces at the window, so the young deputy from the sheriff's office decided to stroll around outside. But all he found was some local brats playing a joke on their parents through a window on the other side, and two or three cars leaving early. He was worn out anyway with all the traffic work the last couple of weeks, on top of the usual troubles, and now pretty soon it would be hunting season. He liked to hunt some himself but was not looking forward to that, from the law and order point of view.

"I'm just in freshman astronomy and just a few weeks into that," Chip was saying to Brit and the black-bearded Hebrew scholar, the one genuine Ph.D. around, who'd been living with wife and child in a cabin for several years. "Of course everybody's going on about black holes and the big bang theory now, I guess they have it in kindergarten.

One bigshot I read about is saying the big bang doesn't work out mathematically. As I understand it, that would be like a balloon with specks all over it blowing up, so the specks all fly out away from each other. But apparently then they'd all be homogeneous and he says they're not; I don't know if anybody else agrees with him. Everything's flying apart all right, only the number of galaxies is about ten to the fourteenth power, the ones we know anything about . . ." The caller was summoning everybody for the big circle in "Shoo Fly," the last dance. Penny came over and wanted him to join but he shook his head, not paying much attention. "Seems the probability of life somewhere out there is enormous, about a billion to one is one guess. Of course we'll never communicate with it, the sci-fi stuff is for morons . . ." The scholar, in red flannel shirt, agreed in enthusiastic despair: hopeless, like most of what passes for civilization in our century. "For one thing we're coming into another ice age pretty soon, probably about ten thousand years they say . . ." Brit said he didn't think he'd wait. The bearded one with a sudden look of pain, as though just then stabbed in the groin, beat his brow with both fists and cried out that he couldn't stand thinking about all that out there, it just threw him completely, when he looked at the stars he wanted it to be nothing but a painting.

A new burst of laughter came from across the floor where somebody had fallen down. Louise, with the enemy gone, was bouncing and merry again, only a little out of breath, not bad for sixty-seven. Chip said he wished he could go farther in astronomy but didn't have a head for that kind of math; maybe geology; except he was getting bitten by French literature that year too. Earlier he'd told Brit the rumor was true, his grandmother was going to sell the place there; she'd lost practically everything in a series of theatrical flops and had hardly spent any time in Vermont for several years anyway, besides she didn't want to be on the kind of road they were putting through now. He was going back to college straight from the barn, didn't mind the rain, maybe Brit would drive Penny home?

A soggy maple leaf blew against one of the dark windows and stuck there the rest of the night. Who knows what yearnings may subsist in a dead leaf, or a star? Well, two or three of the latter-day immigrants in the vicinity thought they knew; they had recently gotten into such things, heard vegetables crying out in pain and were in communication with other worlds and centuries. Thefts were reported from three cars outside the barn dance that night.

7

That's not my name. I'm Phil Johnson. What do you want? I never saw you before.

Over and over the words had been spoken in dream, sleeping or waking the same, only lately with so many evenings to spend alone in the cabin among newly heard sounds of the woods and the few books he had managed to acquire, the dream tended more and more to slide over into triumphant resurgence, nay, more—but watch it, that's rhetoric, even Grandad the Bishop dropped that toward the end. Make it simply "or rather"; yes that's better—or rather a whole new aura, power, authority (which?) in the healing profession that he was born to and had never, never in his heart betrayed. Healing or helping? Must decide. Many more crook healers around than there were five years ago, don't want to get confused with that kind of charlatanism; on the other hand "helping" has become rather pompous, has it not? as well as also smacking of neurosis, not as extreme as the other but still, there's something offensive in the sound of "the helping professions." Makes for distrust; the people who speak of themselves that way, especially women, are bound to have something wrong with them. "He who helps," however, sounds quite pleasant, though obviously too modest for his case.

Don't underrate yourself, you who have so much to give. Picked that up in postgrad psychology course and what a useful aid it had often been—he had six balked suicides to his credit, five he was sure of—and how appropriate now. Yes, speak rather of "guidance"; dignified, unpretentious; used as job title by a multitude of fools and incompetents but never mind, on the better mousetrap theory it will do very nicely. "The world will beat a track to his door." How he had always loved that sentence, even as a little boy, and now, after five years of its being somewhat obfuscated, it came back to him with such freshness, he could half fancy a waiting line out there in the dark all the way down to the Hortons': of people in desperate need of his counseling, as that poor child Mercy Grout had been.

To whom else could she have told that sordid tale of her adventure

139

and escape, terror, self-loathing?—horrible really, and really what put him on his feet again, started it anyway. The sleeper awakened; and oh the refreshment of knowing oneself so needed and so good at it. Surely in entering her poor abused body, brief and unpremeditated as the act had been—but the truest words and gestures of divine therapy are always so, are they not?—he had made the healing wisdom incarnate, therefore viable for so crude a mind; comparable in short to our Lord's use of bread and wine. Not that it would be advisable to go quite so far about it every time; indeed in that instance it might be called an accident, so at least semi-human.

My name is John, I mean Phil Johnson, what do you want, I never saw you before. There's been some terrible misunderstanding, go away, go away. I wasn't a bomber pilot, I never flew a plane in my life, I'm a holy man and a pacifist. Buzz buzz buzz. What was that? Just the Boston to Albany, same time every night. The dark night of the soul; another old favorite; make a note of it. Many excellent ideas for sermons swarming in just now. The camel going through the needle's eye: never mind new translations, they take all the beauty out of it. I am the camel and in all humility I know that any day now, even tomorrow perhaps or next day, the tiny aperture will show itself and the miracle will occur for him who through error and suffering has become worthy, i.e. myself. True, Jesus said the rich man couldn't, not the good man could, get through; better think it over, adaptation possibly too baroque.

"That's not my name. I'm Phil Johnson. What do you want? I never saw you before."

It must be the dream, but is not. Perhaps if he says it again it will turn out to be after all. Instead there rips before his eyes, fast as a squadron of enemy fighters, the never-ending succession of more and more expensive *things* that were this boy's whole spiritual sustenance from babyhood. It was Friday, and lunch hour at the sawmill. The black sedan didn't come all the way up but stopped just by the turnoff from the main road. Old Cobb Grout, owner and boss, had come into the shed a few minutes before, even more irascible than usual and that was going some. "They're asking for *you*." Hands shaking; stop that; quick, get the saw turned off so you can hear him and not lose an arm. "What did you say?" he yells, then gets to the switch, so the roller thirty feet up the carriage to his right and the young man filling in that day as cutter, up the other way, stop their machines too. A final log rumbles down the roller's ramp and comes close to spinning off out the open side of the shed beyond. It had turned cold that week, they were all in their lumber jackets though not with longjohns yet; you'd think there could be some way of closing in the shed in winter. Through the other opening at the cutter's end, and through the light smoke from the slab fire, he could make out the two figures in the car. "What in blazes do they want *you* for? They're the ones ran off with my granddaughter and held up the store the week before . . ." The two outside men, on the truck and forklift, were out of it but the three others were hanging in, gaping, stopped half way to a lunchpail in one case and to cars for those who lived near enough to go home to lunch. The usually welcome quiet, with saws, conveyors, sawdust blower, everything stopped, was like a signal of doom. The old man had come through one stroke a year ago and looked about to have a worse one.

"Ah . . . that must be it. Yes, you're right. I saw them one evening before all that, at the store. They must be after Mercy again. Must think somebody here could tell them where she is."

"You go find out," Cobb Grout raged, "and I'm callin' the sheriff."

"Look, Cobb . . ." He wiped the sweat and sawdust from his face with the back of his wrist; thank God his arm, his tennis arm, was still there; he was glad to feel assured of that. "If I were you I wouldn't do that. If I can get them to go away, say she's off visiting . . ." He went on in a low voice, his back to the other listeners: "You know Mercy seems to have gone off with them of her own free will, because she wanted to. Better let sleeping dogs lie. You could ruin her name for life. I'll see what I can do."

Lucky little boys may get a costume for Christmas, cowboy, Indian, policeman, spaceman, superman; Jeff Smith got eight at one swat, and soon every toy vehicle on the market and every game and the newest, best equipment for half a dozen sports though he played at none; the minister next door showed him how to fly the fine store-bought kite and that was the only time it flew. Throw rocks at passing cars, more fun, at twelve take out one of the family's Cadillacs at night and run over the minister's dog. Let's be friends, Jeff, why did you steal my typewriter, run over our dog? I wanted a new motorcycle. TV in every room over there, air conditioning, first CB, new kitchen layout every year, pink microwave oven over your head then yellow under window, parents drunk usually and before long always, complain to police they're afraid of their own son. He's using drugs, how terrible, and well, yes, maybe pushing them a little, kicked out of five schools, set fire to an empty garage down the street. And on and on. Two can play at this game. My name is Phil Johnson. I never saw you before.

"And never saw this guy before either, huh?" Leering, grey, sick, weaving on his feet, he holds up the well-worn clipping, same as the one burned one night in an ashtray in Canada: the lovely funeral or rather memorial service, the fine, dedicated features of the departed who is being eulogized. Why, the boy must be twenty-three or four now, how time flies, only yesterday the fatherly neighbor for whom all human souls are fellows in Christ, never to be given up for lost, was teaching him how to use an awl and a level, both subsequently ripped off.

"No. Was this a friend of yours? It says Michigan. I've never been anywhere near there."

The young man's eyes were sunken and red-rimmed; except for that bit of color he might be a slug under a wet log. Poor soul. Lost? Oh, never think that, but under the circumstances . . . What he wanted was simple; if it hadn't been he probably couldn't have gotten through the sentence. It was just that the other's girlfriend worked for that man Pace at the Nelco office in Waterville and Jeff wanted the combination to the safe and the outside key. That was all. Guns and powder can get you in trouble on a little main street like that.

"My wife does work there, that's true, but if you think . . ."

The piece of newspaper was jiggling before his face again. "I'm giving you till this time tomorrow and that'll be it. I know this place is closed Saturday. You better just be here, by yourself, with what I told you."

"You want to know something? You're stoned, my boy." That feels better; the old guidance touch. "You don't know which side is up. Whoever you are, my advice is . . ."

"Cut the bullshit. I'll see you tomorrow." This time he literally pushed the newspaper into his victim's face.

Johnson told Mercy's grandfather that that was it all right, they just wanted to know where she was but he was pretty sure he'd put them off. The great saw, whirling before his face like a thousand suns, resumed its awful screams; lost souls, damned ones, flew under the blade; no, it's the just, the pure and innocent, riding the pine log to their doom; in Nazi camps they had walls to keep their screaming private, from your cockpit it's neat and clean and you don't hear anything either, not the bomb, not the screams. You don't see any legs or arms or heads flying around. Here in the mill you see and hear everything and everybody sees you; murderer, you dropped that thing, I saw you, you killed my old father and my children, I can't even find the pieces of them, you burned our fields, you wiped out our village. "Move over, Johnson, for God's sake, you're goin' crooked, you're shakin' like a poplar. Never mind, Cobb won't know, he went home, you take care o' that fork out there and I'll finish this load. Yeah, I can do it with one arm."

Just in time. He went out and pretended to check on the hill of sawdust that would start being trucked away, sold to farmers for horse and cow stalls, next week; then got the forklift going on the fast-mounting pile of planks.

He didn't even know what town to look in, had no idea where she might be living but seemed to remember her mentioning a man called Cheezit; he'd heard about him and his restaurant, in Waterville he thought that was. But the proprietor wasn't in, might be back later, everybody very busy getting dinner ready for a flock of weekend customers. He went to a phone booth, started dialing, stopped, drove a few miles to another. The scenarios became clearer. One: tell Penny, get the key and combo and tell her to empty the safe. And what do they do when they find it empty? Old fool, off your rocker, go put yourself in the Compton Retreat with Leona Horton who by the way has been making phone calls about you, not that anybody'd listen to a certified mental patient. Two: call the sheriff. Three: call Mr. Pace, that could be anonymously, tell him a holdup is planned, etc. Four: combination of one and three, give Jeff the key and combo *and* call Pace, let him handle it, so that's without nonsense of emptying the safe.

Five, gets rid of possible argument and unpleasant words with Penny:
say he has an important document (what? she wants to know) he needs
to put in office safe for the weekend, she can just give him the key and
combo and he'll run over with it, then call Pace, or sheriff, or something.

Stops at store, not Boonton, the one nearer the ski area, buys envelope and paper, will make it look like important document, can't believe he is stooping to such childishness and has gone so far as to put
ten cents on the counter; however, jumping from that plane didn't feel
much like real life either. Keeps the envelope, thanks the woman, goes
into phone booth outside.

"Hello . . ." That was Carl's voice, in Michigan; sounded considerably aged, maybe things haven't been going well. Silence is worse than
screams, yet hangs on listening to it and to the dread "Hello . . . hello
. . ." until operator says Signal when you're through. Mother was alive
for the memorial service, the clipping said so, but may well have
passed on since, poor lady, such a blow, losing a favorite son like that
and the body never even found. He'd thought of it often and how good
he would have been at consoling her—one of his specialties on the
parochial side. Meanwhile there might have been certain burdens on
Carl, financial and other, she might have had to move in with him and
his family, or did the news story say she lived in a nursing home? He
hadn't noticed; it probably didn't say anyway, if so, who was paying for
it. Do Carl good, make a man of him, he always did love being praised
for virtue since he wasn't much good at anything else; terrible at tennis
and most other sports. I think you married me, Margo said once—the
only bitter remark from her that he remembered—just to please your
mother, by not bringing a better-looking woman into the family. How
absurd women can be; he hoped for her sake that Margo had come to
be ashamed of those words. His mother, ugly, dumpy, yes, with atrocious taste in clothes but that's comforting in a mother, and so kind, so
giving, always thinking of others, never said a word against his first
fiancée, except to hint once that she might be a little worldly for
church and university people like themselves.

Signal when through. The receiver was like a heavy rock in his hand
and putting it down left him feeling suddenly very tired.

Six: light out, head south as far as gas and cash last, start over, make
a whole new life. As he had already done once before, jeered the dead

telephone. Nevertheless, he started, drove twenty-five miles to the interstate and south one exit before a cop car looming in his rearview mirror reminded him of something rather awkward. There were other drawbacks too but this one was decisive, although as senseless as a quasar for any real bearing it had on his life. He was going to have to be a witness in a murder trial, within a few weeks most likely, and his disappearance would be officially noted; he might even be tracked down—for something absolutely fortuitous, that had nothing whatever to do with any thought or action of his, past or present. The injustice of being so persecuted, robbed of all moral prerogative, by a mere whim of chance, at a time when forces that did—or might be said to—relate in some way to the person God had willed him to be were pressing so cruelly on him, made him strike the steering-wheel and groan aloud, "My God, my God, why hast thou forsaken me?" Make a note of it when feasible, put together with dark night of the soul; so often we repeat such phrases without taking in their true import.

He left the highway, relieved to see the police car continuing south, took it back the other way, retraced his route. But found his hands shaking, as badly as that afternoon by the saw, at the thought of sitting alone in the cabin on this particular night, listening to every sound outside in those dark woods. The dark night is not only of the soul. Rephrase; point up.

Seven: have a vision; Saul on road to Damascus; many other saints at similar turning points, after which persecution and forces of evil generally of no consequence, or a blessing rather, giving access to the Light.

There was fog everywhere in the valleys that night, along the stream beds, making driving hazardous and carrying a vague suggestion of an eighth alternative. But up the hill the fog thinned and a little past Ellis Horton's farm stars and a crescent moon shone in marvelous clarity. He stopped, got out and was dumfounded by the billowing glow on the waves of haze below; a perfect setup; he was seized by a thrill of anticipation. He had had a vision once, when he was about fourteen, it might have been what had decided him to go into the ministry; he must try to remember; and the stance—what could that have been? Or no, concentrate more on the beauty of these peaceful fields and the celestial glimmer over the mists of mortal travail. Now it was not just his hands trembling, he was shaking all over. Instances of fearful illumination raced through his mind; better not be struck blind though, that would be awkward; still, if it were the only way . . . Instead, a fearful weight began to press on him, increasing by the second, as though all the stars, lightless, were converging as so much dead matter to crush him in the dirt. With agonizing effort he dragged himself back onto the driver's seat and fled the awful spot. There might be a buried meteor there; he had heard of such phenomena and their peculiar effects on the laws of gravity.

For once Lem and Hannah Palz had missed the monthly square dance. For years they had made a point of going whenever possible. They enjoyed their neighbors and square dancing, and the general good humor and chitchat even with those of the neighbors they didn't particularly cotton to or see eye to eye with on some rather funda- mental questions. But they weren't in a mood for frolicking that week. Like Brit and Louise Horton, only with some extra reasons, they felt life closing in and the land they loved shivering like a wild thing about to expire. They too day after day had listened to the chainsaws coming closer, and tried to drown them out. The road was going to cut right through the middle of their sugarbush, the second best in town after Ellis Horton's. And they too would have enough maples left for a modest living but wouldn't feel the same about them, in sight of the Nelco development already being staked out, and kept making little excuses for not getting in the wood supply for the sugarhouses next March, though it must be done before snow and every other year had been by early November. Most other farmers tried to do it in late spring so the wood could have a year to dry but the Palzes were rarely that well organized.

There was a chapter on all that in the book they had come to curse themselves for, each blaming himself more than the other, Hannah more bitterly. Stupid innocents—hadn't they known that invasion of privacy was the world's number one titillation, ahead of sex, these days? and they had gone on playing into the world's hands in the aftermath. The little improvement in their bank balance was by now nearly wiped out, but no amount would have been worth it.

Of their domestic colony, the best to be said now was that it was nearly wiped out too. Their own plans were too uncertain; the remaining few were supposed to be looking for other arrangements. The cop who had come in none too affably that night had found only a small gathering of five or six ordinary-looking weirdos, with musical instruments including only one guitar, and no marijuana, at least he couldn't smell any, not to mention the heroin he thought he should look for as well as he could without a search warrant. Instead he got a lecture on cottage cheese from a young woman who was fussing with six large disgusting cheesecloth bags of it, like elephants' balls, hung from the ceiling in an ex-shed connecting the house with a made-over outbuilding, and a counter-lecture from a blond-bearded character who disapproved vehemently of all dairy products. Another, apparently an adult though of childish proportions and petulance, claimed to be living on nothing but imported bean sprouts and was equally heated on the diet question. The argument was clearly chronic and all were glad to have a new audience, if not umpire. A baby's squawling and screeches from an older child or two emanated from the farther structure. "Yes, yes, you've got a point there. No, my digestion is fine, thank you. Now Mrs. Palz . . ." At that a mongrel puppy urinated beside and partly into one of the cheese pans.

Hannah was unstrung, even more than usually in late weeks, her husband annoyed. They had been just about to try out a little Homage to Debussy, an arrangement by Lem from three of the easier piano works, for the instruments at hand, which were, besides their own two: violin (terrible), flute (so-so), and clarinet (very gifted but arrogant and uneducated). It would be the last group performance in the house, no point going on with what had become chore if not farce, but Hannah had wanted to run through it for Lem's birthday. As a further birthday present, when they were getting up that morning, she had brought herself to admit she was drinking too much and promised to stop it, as she had done until a nip before dinner; a fine dinner, the first she had applied her high culinary skills or any thought whatever to in weeks. The rest of the household, whom she would have liked to invite for amity's sake, were not candidates for such stuff as quenelles de brochet (the pike, caught by Lem on a trip to Canada late in the summer, hadn't lost too much from freezing) and quail in port and a Château Mouton-Rothschild '59 that had been in their cellar some fifteen years.

A private party, a finger lightly lifted against chaos of whatever mode and provenance, and scarcely a fitting prelude to this intrusion.

The cop was not one of the young deputies but a man toward sixty, of long and impressive history on the force, who had been very sympathetic with them a few years earlier when their house had been broken into.

His eyes had a different glint now. The parents of a girl supposed to be living there wanted to bring charges against the Palzes for getting her into some kind of whacky religious business and a phoney marriage connected with it. He couldn't remember the names of all these sects, consulted a paper from his pocket—no, not Reverend Moon, that was a different complaint, not Scientology—what a name!—or that little millionaire oriental who made all the hoopla at the Astrodome in Texas. Boo Boo Sam Dah, that was it. The parents had a lawyer, working with a de-brainwashing organization. He'd better talk to the girl. Was she there? Had there been some kind of marriage ceremony in the house? No, the two had moved out in September, maybe to live with the Boo Boo group, they hadn't said.

"But they did live here with you?"

"For a while, yes," Lem said. "The boy did some carpentry for us and is quite a talented bassoonist."

"And the wedding was in Waterville," the cottage cheese girl put in indignantly. "I went to it. It was very tender and deeply felt, everybody wore wildflowers—of course there wasn't much left around but goldenrod and that white stuff, getting kind of sick that late in the year. But it was just sweet."

"That wouldn't necessarily make it legal."

"Well who cares, except her stupid parents. I don't know *any*body who . . ."

Hannah hushed her with a glance, not lost on the officer, who kept looking around the once low-ceilinged farmhouse room, now two stories high at the music end, for some kind of evidence, if only wildflowers, to justify his call.

It had struck him as a very homey and interesting, if unusual, room three years earlier. He liked fooling around at cabinetwork himself and had asked many questions then about the harpsichord and organ Lem had built and the attached couches, also his work, along two walls, upholstered in woolen stuff woven by Hannah; he really went for that, it was in a lot of colors and he'd asked his wife later why she couldn't get busy like that instead of buying all that expensive shiny stuff for their sofa. He'd also liked the two stone fireplaces facing each other—two! never saw that before; wanted to know about structural supports and how many partitions had been taken out to make such a nice big room; was intrigued by the old cast-iron New England weathervane in the shape of a flat cow, not on the roof but hung on the wall like a painting, plus a whole lot of funny-looking gods and pagodas and things from their travels—in *Asia*? Yes, Lem had been on concert tours on several continents, before the accident of course—showing the mutilated hand, as though indifferently. And this big sunbeam thing, over one of the fireplaces? No, that was French, 17th Century, they'd picked it up in a junkshop in a little village. Yes, they still liked to travel when they got a chance.

All this the officer had told his wife, saying that certainly was the kind of family you like to meet, nice married daughter had been around then too, you go in a room like that and you feel you've really been places, seen the world, had new ideas, and why couldn't *they* think about going somewhere before it was too late. He'd been crazy to go to Alaska ever since he was a kid; probably different now with the pipeline and all but still, there'd be plenty of ice and mosquitoes left. And the books! must be two or three thousand, do you suppose they'd read them all? His wife reminded him that their son and his family had come home broke and in a vile mood from their summer camping trip in Oregon, two of them sick from polluted water in some campground and the kids quarreled all the way; exactly as happened to the same family doing the same thing again in the summer now just past.

The books were still there, up to the ceiling on both sides of the ex-shed where the cottage cheese was hanging.

"But Mrs. Palz, you *are* a communist, I mean were at some time, weren't you?"

Then it was the bomber girl recently arrested in Compton, quoted as saying nice things about the Palzes and that she had hoped to live with them. Then the couple who *had* lived with them and had stolen Thelma Nesbit's Boonton Collection. Each item was a little brushfire of innuendoes taking several minutes to burn out. Then back to the Boo Boo affair. "You didn't influence them to join that movement, I suppose? For instance that statue over there, that looks like a Buddha, from the pictures I've seen . . ."

Lem was a small-built, lean-faced man, of unusual physical strength and fitness for his age and a low threshold of irritability, further lowered by the atmosphere in the household lately. Their own children were complaining, saying they didn't like to come home to visit any more, with all the yakking and no place to be in peace, although the extras cooked and ate out in the other building. There was no denying that both music and conversation had degenerated. They had lost their two best performers, a violin pupil of Lem's and a clarinetist, to Marlboro and a good timpani man to Hollywood. Two of those remaining went through the evening's fare as a kind of duty to their hosts: a misconception, it would have been better without them—impatient to get off to friends' houses in that village or another and blow their minds and the countryside comatose with amplified rock. What had started with no prospectus or deliberation, just from a chance concatenation of good feelings, had turned into as much a shambles as if it had been an institution. He was in no frame of mind for any extraneous nonsense.

But at the mention of the Buddha he burst out laughing, not harshly but in a sudden shift to genuine, wholehearted amusement. "First we're communists, and then that! Oh, I love it. Goodnight, officer, always nice to see you. Drop by any time."

By the door the cop stopped, noticing Penny, who had appeared deep in a big book the whole time. The introduction was made. "Johnson. Johnson. Oh yes—that Long Trail affair. Funny, we had a phone call just the other day about somebody by that name—from a Mrs. Stowe in Compton; ever hear of her? Of course we get a flood of nut calls nowadays, you'd be amazed how many. But what a coincidence, your happening to pass by that spot too, Mrs. Palz. I'm afraid it's going to be a strain for you, having to testify, but we can't help that, can we?"

Leona had phoned the Palzes too. She'd heard that *Mrs.* Johnson— Mrs., ho ho!—was often at their house and had they seen that morning program with him making an anarchist speech on the steps of the Capitol, under another name? Imagine that dim-witted brother of hers taking in a tenant like that! By chance Lem, who rarely watched TV at any time, had seen it, just by way of distraction while taking a hotpack treatment for an attack of bursitis in a shoulder, and had to admit he was struck by the resemblance when Johnson came, really came crashing, in, a few minutes after the cop's departure. He had never come to the house before, and not having been along on the ill-fated walk in his company, Lem had seen him only once or twice from a distance.

"Yes, she's here. Come in. We were just going to play . . ." They had in fact started playing the Debussy, but the new arrival looked so seriously stricken, the instruments were put down and several of the company hurried to keep him from falling and help him to a couch. Penny was the last to move or speak to him. "Are you all right, Phil? What's the matter?" She could imagine plenty that might be, to be topped off by his passing the police car on the road just now, and was delighted to feel so detached from it, as if she had never been and could not possibly be, in anyone's mind or dossier, involved in any difficulty of his.

It was Hannah, although she hadn't much taken to him on the walk still less at its bloody climax, who tried to make him comfortable and felt sorry for him, shaken and sick as he looked just then. Could she bring him a hot drink of some kind? a cup of tea? A mild stroke was what came to mind, but his pulse was fairly normal, and as he began to resume color and composure and urged them to go on with the music, she was mainly relieved that Chip was not there that weekend or at least not coming till Saturday if at all. He was the other darling of their hearts, along with their own brood—their "faun," the least knowable of the lot but no less loved for that. Together with the Hortons they had slid into this doting-parent role when he was small and his real parents in their remarriages had less and less time for him, on one side at last none: his mother had been killed with one of her gigolos in a car crash on the Riviera when Chip was eleven, the summer Hannah nursed him through the mumps. She had assumed for some time that he would be in for rather more than the usual sexual mess and error at the start, so was just slightly repelled, not too upset, by Penny's flamboyant play for him. But she hated any domestic distress and was already jangled enough without having to watch this poor man be tortured under her roof. Let the inescapable trouble of that ill-matched pair burgeon out of her sight. Indeed just then she wished everyone there and their rude, messy children out of her sight, for good, except her dear, wonderful husband. They had made a long mistake, out of carelessness, as if enough ugliness and turmoil weren't pounding in without their help. They must find each again, alone, quietly.

And in a way did in the next half hour, playing as though only for one another, she on the viola she had gone back to after the accident, when she ceded the keyboard to Lem. He had of course to skip and fake a good deal in the bass but was skillful about it; it was the index and third fingers that were gone and he took a little ironic pride in the trill he had perfected with the fourth and fifth. They could enjoy what they played. Only with the others there now the repertory had shrunk; anything later than Brahms was too difficult for them; in the contemporary works Lem and Hannah wanted to try, in particular one by his old friend Messiaen and another by a younger Austrian ex-student of his, they were hopeless, couldn't read the notes. The Debussy was borderline in that respect and a bum steer in all others. They could read it but didn't go for it, knew the composer's work in general only as TV background slop, and after the short opening Prelude left off their scratchings and tootings and listened, two of the three with some faint show of pleasure, as Lem and Hannah put aside the ill-fated scribbled score and proceeded on their own, in abrupt removal from any company either present or lingering by impact.

What they embarked on, rather to their own surprise as they had done nothing like it for quite a while, was the old Debussy potpourri or "devotional spoof," put together originally for another birthday, not in the family but of an old music-loving lawyer friend in Compton; the fragments making it up had varied from time to time. The signal for it this time was Lem's pulling the snare drum into his reach and the cymbals to Hannah's, in case they got as far as the bumptious street section of the "Iberia" and were in good enough form to manage some extraneous whacks. They did, and were, in spite of an occasional grimace over some failure of memory or a little trouble with the fast pizzicati. But Hannah, though out of practice, happened for no clear reason to be playing unusually well. Their version of the grave "Dancers of Delphi," always the opening, in which the illicit viola had to be sneaky in its contribution, just a filling out of inadequate piano bass, set up an ache of ancient silences. The slow notes wove woodland water scarcely sufficient for drops over rock to a pool still and bottomless as human memory below. It was all a waiting, as by some Grecian urn impatient for closing time at the museum or the pool for the next drop.

It was the heartfelt best the two players could do under the circumstances, indeed no spoof but there was some protection to their privacy in hanging on to the word. A few bars of ragtime from "General Lavine" led to the first movement of the late cello sonata, the viola up an octave when necessary but the loss of the deeper sonorities was not much more damaging than freezing had been to the pike, and it was home base to them both, they had played it so often. But then to Hannah's special delight first and slight apprehension secondly, Lem swooped into the best-known measures of the faun Prelude, and more surprisingly to the great upreaching theme of the last movement of "La Mer,"—called "Dialogue of Wind and Sea" in nice decency of restraint and not very misleadingly; the piano could only give a reminder of it but as written, that first stunning unison of flute and oboe could hardly be heard as excluding man's unanswerableness from the dialogue. Wondering, she was able to sketch in the strings' full-force accompaniment to the repeat, a little faster, of that grand lurch of a cry and its staccato falling-off. Why, out of the dark store of this man's unthinkable taboos, why on this particular night?—a return present to her, or a sudden self-pitiless facing of loss beyond limbs, beyond sonorities; yet Lem was altogether alive and brought out these few strains from the depths as in no more than a splurge of high spirits and love of the music. "Quelle merveille!" he murmured. They closed with a swatch of the Debussy known and loved by all ad nauseam, the public-airwaves cliché of the age, musical impressionism at its most graceful long since vulgarized into a dead duck, hideously without voice, and that too breathed true. They were themselves electrified by it.

They were still exchanging a little smile as quick and fragile as their closing notes, of renewed rapport and promise, of some crucial, featherweight past between them on the verge of recapture, when she reached for the half-finished highball beside her and swilled it down.

"Bravo! Bravo!" cried Phil Johnson, to the embarrassment of Penny who knew that wasn't the custom. But Lem and Hannah seemed pleased, and were pleased too by the man's looking considerably revived. "That last part," he said, "was just like something I saw on the way here. The moon, you know, on some fog it must have been, down below. What a coincidence." There was no sarcasm in Lem's glimmer of response, just a quick suggestion of the benevolent old leprechaun. "Yes, that was the idea. It's called Moonlight. 'Clair de Lune.' " "He doesn't seem to stay in the same key much of the time, I mean within the same piece—I realize you were doing several different ones. But then where does the shape come from? or isn't there any? I should think that would be pretty risky. Is that what they mean by atonal?" The clarinetist, on his way to the door, mimed disgust at the overheard naiveté.

Penny, as Mrs. Johnson, could scarcely join the exodus to the village as she usually had and had to hang around, pretending to listen to a Schubert record while some courtesies were exchanged. The black-bearded Ph.D. from another hilltop stayed too, and two or three of the Palz menage. Hannah quietly practiced a part in a Stravinsky ballet score in the corner. It had felt so good, playing, more than any time in weeks, she had as good as erased the policeman's visit and wondered who had emptied her glass. The sweet-faced witch girl, with a recalcitrant two-year-old on her lap, told Penny she was learning fast and getting much better at the incantations though the concoctions were still difficult; there was a coven a few miles away that she hoped to be eligible for soon. The child was not exactly hers; she had, she thought, technically given birth to a little girl who was around somewhere but human resources must be pooled, all must be parent as well as child to one another.

Johnson consented to a beer. "And are you enjoying life in Vermont?" Lem asked as he handed it to him. Yes, the face and voice seemed unmistakable, though the speaker of ten years ago had been all flash and vigor; whatever made him change his name must have been rough, to bring on such haggardness. Or it might be just his current lovelife imbroglio. Whatever the case, Lem had seen many stranger and was not much interested; it was not in his sphere of curiosity, just so the man wasn't a criminal and he felt reasonably assured of that, merely noting that his eyes darted about the room and seemed to see nothing, neither orientalia nor musical instruments nor home-woven upholsteries. The short spate of questions about the music must have used up his supply of interest, or been just by way of decorum from an interloper. The eyes appeared to focus a moment on the cow weather-vane, so that Lem for politeness' sake remarked on its construction and origin, but Johnson then said only, "Oh yes, very interesting," without attention, as Hannah had described him doing about everything she and Brit had pointed out to him on their walk. Lem didn't mind that

either, it was just unusual; most people on first entering that room were
driven to comment, however perfunctorily.

"Tell me"—this came bursting from Johnson, who with no preamble
or apology was pointing to his host's left hand—"was it very hard?
losing what you had lived for, like that?" So he was not altogether
unseeing; on this question his interest sounded desperate and uncon-
trollable.

"Yes. Of course. It was hard on Hannah. And now . . ." He glanced
over to where she leaned toward her music stand, as though studying a
phrase, and as though her earlier fidgets had blown off without a trace.
As perhaps they had but he knew she had lost her place and would
start nodding soon; he had been wrong not to veto the wine he so
prized and enjoyed; he must take the viola from her before it fell. The
booze, extended to mornings lately, was not going to be stopped by a
birthday promise, or the pills that she still deluded herself were secret
from him. "Her nerves are on edge, more than then. She imagines
things. I must get her away, to Europe or somewhere for a while. She
can't stand the road machines. Or the police. You'll understand, you
also were questioned, about that same loathsome crime." The vowels
in *also* and *loathsome* came out as strongly European, something rare
enough in his Vermont-inflected speech as to sound like a deliberate
announcement or reminder of some kind, which it was not. His dark
grey eyes, alight most often with vague, gentle kindliness and a rather
distant humor at the human spectacle, could turn extraordinarily piercing. "Or . . ." A shrug and a brief glance around the room filled out the
analysis. "And you, you have read philosophy I'm sure . . ."

"Oh . . . What makes you think so?" This both flattered and on
guard, even alarmed. "A little, of course. Why?"

Lem's shrewd smile overlay ancient courtesy to the stranger, more
than any specific judgment of this one, about whom he was sure now
the madwoman had been right. It was still no concern of his, he merely
perceived the fact. Smiling a little he said, "We who have been
through such deaths recognize them in others. I was in camps. German
ones. And French." The tone was light; he would not elaborate.

"Well then perhaps you can tell me . . ." This too came bursting out,
the pent-up need and pain no longer containable, the unspoken end of
the sentence perfectly clear to them both, though to only one an echo
of Tolstoy. *What to do, what to do.* Oh how often, from what a variety

of souls the man of God had heard it; with what skill—or innate illumination?—he had nearly always found the words to soothe and edify.
Very strange indeed it was to be in the other chair, the cryer-out from
the abyss, not appealed to but appealing, in such sore need. For a
second he felt his fate hanging on the light from this mysterious stranger's eyes: the answer! he saw it trembling there; what would it be?

He braced himself for tremendous, possibly humiliating insight, even
reprimand.

"Please," he blurted out, "don't be afraid of hurting my feelings. It
might, I'm not, I need . . ."

But Lem was not in that line of work. He sat down at the harpsichord and strummed, absently. "A nice piece, this. Do you like music?"

"Rescind! Recant! Repair!" shouted the cottage cheese girl, appearing from the library-pantry wing in beaming elation, as though suddenly in possession of good tidings for all present. "Get into the Sixth
Circle of consciousness! Don't delay!"

"Oh Gladys, shut up!"—in fierce irritation from Hannah. "We're all
sick of your nonsense." But she rescinded and recanted a trifle. "Here,
quiet down and get your flute and let's try practicing this together."

Instead the girl, locks like tangled old boat lines in a bad sea and the
boat itself scarcely seaworthy, began dancing by herself, in wide pa-
rabolas of flat-chested torso and limbs hurling forth exclamation marks.
Her joyous expression had turned a bit sly and ominous. "A nail!" she
cried as she spun and swooped. "Bring me a nail, to keep it shut."

"She gets coffins on her mind," murmured the novice witch toler-
antly. "And hasn't been doing her share of the work lately."

"Yes," said Johnson, "of course I do, on nothing like your level.
You'd find me pretty ignorant, I'm afraid. But we used to sing a great
deal in my family. My mother could do most of Gilbert and Sullivan by
heart at the piano, and we'd all take turns in the roles . . ."

The recollection changed him dramatically, breaking down caution
and indifference alike and bringing such a flush of human warmth to his
features that Lem, smiling, picked the volume out from the shelf by
him and opening at random started to play, in delicate burlesque.
Johnson, shy, amused, titillated in quick succession, while Hannah
plucked alone in her corner and the Sixth Circle wheeled at his back,
hummed a few bars, as though to go no further. But before he knew it,

his quite vibrant baritone taking over irresistibly, he was launched on his once-famous parlor comedy routine. "I'm called Little Buttercup, dear Little Buttercup . . ." Hannah and the dancer were astonished out of their respective swoons; the scholar and his wife and child, who were starting home, came back in, though it would make them late for their TM; faces of various ages appeared from beyond the cheese bags. Penny stared at her nails, finding it impractical to sink through the floor. ". . . though I could never tell why. Still I'm called . . ." Now he was acting it out too, with lift of brow and tuck of chin, while the resonant voice, not altogether untrained and far from clumsy in its modulations, swelled or hushed in a mimicry verging more and more on a cry from the deeps, though the singer's eyes stayed agleam with a devastating invitation to laughter. ". . . sweet Little Buttercup I . . ."

Lem, accustomed to strange revelations through music and who could enjoy any excellence in it short of blatant vulgarity, finished with a deft little flourish and with a laugh laid a hand on Johnson's shoulder. "An old hand, I see; very well done. I return your Bravo. We must try other things some day. I have some Campion here just right for your voice." Most of the others, joggled out of their confusion, decided to laugh and applaud too. Hannah, glad it was over, had to admit the man had a decent voice and an instinct, however long unused and misapplied this time, for public presence. For all the grotesque of the thing he had been close to infectious, with just slightly better judgment would have been; the real old ham, out of practice so a trifle manqué, that was it, and that was the nature of his intense sparkle of gratification after the act, minus the manqué.

So ended, to their view, the visit begun in, and evidently occasioned by, some nearly mortal travail.

The sparkle lasted almost to the Johnsons' cabin door, though from Penny he got neither praise nor any other conversation; she had heard him sing such stuff before, long ago.

"Penny, I have to tell you something. It's why I went looking for you there—you'll forgive me for that, won't you? You know I don't want to be a tether on you, I know you have to live your own life. I haven't questioned you or tried to interfere, have I? Only . . ." They were outside, in the murmurous and awful night; he pretended to be fumbling for the key. "It's just that I have an important document I thought it would be wise to keep in your office safe for a while. If you'd give me the key and just tell me the combination I could run over with it in the morning . . ."

"For God's sake, what important document could you have? You're getting delusions. Leave me alone, I want to go to sleep. Sweet Little Buttercup! You old fool, couldn't you see they were all just laughing because you were making such an ass of yourself? Did you think it was your mother you were singing for?" A few minutes later a key, with a scrap of paper stuck in the hole, landed by his feet like a dog biscuit. "Go ahead, pay off your little goons. It's for them, isn't it? It's none of my business, I'm leaving anyway, I have other plans." In the midst of brushing her teeth at the small iron sink that served as washbasin too she added, in a more familial voice through the mouthful of lather, "Those crooks, I'd be glad to see them get it. Pace was making a bunch of phone calls today, being cagey of course but there's something that stinks about everything they do. Somehow he's got that right of way over what Brit calls his woodlot—remember? no, you wouldn't. So they're going to start working this end of the road again. No, that's all right; after I lost the fucking key a couple of times I had a spare made. It's my goodbye present."

8

He served doubles repeatedly Saturday morning, and in general was so off his game he knew he should withdraw and let his partner's young son, who was waiting around hoping to play, take his place. Instead he proposed changing partners for the second set. "It's just not your day, Phil, we all have them like that. Well all right . . ." The group of men he had taken to playing with were neither friendly nor the opposite; they asked few personal questions, seemed to know each other as little as they did him, existed for each other on the courts exclusively. They played hard and well and were civil; that was enough; occasionally between games or after an unusual shot good or bad somebody would make a joke. He did better in the second set so felt all right about hanging in for a third. Wet leaves on the courts were the problem that late in the season, not a waiting line; they could play all day if they held out and wanted to. A single brown leaf tugging from its twig distracted him mightily, so did weekend traffic slowing up now and then along there, for people to watch the game or case the motel. He likened himself to a cat for watchfulness and felt a little puff of satisfaction with the unaccustomed stroke of simile, forgetting what occasioned it. Somebody suggested that at "their" age they shouldn't overdo it, could get a heart attack, tear an Achilles tendon. He was by far the oldest of the group, though on good days also the best. He sat out a set at last and spent the time looking at his watch almost without interruption, starting at 10:57.

It was twelve miles from there to the sawmill and not a fast road. At 11:15 he was invited to play a set of singles, "if you have time, you seem to be worrying about an appointment or something." Now it was the second hand he watched, and a certain remaining leaf on the maple branch across the court, then an actual grey-striped cat that appeared on top of the cedar fence along that side of the motel drive, stalking a bird or chipmunk perhaps. He had no idea who was making the proposal. If the leaf fell in the next ten seconds, or if the cat jumped on their side rather than into the drive, either one, he would play. "Well, what do you say?" It was the boy who was asking, young man rather, about his son's age. Would he have finished college by now? or dropped out? where and what kind of person might he be? The questions would have had the same weight if they had concerned the young stranger beside him.

The leaf hung on. The cat jumped on their side.

On his second try at the phone early that afternoon, to the former Banks house where he knew Jim Pace stayed when he had to stick around for a night, there was an answer. "A break-in at the office? tonight? Is that what you said? who are you? why are you calling me? how do you know about this?"—angry; flustered; probably about to take off for somewhere and thinking he'd have to change his plans. Johnson hung up, feeling himself on the side of virtue but demeaned and foolish. No reason to think the frustrated hoodlums—no, hoods: watch those archaisms—would try it that way; still, needing money badly enough they might, while also carrying out the threat against him personally. Therefore, said logic, since the call had no bearing on his own imminent exposure and ruin, it had been a disinterested and thus virtuous act, Q.E.D., whether of any practical consequence or not. Besides, on the faint chance there might be some, a little hope could lie there; setting one gang of thieves to catch another is not the Christian approach, but Jesus too had His practical side; if only he could get his hands on that newspaper clipping in the process.

An hour later he phoned Michigan and that time stayed on the line. "Carl? Carl?" Ah, that heavy breathing—gratifying somehow, rather exciting; it sent a tingle of life through him, as if he were indeed returning from the grave; made everything in that instant seem worth while, whatever everything was. He laughed into the receiver. It was his foster-brother who sounded the more defunct of the two, when at last he managed to gurgle something. "I can't explain now, Carl, I'll tell you the whole story later. But you sound funny. Are you all right?" Gurgle; apparently not; maybe he'd had a stroke, poor fellow. However, some faint halting words did come, from that other planet. Oh it's fun coming back from the dead, you should try it some time; don't say that to Carl though, not his type of humor; Margo might appreciate it, she used to laugh at various things he didn't at the time find particularly funny. Please, don't tell Mother just yet, or was she . . . Yes, she had passed away shortly after the service for him, had been failing before, never got over the blow. No, Margo wasn't at home, had gone to

Minneapolis for treatment but seemed to have left there, hadn't been in touch for a while. Son drifting in Europe, they didn't know where; daughter still at home, poorly, in bad mental shape. "Well, can't you help her? get her to a psychiatrist?" That breath again: an accusation? ignoble but Carl might be capable of it, never was very responsive to others' sufferings, lacked that kind of imagination. Which could also explain his few words coming over so thin, little teletype pinpricks. Now it was not leaf or cat but a lone fly in the phone booth, unsteady of wings and legs, woken from torpor, that held his attention. "Carl, tell me something. How do you think it would be taken, I mean by people in general, if I went home? What? You'd have to think about it? Well all right, I'll call again, just don't say anything in the meantime. Promise. There's a fly buzzing in here, I guess you can probably hear it . . ." He didn't think his brother had hung up; it sounded more as if he had collapsed and knocked the phone over.

The play, he learned from mimeographed handbills in all the store windows, would start at eight, in the highschool auditorium. He got a seat on the aisle far back and was in it only as the lights went out, to avoid recognitions and encounters, not that he had much acquaintance in that crowd. Cheezit the restaurant man, as director, came out first and got a big hand and a lot of laughs talking about community spirit and the Green Mountain Boys—some of this in a broad parody of Vermont speech that might have stepped on some toes there but seemed not to—and how lucky they were to see this fine play there where they were all friends instead of in some Broadway theater, and of course contributions welcome but all you fine folks more so, with or without. The leading lady, by the way, Margo Philipson, was a new-comer in town but he'd bet his bottom dollar they'd all be wanting her to settle down and stay a good long time once they'd seen her on stage.

Johnson had caught sight of an extra cop near the intersection at the center of town, a few doors from the Nelco building, but no sign of disturbance. Pace would presumably have alerted the sheriff's office; he had driven by it himself three times in the course of the afternoon but something on the order of a leaf or a fly, once actually a wasp on the inside of his windshield, had deterred him each time. He could walk out on the play and still do it, of course, but the reasoning behind the idea, if any, had become a hopeless tangle, in which neither sequence nor purpose was to be traced. In any case he now felt ejected from the whole matter, as decisively as five years earlier from a certain small plane, by the sight of his wife up there slowly moving about a livingroom remarkably like theirs in its furnishings and with a rather dreamy, more than thoughtful, look turning on one light-switch after another, exactly as at dusk every day in their twenty-four years together; or almost exactly. In this near-replica of their parlor in Michigan she was not moving like a woman in pain and wearing a steel-frame truss, or any, and her voice and expression, when at last she spoke, instead of the old habitual resignation and self-effacement betrayed a positive rejuvenation that cut him to the quick. He had noticed something of the sort at their brief meeting at the Hortons' but had managed to put it down as an error on his part, due to shock. "Oh Harry," went her soliloquy, "why couldn't you have come home on time? You know how I hate being alone after dark, and just today of all days, with these strange phone calls . . ."

How grossly unfair, for her to be enjoying herself so and captivating an audience into the bargain. His entire source of moral stamina in these years had been his daily spasm of anguish over the suffering he was causing her; he had pictured it quite vividly at times—the sighs and tears, the aging flesh, the brave little replies to condolences, the lonely appearances at church—and that he could do so had sustained him through several years of bliss. The whole scene up there, lights, props and all, and the audience too, might have been mounted for the sole purpose of robbing him of that support, just when he needed it most. It was too cruel; he would not have believed it of her. However, seeing himself enter the stage door rear, take off hat and coat and prepare to hear her lament, he decided to forgive her. Come to think of it, he really must; wrong had been done on both sides; hers was just looking younger and happier than before she was the victim of his.

The Harry she was treating as a husband—in *their* livingroom!—was not nearly so magnanimous, and not a good actor either. Furthermore the play, a murder mystery, was as stupid as she had said, although without knowing much about the theater in general, he had an impression that Mr. Cheezit must have done quite a skillful job of directing, for things to keep moving at all. That and Margo's strangely compelling voice and command of the stage. He had never taken much account of it, nor often stolen time from his work to see her acting, but it was true that in their younger years she had been in quite a number of plays, in college and later at the local university theater. They might even have met after one of those shows, he wasn't sure, in fact hadn't the foggiest idea when they met or first went out together. There was now a villain on stage, pretending to be a friend—hold it, Margo, don't trust him! I have an important document, I mean something I have to tell you— really in cahoots with the drug ring that for some reason or other has planted the stuff in her, or their, or our, house and is now trying to get it back. She doesn't yet suspect; violence is imminent; she holds it off with a speech about her flower garden, delivered with such pertness and charm that the audience, which seems to be most of the popula- tion of Waterville and surrounding countryside, is induced to fall for the otherwise idiotic suspense, and just then the screams of more than one police car forced the actors to stop until they had passed and brought a howl of laughter over the hall.

Johnson sprang up from his seat, but seeing that nobody else was so aroused and that he was making himself quite conspicuous, quickly sat down again. The loudest laugh came from a man in the front row, who craned around to share his outlandish amusement with the rest of the public and turned out to be the sturdy, baby-faced, middle-aged fel- low, or country bumpkin, he had also been introduced to that day at the Hortons'. Margo, busying herself with a vase of chrysanthemums, was the only one of the cast who didn't fall out of role and simper, in helpless reversion to real-life identity, during the interruption. There were then only two short speeches left before the intermission, not time for the foolish grins to fade and any shred of illusion to be re- stored, but either the leading lady or the community spirit noted by Cheezit made for a grand burst of applause just the same, in which the noisiest clapper and sole yeller of "Hooray! Hooray!" was the uncouth character in the front row.

Johnson pushed hard against the crowd and with some difficulty found his way to what served as greenroom. It took him another two or three minutes to wedge in beside her and the intermission was to be ten in all. He skipped the congratulations.

"Margo, tell me where I can find you. I have to talk to you."

"Hello. How nice to see you." She smiled, as poised as though still

on stage, and turned to others including a local reporter who were
trying to speak to her. Close to, the heavy make-up made her look like
a cheap oversized doll. The fact seemed to amuse her, if she was aware
of it; more likely she was still in the grip of her part, and he touched
her shoulder, restraining a violent impulse to shake her out of it and
bring her to whatever self she might now possess, as the others had
been shaken by the police sirens. Like sounds heard on an operating
table, inchoate voices and mass shuffling of feet swelled and subsided
beyond the curtain; the footlights came on; she moved away, ready for
her entrance, and he followed until he was actually on stage and had to
be yanked back as the curtain rose. "Margo! for God's sake!" That was
certainly heard out front. She responded with the merest shooing mo-
tion of the wrist, as at a fly in a phone booth, her attention all on the
lines she was about to speak, and was speaking as he found himself
being dragged with overwhelming force and speed to a back exit.

"You leave her alone, see?" the man said in a furious whisper, "if
you don't want your head blown off. I know who you are, you two-
faced lyin' spook, I seen your picture tucked away in her drawer till
she took my advice 'n' tore it up. Tried to play dead, did you? Go
ahead, *be* dead, ain't nobody around here goin' to be sorry." With a
grip on the collar he had the much taller man on his knees at the top of
a stoop, overlooking the parking lot. "You got any message for her, you
can send it through me. Just ask for Walt Hodge, that'll be all the
address you'll need." Like a misbehaving puppy, Johnson was then sent
flying over the steps to the asphalt, while the door above banged shut.

The police cars, he learned shortly after coming to, had been heading away from the center to where a bunch of panicked horses were
obstructing traffic on the highway. His informant at the drugstore said
some out-of-town vandals had been seen letting them out and had done
some shooting too but he didn't know what was happening now.

At the cast party afterwards, at the back of Cheezit's restaurant,
Walt was cruelly tempted. Hadn't had a drink in six weeks, whiskey
and beer were sloshing around the table and being all dressed up like
for a funeral made it worse. It wasn't sad and sorrowful any way but

those two, the clothes and the temptation. Everyone there knew and liked him—the highschool teacher who'd played the villain, the druggist's wife and daughter, Doc Macklin who'd been dragged along out of the audience for friendship's sake, and several more. The transformation of Walt Hodge had been making the rounds as quite a little story lately, and the old doctor felt especially benevolent about it, having been called out of bed by Brit Horton the night of the mattress episode and taken a good deal of cussing out from the patient for two weeks afterwards. He'd also doctored the Bankses for three generations, known Walt from boyhood, and if he didn't do a better job of killing himself next time, would have predicted an early death by alcohol.

As might still occur, he was thinking, observing the disgust on that rugged face at the taste of gingerale. For the time being the coincidence of the doctor's having helped save the other life, that of the lady from Michigan, beyond a doubt the agent of the miracle, gave him such limited assurance as he ever allowed himself, that his own life was not altogether wasted. He had seen too much of the human picture to suppose for a minute that the strange alliance could last very long; even without what he had sensed from that evening's performance, a certain cultivation of mind in Mrs. Philipson, whom he had seen every day at the hospital, was going to make that impossible. Nevertheless, he felt more than relieved, positively delighted, to see Walt's hand, which had been moving through agonizing conflict toward a bottle of whiskey on the table, come wrenching back in triumph, to be clasped a moment in quite loverly fashion by the prima donna at his side. Too bad, too bad; it might have worked, if only that skinflint and tyrant Ned Banks had ever thought of letting his ward, long ago, get some education, instead of keeping him under his heel as a slave laborer and forcing the mentality of a slave on him too until it was too late.

The next minute, though, the ex-slave was regaling the table with a mimicry of the psychiatrists he'd recently had to ·do with, and Dr. Macklin, joining in the laughter, half wondered if he might be wrong.

" '*Good*mornin',' they says with that mean look"—the bushy blond eyebrows went into a slant of cagey suspicion—"like you was set to bring on a thunderstorm and gonna deny you did it, that's how they're learned in them sickeatrical schools to make you feel, 'and how's our cheerful de-pressurizer today?' or presh-*shun* it could be. I told 'em I wa'ant none o' them three things startin' with *theirs*, where did they get that right of ownership, an' that gets that smile on their foxy faces like you never seen on man nor beast, it's particular to that one species—you ask Doc Macklin there if it ain't, he knows 'em." Walt's nostrils seemed to thin down an inch apiece, under the knife-edge insinuation he threw into his naturally rounded, ingenuous features, now further contracted by a fleeting hint of superiority and phoney familiarity combined. " 'Attaboy, Walt,' they says—no point tellin' you which says, they all got poured out o' the same bag o' beans far as lingo's concerned—'you go on showin' that fine independence o' spirit an' we'll git you outa here a sane 'n' healthy man.' 'Then it'll be no thanks to you,' I says. 'I'd as lief cuddle up to a porcupine as have you jabbin' yer dirty little minds into my private business any more.' That gets the real know-it-all workin' "—his face took on a custard-pie smear of vast condescension—"an' they say it's been a highly successful session. 'Once we get these hostilities into the open we'll really start cookin' with gas.' 'I sure hope so,' I says, ' 'cause I can see you fellers need all the encouragement you can get. The only cookin' I can see we might get down to is if you got any figsations you want to talk about, I'll listen an' we'll reverse the charges.' That was just to be polite. I wouldn't 'a' listened for a Guernsey heifer, supposin' they'd accepted the offer. I'd sooner sniff the underside of a backhouse than what that breed's got packed in up here." He tapped his head, then shook it mournfully, in pity for his fellow-man.

"One poor cluck in my room there, been married twenty-six years, they was tryin' to make him fall outa love with his wife. Some bigshot way back, sort of a George Washin'ton in their business, name o' Floyd—what? okay, Froyd, don't matter—seems he taught 'em that's an awful powerful disease, gettin' stuck on one other person like that. Wouldn't let her come see him an' the poor feller got worse 'n' worse, he'd be cryin' for her all night."

The schoolteacher, a sunrise-hued cherub in his forties, who had been going eight years to one of those same shrinks, objected, with the congenial smile called for by the occasion; the slight evil corner of the smile was just a lingering carry-over from his stage role, as hard to relinquish now as it had been to stay in during the interruption on stage. His amateur acting and the villain role in particular had been on the urging of that medic-confessor, as an antidote to his innocence complex. He told Walt he was unfair, after all he hadn't been there for *no* reason, had he? and he certainly looked fine now, so they must have done him some good, whether he wanted to give them any credit or not.

Walt apologized, with dexterity amazing to the doctor, who had thought he knew him so well. Laying his huge paw on the teacher's little pale equivalent across the table, he said, "Ain't a one of 'em could give a body the shivers like you did tonight." The teacher glowed. "To our villain!" cried Cheezit, raising his glass at the end of the table, and after a round of high-spirited toasts, conversation reverted to the play and then local rumors, of the hotel next door being sold and the horses up the road that night and one thing and another, all in very jolly and friendly mood. Margo, when asked, said she really had no idea if she'd be staying on there, she hadn't come with any such thought, she'd have to see. Walt hadn't had a chance yet to tell her about throwing her long-gone spouse out the door and when he did she neither scolded nor praised him for it but just looked thoughtful, as if she'd known for a long time, long before knowing Walt or setting foot in Vermont, that that was the way it would one day have to be.

But Dr. Macklin had not been far wrong. They were not exactly quarreling a little while after leaving the party, just fighting back tears and feeling smothered in feathers, it was that confusing. Yet only the day before they had walked in high meadows a few miles away, not the old home he wanted no more truck with, where a tumbledown shack was for rent or sale, with a view nearly as grand as the one from Ellis Horton's place, and had kissed on the rickety porch as though in a promise needing no words. The place was going very cheap, most people wouldn't think of fixing up such a shaky little ruin, but that was work after Walt's heart and he explained in detail what he would do and how, if it were his.

"It ain't on account o' *him*, is it? Yeah I know, you come here lookin' for him, I guess you didn't know he had that floozie along with him and she's prob'ly why he played that whole fool bastard trick on you. But that can't be it now—not *now*, Margo! It's you got me into prayin' an' goin' to them meetin's, I was tryin' to be good enough for you, so you wouldn't think I was just a bum—like I used to be, I'll admit that, but I ain't any more."

"I know, Walt, my dear darling, and I admire and love you for it.

And of course it's not him—I don't hate him, he's just a funny kind of nothing to me. But I just can't pray with you. It's gone out of me. I can't *believe*, the way you mean. You wouldn't want me to go and pretend, would you?"

He glowered so, she was reminded for a second of her fear of him, the first night. "Maybe you think you'll be a bigtime actress, just because you done so good tonight, an' I wouldn't suit, to be along with you. One o' them TV stars maybe . . . " That was unfair, as her laugh told him and he knew anyway; she'd done it once, for fun and because of a debt to Cheezit; had no thought of ever being on a stage again. "I gotta have the Good Book or the booze, one or the other. Right now I'd ruther it was the book, but not without you feelin' the same way. I can't. If it was just me I'd say all right, but the preacher says no an' I can't go against him, that's the word o' the Lord he's sayin' outa his mouth, not some two-bit in-dee-vidjal opinion. Just last Sunday he says, if one o' us is livin' with somebody, husband or wife or however, that ain't believin' the true gospel and comin' to meetin's too with the truth in their hearts, then we're sinners along with 'em an' we better expect to pay for it in hellfire till kingdom come. Margo! ain't you never imagined what that's like?—hellfire!—down there, forever 'n' ever."

"Amen," she murmured sadly, in the echoing cavern of her whole life; then with more heart, "That's not what Saint Paul said, he said just the opposite, that if a man or woman . . ."

"Don't say that name! He talked about him too, an' how we wasn't to open that part o' the book, because that was the devil talkin' there to fool people, pretendin' to be an apostle o' the Lord."

She turned away. "Try to forgive me my need and my stupidity. I never meant to do you such wrong." And for the first time her body froze at the touch of his great hands, that were rough only in texture.

"The Lord is my shepherd I shall not want he leadeth me beside the green pastures." He was saying it faster and faster, on his knees beside the bed they had shared through the one perfect month in either of their lives. "See? I know the words now, I learned 'em just for you, leastways in the beginnin', an' now you don't want to hear 'em or say 'em with me. Or the Lord's Prayer either that you taught me yourself. As we forgive them as trespass against us, lead us not into temptation but get us out, no, deliver us—that's a real stout word, *deliver*, like a package, an' that's what we are, just a bunch o' dumb packages for the

Lord to drop off where He sees fit. Deliver us from evil, it says. Oh Lord, Lord, I never spoke against you, not in my heart I didn't. How come you want to play so dirty with me?"

From around the now quiet corner and up the highway maybe a quarter of a mile there were sounds of commotion and soon a police car was zooming that way again. He felt guilty. He was good with horses and should have gone up there to help round up the runaways instead of blabbing his head off in that restaurant. Maybe that was why he was being punished so, though it seemed kind of quick for the Lord to have found out.

"Walt, you're not going to . . ." She didn't dare say the word whiskey.

Anyway he was dressed and gone, without looking at her again. She heard the front door slam. It was true the inn was being sold, and the new management would take over soon.

All evening Brit had been puzzling and stewing, hardly paying attention to the programs at all. He'd just learned late Friday, first from Jim Pace who stopped by to commiserate as it were and then by checking that deed and others to adjacent properties in the town records, that his precious woodlot was not twenty-seven acres but twenty-five point one and its boundaries were not where he had thought. At ten Louise turned the TV off and with a new sword in her heart was saying well, those old deeds were often whacky, they'd heard of plenty like that, they'd just have to accept it and forget about it, when the unknown car whirled in, slowed a second and then went careening up toward the Johnsons' cabin.

Nobody was home there. Brit had seen Penny leaving on foot with a heavy knapsack long before dark and Johnson's old car hadn't been around all day. The shots were through one of the car windows as it roared back down: an automatic, that was, or more like a semi rigged up that way, maybe that M-16 a nutty city hunter came around with one time; didn't sound like any gun he was used to. Louise tried to hold him back but he was on the steps with his rifle when the green Pontiac with New York plates blazed by and paused again. "Naw, this isn't the place!" the driver yelled and it was off up the road at the same crazy speed, throwing up a spray of gravel. He'd recognized two of the motorcycle gang, from the time in the store way back and again the night of the square dance through the wet windows. Chip had come by alone that afternoon and said he was just there for the night and to get some things. Louise tried and cried and couldn't stop Brit. That was the direction the maniacs had gone in and he was backing his old station wagon out and about to follow, with the rifle, whether or not it made any sense for one old man alone to be doing anything of the sort, when Johnson turned up and said he'd go with him, so Brit hurried back for his shotgun and they were off. Aside from some bad bruises on the face, Johnson was looking more wrung-out and peaked even than after the September affair and Brit figured he wouldn't be any more help than he had been that day but he couldn't be choosy.

The Pontiac wasn't in sight at Chip's shack or by the closed-up big house beyond but they could have driven it back of the barn or in among the trees a short distance. Brit stopped a little way off and approaching the coop on foot, with Johnson behind him, heard a wild, unfamiliar voice that had to be Chip's yelling in a half-strangled kind of way, "No, I'm not going, I won't!"—something like that, as if he were being held down. As he was, only not the way they'd envisaged. The door was unlocked and when the two men rushed in they found Penny kneeling on top of him on the floor, naked from the waist up, right fist raised as for a blow, her face smudged with tears and contorted by rage and frustration. It became more so at the intrusion, though she did roll off and get to her feet.

"How dare you follow me and break in on me?" she screamed at Johnson. "You horrible old man with your wrinkled skin! hypocrite! I loathe you, I wish I'd never laid eyes on you . . ." For sanity Brit was thinking he'd take Leona over her any day and maybe even the gang of junkies they'd come chasing. Chip said the car hadn't been there, it must have gone up the other way at the fork: to the old Banks place that would have to be, where Jim Pace was staying that night for some reason, which he usually didn't on weekends; the Hortons had seen him drive by.

Chip, jumping at the excuse to get out, in spite of Johnson's not relishing his company, in fact looking as if he'd as soon sit with a rattlesnake, grabbed his own gun and piled into Brit's car with them, leaving the still topless girl in a heap on his cabin floor.

They lurched as fast as the station wagon would go, back to the fork and after a short pause for debate there, up the other way, in strained silence at first except for Brit's muttering, only to ease the tension perhaps, that if that gang were shooting at Jim Pace they ought to get a medal for it. "Stickin' our fool necks out for that sonuvabitch!" But they kept going. The question at the fork had been whether to get to Brit's telephone instead and call the sheriff, as seemed the only sensible course for their own health and happiness, but before any law-enforcer could get there the trouble, if any, would be over, whereas their just turning up on a peaceable social call might be deterrent enough. To Brit's surprise, it was Johnson who was most vehemently for that choice, saying with fierce and peculiar exuberance, "No, no! We must let them see us, I know what I'm saying, I'll explain later!"

Leaning forward from the back seat, Chip managed to bring out, in a voice not much more at ease than when he was being sat on, "Mr. Johnson, I'm sorry, I mean I know you don't care in one way, she told me—I mean how it wasn't a real marriage you had and all that, but I just want you to know . . ." He might have been addressing the rear of a public statue, one that might turn and spit fire. "I guess I was stupid but I mean I never thought she was that serious about it, wanting me to leave college and head west with her and everything. She says you're kind of her guardian so maybe she told you about all that but I . . ." No spit, no fire, only ominous rigidity in the back of that skull. Just to change the hopeless subject and atmosphere, Chip bumbled on with a few nervous words to Brit about their last visit together to the house now in sight, for poor Walt Hodge, "and now look at him, with a job and that bangup ladyfriend and . . ."

That touched the switch. The statue's head jerked sideways and the hollow, tight-jawed command shot from it, "Shut your fool mouth, you young idiot!"

The green car was there all right, facing downhill ready to get away, with the driver at the wheel and his three pals doing something around Pace's convertible parked on the grass nearby. The house door was wide open, the lights were on and Pace was nowhere to be seen. Brit blocked the road, got out and strolled slowly over to the window of the Pontiac. "You lookin' for somebody? Maybe we could help you. You

mightn't know your way so good around these roads." Chip was beside
him. The young man at the wheel looked too far gone to understand
the words or anything else; jaw hanging, eyes wallowing, he seemed
ready to slide to the car floor, until the bullet crossed in front of his
face and between the two heads outside. At that he pushed his way out
past them and ran for the Cadillac. "Come on, get outa here," he was
yelling, but on the way he whipped around and was aiming a pistol at
Chip. Brit, quicker with his gun, had it up and was about to get him in
the arm when Johnson, with a great outflung gesture of both arms,
stepped in front of the barrel. "In the name of Christ, stop!" he cried
out. "Jeff, I want to talk to you, I'm your friend!"

The shot missed by a hair and Chip was running to the back of the
Cadillac, taking advantage of a diversion in the ranks over there, said
ranks being in worse shape than Jeff, by a good deal. One picked that
moment to fall unconscious if not dead on the grass. A second, not
much steadier, suspended operations to try to drag the fallen one into
the back of Pace's car, mumbling, "The stupe, I told him he had
enough." Jeff said no, one of the horses kicked him, and tried to help as
well as he could without letting go of the pistol. The third, in a fit of
euphoria, started letting fly with the automatic up among the bare
branches of a huge maple, once the pride of the Banks lawn. He
seemed to have forgotten the current engagement altogether. "Look at
'em! I always said horses could fly and there they are, the sky's full of
'em. One down—I got him! There goes another, watch it, he's gonna
dive!" So Brit was able to run over and help Chip pull the Nelco
magnate out of the trunk of his own car and get the gag out of his
mouth and the rope around him partly untied, before the order of
battle was in some measure restored.

At least the character with the M-16 or whatever it was, a sawed-off
thing powerful enough for an elephant gun almost, came down to more
terrestrial aim, whether consciously or not; Jeff was set to get anybody
who tried to stop him from driving off in the Cadillac, their original car
having no way out but into a steep ditch, and Pace, who had snatched
Johnson's gun from the ground, was hollering that if they didn't leave
that new model of his alone they'd all be dead. Chip, never a fighter
and who couldn't bring himself to see the whole business as anything
but a bad joke that would soon stop by itself, was about to shoot at a
front tire and Jeff to return the favor more or less at his head, when

Johnson once more stepped magnificently into the line of fire. Once more his arms were outstretched, his beard gleamed almost white in the moonlight, and his stirring voice resounded over the mêlée with the conviction of centuries.

"Jeff!" He walked toward him, the erstwhile neighbor-child being by this time at the wheel of the Cadillac, with the motor going. "I'm your old friend, John Philipson. You were right, I had to lie to you yesterday. Never mind that now, or anything you think you have on me. That's all past and I'm making it public knowledge right now, so you can forget your little blackmail scheme and we'll start fresh, you and I, like two decent human beings. How about it, Jeff? You *can* be a decent human being, I know it's what you want to be. Drugs, stealing, guns—that's not what you want. We all make mistakes . . ."

That got a jackal laugh. The troops had meanwhile staggered into the car. Let them go, was Chip's thought; good riddance and they'd be caught quickly enough. Pace would see to that. He could tell from Brit's face that he was taking the same view. So the two of them stood back, in relief at the harmless ending, as the shiny vehicle ripped in reverse over the leaf-strewn grass and down a steep bank to the road, bypassing the two other cars. "Thieves! Murderers!" Pace shouted, and was in the act of firing at the driver when Johnson knocked the gun from his hands, crying, "Peace! enough of this violence! let me talk to them . . ." The bullet hit Brit instead, and to the tune of the automatic playing through the back window and bestial shouts of something short of triumph, since all the expedition had netted them was one stolen car in exchange for another, Jim Pace's beloved possession, very like the ones that used to grace Jeff's family's garage in Michigan only of course up to date, tore off into the starry night.

"Brit! Brit! can you stand up? Hold it, we'll get you to the doctor." Pace and Johnson were both bending over him. "Let me feel his pulse, get a sheet . . ." He came to as they were tearing one up and trying to get his jacket off, to stop the gush of blood below his left shoulder.

"For Chrissake . . ." The words came hard, he was fighting for any breath at all. "Leave me alone and get to that boy. He's the one's hurt."

They had forgotten Chip, and Brit was right. He had turned his back in disgust at the departing samples of his fellow-man, and the one with the fancy rifle job, perhaps trying for the sky again, had happened to get him in the spine.

The casualties on the other side occurred some twenty minutes later. Either the gang didn't know the best route away, or thought Waterville the nearest place to pick up a different car before the cops got after the Cadillac, or couldn't resist seeing what was going on with the horses they had let out to keep the law busy while they went on their other errand. In any case one police car and a small group of people were still out by the corral, and the last two horses, with a stocky blond man leading them, were half quieted and nearly at their gate, when a blast from the car horn or the speed-shriek of the car itself threw them into panic again. The man was knocked to the side of the road. One horse flew over the car hood and through the roof, before the convertible turned over, horse and all, and crumpled into the shape of a piece of old Kleenex against a telephone pole.

The human remains on what had been the front seat caused general stupor and one case of vomiting. The two passengers in back, who had been cushioned by the body of the horse, were dead when the ambulance arrived.

"Margo, I'm asking you again. I don't think you were quite yourself when we talked the other day."

It had started snowing before dawn and the thin flakes were still falling, piling up in little patches on the inn porch and coating the railing. With her small valise packed and ready beside her in the front hall, soon to be bustling again with skiers, she had been watching it through the glass top of the door.

"Oh dear, I did hope to learn to ski, or try to. I suppose it would have been ridiculous." She smiled, more in a little play on wistfulness than the real thing. It was a certain fatigue at the moment that made her not welcome the trip. For a month she had taken all sorts of pickup jobs, at the restaurant and cleaning house for well-off weekenders and as saleslady off and on at the pottery store, to get together enough cash to leave with. "But isn't it pretty? I do love watching it. I hope the roads won't be too bad."

"You're not, you can't be, going off with that lout I saw you with—?" He didn't mention having been thrown out the back door of the high-school auditorium; it was not the kind of episode he chose to remember and he had managed not to most of the time.

"Walt? Well it's not really your affair, is it, John?" She still smiled, sweetly and quite distantly. "But since you ask, no, he's made other arrangements. Maybe you haven't heard—he's quite a hero around here now, since that terrible night, of the accident and everything. He had a broken arm and a lot of cuts and bruises, and still he was the first one to get into the wreck, to see if anybody was still alive. And before that he'd rounded up the worst of the horses, the ones nobody else could handle." A weight of sadness came on her as she looked out into the gently descending snow again. "I can't get over its being Jeff in all that mess, ending that way—the puzzled, sweet-faced little boy he used to be." She might have been about to say *do you remember?* but put it differently. "I remember the time you told him he looked like Tom Sawyer, and he said he didn't know any Sawyers and his name wasn't Tom. He thought you were making fun of him." But then he'd said maybe he'd seen a TV show called something like that and if he had, it stank, was the boringest thing he ever saw. John didn't remember. They'd spoken of Jeff's death before but only in its public aspect; the events preceding it, both immediately and by a span of years, were best left, in the view of one of these two, to be cloaked by time.

"You haven't asked how I happened to come here. It was through him—Jeff. He recognized you somewhere around here and told his mother and she phoned me. I didn't realize then . . ." But she wasn't going to bring up Penny or Penny's visit to her the day after the gun-fight and the accident. ". . . how different everything would be, after that extraordinary operation."

There was very little that Penny hadn't told, about Chip Holloway too though not the nature of his injury, which wasn't known then. The visit had been longer than intended. The girl hadn't a ghost of a plan in her head and was so wrought up, Margo had to keep her at the inn for the night, with a consequence that made her regret it. Penny had decided that men of any age were vile and not that much fun anyway, she was through with them, and in fact could see now that it was Margo she'd been in love with from the beginning; it was just the tyranny of conventional thinking that had made her run off with the wrong partner in that marriage. Unfortunately her recent outdoor years had done wonders for her muscles; she ripped her motherly confidante's nightgown, wanted to spray her long hair back and forth over her belly, and in short made quite a tempestuous scene before accepting her second amorous defeat in twenty-four hours.

Nor would Margo now speak of her trip to Boston with her new friends, Louise Horton and Hannah Palz, to visit the Holloway boy in the hospital. Not that tact, where she owed none, imposed any such reticence. She had heard no coherent account of the fracas that had brought such grief and was not tempted to draw one from her present caller—or suitor, more precisely; he had already told as much as he cared to about his peace-making efforts that night. The marvelous leap from the ledge, among the autumn leaves, that she might have thought she had dreamed if Walt hadn't been there seeing it too, she hadn't been able to recall aloud to Hannah and Louise either, surrogate mothers both of them, stricken past any such reminiscence that day.

"Oh, you had an operation here, did you? I did notice you seemed to be looking much better." It was said in haste, indifferently. "Margo, you must listen to me, for both our sakes. I need you."

"In what way? You didn't, for five years."

"Have you no forgiveness in you? We need each other, to make a life again."

She sat back, comfortably relaxed in one of the wicker armchairs brought in from the porch for the winter and scattered every which way around the dilapidated lobby. She had kept the cheap reproduction of a grandfather clock going during her stay, and glanced at it now. "Cheezit should be here in a minute. He's driving me to the bus in Compton, he has to go every day to market." She looked back at the tall man standing before her, as though already in the bus terminal and being asked a question by an impatient fellow-traveler, one not without some vague interest, extremely goodlooking too. The haggardness and state of nerves that had made him look so enfeebled the night of the play were gone, vanished; refreshed by multiple reliefs—Penny's departure not the least, Margo could have guessed if she had bothered— he seemed very nearly his old imposing self and quite ready to be charming if given a chance.

"It would help you look respectable, I can see that and how important it is to you right now." He would have welcomed bitterness in her voice, as something to rebut, but there was none; he could as well have jabbed a sponge fresh from the sea. "It always was. You couldn't even face a simple divorce. My goodness what trouble you went to, to avoid it. I suppose you landed in the wilderness, and in the dead of winter. Wasn't it awfully cold?" The sponge, sunlight running in its pores, was mocking him, as no such creature should.

"There were reasons," he retorted. "Things you don't know."

"Drugs? to keep in with the young? not look like an old square? You don't need to worry about that now. With your history you'll be very popular."

"We took, that is I took, very little. For a short time."

"And found your consciousness expanding? I'm so glad."

"You sneer! You talk like an ignorant child. I think I can honestly say that I *have* expanded my consciousness, through everything that has happened, and any suffering I may have caused you, or others . . . Yes, I know about Carl's stroke, I phoned. I can see that my, uh, actions may have put some burdens on him, but he always did like being the good one of us two, you used to say so yourself, and he was probably heading for some such trouble anyway, poor fellow. I'll try to do something for him as soon as I can, when this stupid murder trial is finished. That'll be early March, they say now." He frowned, at that last irrelevant hurdle; it entailed certain complications, because of his switch of identity, but powerful friends from his past were eager to help, now that his romantic story was out—minus, for general consumption, the romance: he had simply fled from worldly attachments, to the wilderness, as saints are prone to do; it was going to be all right. "Look, Margo, I can be more help to people now than ever before, I'm sure of that, I feel it, here"—he thumped himself in the neighborhood of the heart—"and if you will help me, my dear, to help, to heal"—which?— "as you always did, can't you see how we'd be healing one another too? It's not just my need. It's for you . . ." It would have been preferable if she had avoided his eyes. His voice went matter-of-fact, with a touch of petulance. "You didn't tell me the other day that you were planning to leave so soon."

"I wasn't. I hoped I could get Alice to come here with the baby— well, not baby, he's two and a half. She needs so to get away from there. She's in worse shape since . . ." Since her father's hoax and reappearance had made the front pages even in Detroit and Chicago;

that was when the phone calls from her started. "So I was delaying, and sent her all the money I had for the trip. But she wouldn't, and now I think she must have lost her job. She seems to be home crying all the time. I could tell last night that I should go right away."

"Well then"—a youthful eagerness flared up—"I could go with you. Or you could both come and join me; I do have a good deal cooking around Boston. But right now . . ." He took her shoulders in both hands, with a smile fit to untie all knots and rarely seen since courtship number one, "if you'd delay long enough to bake us a batch of those cheese biscuits . . . To tell you the truth I haven't had a decent meal since I left home." He made it sound like a week's business trip to England. "How about it? There must be a stove in this place, isn't there?"

For one ghoulish second the inspired appeal, to the wife of old, came rather close to the mark. Then the smile, already held past its normal limit, switched off, leaving a dull glow of both abstraction and command.

A car horn blew just outside. Cheezit was waiting, cheerfully; it was remarkable how much of the time he managed to be cheerful. Margo had already spoken about the insurance money, which she would make over to him for repayment. Now she added, picking up her suitcase since he hadn't offered to, that she would send him half the proceeds from the sale of their house and furniture.

"You're going to sell *my house?*" It passed belief. He had to control himself not to shake her, before a still small voice intervened.

She signaled to Cheezit that she was on her way, and motioned to her ghostly visitor to go out so she could lock the door. "You forget, Johnny," she began, with a touch of merriment above a load of sorrow, for more lives than theirs and for theirs as well, "but never mind. By the way, your old flame Althea, I forget her married name, came to the service for you; I suppose you saw that in the paper. I gather she's been divorced for several years."

"Who? Oh, was that her name?"

Margo laughed. "You knew it a few days ago. Someone you play tennis with here had known her in Florida and happened to mention her, you said."

"Perhaps so. It's hardly what matters now."

As they went down the steps in the snow, she still carrying the small suitcase which he couldn't bring himself to touch, she said in a tone of neighborly chitchat, "You were asking about my friend Walt. He's taken up with a good-humored, motherly widow in his church group, they sing hymns all the time and she has six children who seem to be crazy about him. Isn't that nice?"

Just to occupy his right hand, which under normal conditions would have had hold of her small luggage, he scooped up without noticing it a handful of snow from the stoop railing. It formed into a snowball by itself, and staring after the car that had to wait a minute at the intersection light, he had an impulse to laugh and throw it at the back window. How they would all laugh! she and Mr. Cheezit too. It would make them all children again, the car would come back, somebody else would take care of the consequences of whatever they did but there wouldn't be any consequences, it would all just be fun, such fun— wouldn't it? Even sobersides Carl would laugh, out in Michigan, while their mother smiled ever so benignly from the parlor window, at the dear silly boys in their innocent excitement over the snow.

The car made the turn. His fingers smarted with cold. He looked down at them, surprised by the pain; the snowball had turned hard as a rock and grey. He dropped it and quickly walked away up the street. Of whom was the murder trial to be? He had an impression of having seen the criminal that day in the woods, of its even being someone fairly well known to him, which was scarcely possible; surely his memory couldn't be that faulty. Yet the scene as he tried to reconstruct it, and would have to in public before long, had become strangely confused, and his own part in it shifted from one moment to the next. The sting of the icy ball in his hand had given way to another sensation, of warm blood, not his own but poured onto his skin from someone else's body. Ah yes, he remembered now, he had had that crazy—no, apostolic—urge to bathe himself in it. He must keep all this well in mind; it was bound to come up in the cross-examination. But the not quite unfamiliar face of the killer among the trees, that was not so easy to pin down; he was quite sure they hadn't seen anyone, but didn't see how he could be making it up. He would have to ask Brit or Mrs. Palz if they remembered anything of the sort.

He had planned to go on and visit Brit in the hospital anyway, and had been rather dreading it. But he was leaving that night for Boston, to work in a certain appropriate circle on his status and prospective tactics as a redivivus, and knew he must not put off the call until his return for the trial.

It turned out to be more awkward even than he had anticipated, and for his self-esteem no more rewarding than his meeting with Margo. Brit, recovered from the wound but not from the heart attack incurred at the same time, didn't want to talk to him or even look at him; it was just the way he had been received himself by Walt Hodge one day in September, in a different wing of the same hospital. It took all Reverend Philipson's bedside manner to get so much as a grumble out of him in the beginning. Shrunken, parchment-skinned, he was looking his age at last, and more; the beavers wouldn't have to worry about his traps that winter.

"You fixed that boy Chip all right," he said at last with furious bitterness.

"*I* fixed him? Brit, what are you saying?" True, he'd heard from Louise and the Palzes that Chip had been flown to Boston; the last word was that he was probably paralyzed for life. He had congratulated himself on taking no pleasure in the news, but neither had it lingered long in his mind, with all that was pressing on it at the time.

"He got your girlfriend and you got both of us shot. Don't matter about me, I've had my life, but him . . ."

"That's oversimplifying," said the minister with an air of kindly tolerance. Indeed it was, in more than the sense intended, as they both knew. For once poor demented Leona had been right, but the long tangled background of causality was of little interest to either of them just then. "But I didn't come here to argue with a sick man. If I've made trouble for you, Brit, I'm truly sorry. Certain things seem to come about, don't they? whether we would have willed them or not. I've never found it easy to attribute guilt in human affairs. Even that other boy, Jeff, and his friends—with all the wrong they did and the terrible price they paid . . ." He sighed, smitten by the pity of it. "We have to try to understand. But the main thing now"—he mustered up some semblance of heartiness—"is for you to get on your feet again. And meanwhile I want you to know how grateful I am . . ."

"I might get on my feet sooner'n you want . . . You and your goddam blabbermouth. That lyin', money-crazy Jim Pace, I used to think he was the lowest human specimen I'd ever see, but looks like maybe you got him beat. Git outa here before I have to crawl outa this goddam bed and throw you out. Git!"

It didn't seem the moment for the ex-Mr. Johnson to refresh his memory about the scene that was bothering him. And by that hour the next day Brit was dead.

9

Skiers trickling down the mountain's cheeks; here and there a blob of them halted together; parking lot by the lodge a big dark blotch, sinister, the kind for sinners to fall into though if you dip closer you can make out the models in all their colors and even the racks on top left unclamped for the day, pointing at random like so much else in life. Along the road more motorbugs scurrying to swell the blotch if there's still room or else stop where they may, at the foot of the white mothering mountain whose motto is Ignore! ignore these tiny seekers and suppliants and their arrogant little skills if indeed they can claim that much. But to the butterfly above it is piquant, a change from mere snowscapes however geologically upheaved, and to both men in it vastly gratifying, in different ways.

There were a few other butterflies in the sky, some heading for the mini-airport that one had just left—more skiers arriving, more business, more vacation-home owners or prospects for same—and far up above them all a single long jetstream, luminous in the sun as certain Renaissance angels' wings, proclaimed the new sublimity. In a burst of boyish pride Jim Pace gestured to his pilot-companion, as they passed over the unfinished scar of the new road up from Boonton and the mere bullfrog jump to be made before it linked up with the similar scar around the mountain. There were many other new lines and broad clearings between, and one large structure on the far side was already up, designed to make the facility they had just left look like the peanuts it was. Boonton had seemed at first too puny a name for what this was to be and he had pulled for Mt. Wonder, but had been persuaded that the native touch would be more catchy, by its very irony. The pilot nodded, recognizing for a second his old if temporary and not particularly happy home, and smiled. He might well. It was all over, he would never have to come back, and good fortune in every respect waited for him ahead, in Boston and even, he dared hope, in the country at large.

"Great show, Phil," the Nelco boss had said as they left the courthouse the afternoon before. "You really wowed 'em. That bit about the

187

other face, how did you put it? among the trees, that was some stroke. How do you ever think of a thing like that?"

There might be some topics the two wouldn't have agreed on if they'd pursued them, but Pace, first intrigued by the other's story and then taking a real liking to him, had been the soul of kindness. They'd had several other excursions together and he'd had the plane waiting to leave right after the trial, but there was an unexpected hitch. So they had a final evening together on Banks Hill, after a first-rate French-style dinner at Cheezit's, which in that company the realtor didn't mind paying for."I have to hand it to Hannah Palz too," he said over a first martini. "The way she looked the last time I saw her, I wouldn't have thought she could stand up in court or anywhere else." He put on a gross mimicry of a drunk. "Maybe leaving Vermont is just what they needed. Between you, you made that young defense lawyer look good and silly before it was over. The poor cluck, thought he'd make a killing, that's why he took the case. Moved up from New York a couple of years ago, figured this would be a good place to get big in politics. Matter of fact I was thinking of hiring him myself; I could use a man his age with that kind of get up and go, that's partly why I sat in on some of it, to see how he'd do." He pointed a thumb down at one remaining and very savory shrimp. "Of course I had no idea he'd go for *you* like that. And then all that stupid stuff he'd raked up about the Palzes and thought he'd be sly enough to get by with. And on that hippie from the fire tower too; I wouldn't want to have a meal with him but he's no criminal, everybody around here has known him for years. Ridiculous."

He wiped his mouth as though clearing a deck, as his guest murmured some kind of agreement.

"Well, he's talked himself out of one job. I thought he might find some smart way of handling it. You know, getting a crazy killer off when he's obviously guilty as hell, you got to be good." He didn't add that the State's Attorney, a little unbuyable old bookworm who looked like a handyman until the chips were down, was nearly a double of the lawyer who had caused him two setbacks in similar courts in New Hampshire not long back; he needed somebody on his payroll who could lick that type, in case of future need. "But he threw it away. With your help." They smiled, conscious of being the subject of some nudges and whispers around the restaurant; the proprietor himself was not showing them any particular deference, merely asking in the routine fashion if everything was all right. "I can see now it was all open and shut anyway, he shouldn't have taken it, but still . . ."

A new group of diners acquainted with him stopped to be introduced to his distinguished friend and exchange remarks on business matters as well as the events of that day. Over the chocolate mousse he started to say that he was thinking of buying the Palz property; together with the Holloway place that he'd already acquired it would give him a great leverage up there, for the future if not right away, but the topic was not of much interest to either of them, among so many larger concerns.

"Don't misunderstand me. What I said about the young lawyer and them, the Palz family. It's not that I go for people like that, hell no. I'd be glad to see all the kooks and anarchists or whatever you call 'em run out of this countryside. But it's a free country, you've got to have solid evidence, not jokes like cottage cheese and a couple of guitars or even her being a commie forty years ago though that might be more to the point. Why, he was even going to slip in something about that old history thing of Thelma Nesbit's, what do they call it, the Boonton Collection, that was mailed back weeks ago and would just have brought him another objection anyway." He signaled for the check. "If you come right down to it, our big mistake as a nation has been letting all these refugees like Lem Palz come in and take out citizenship. It's demoralizing. People who've lost everything in those German gas places and all the rest of it, and all the ones from Vietnam now. Sure I can feel sorry for them but it's unhealthy for the country. They bring some kind of death feeling with them, it just doesn't fit in. We're a young country. We ought to keep it that way."

"Now, now." The minister, having greatly enjoyed his veal tetrazzini and noted the figure on the check, was not in a position to sound too censorious. "We can afford some charity. And as you said, Mrs. Palz did acquit herself with a good deal of dignity today."

There was the big Mexican vase, always about to topple; and the boy in the wheelchair; the two bodies beside the Long Trail. And the

court building. "How beautiful it is. I never really took it in before."
Hannah was speaking late that night to her painter friend, Claire Nolan, in New Haven; two of the family had driven her and Lem there
straight from the courthouse. Lem had turned in, in the first of many
strange beds awaiting them; no, second; the last two nights they had
slept at a friend's house in the center of Boonton, their own being then
empty, everything sold, stored or carried to the town dump.

"You remember how we talked about the proportions of that building, when we wandered in for a look, years ago, and were surprised to
find the courtroom upstairs and just offices below. Those lovely white
fluted wooden columns of the portico—or just porch you have to say
there and you can't call them 'grand,' they're something better, more
quieting and natural than that. The squat spire is the only mistake. The
window design is so perfectly right, wonderful outside with the snow
deep around, the shutters almost black, with the small shell-shaped
pair at the top closed. Some country majesty of spirit, of a highly
educated order, went into it, a hundred and fifty years ago, and it
endures, that's what I couldn't come to grips with. You'd think it
would ennoble anyone in it—that's the function of great architecture,
isn't it? And you can imagine how much deeper the harmony of space
and line, and the relation with the green outside too, go in your feeling,
with its purpose brought to such a pitch. I think I understand temples
and cathedrals better now. A moral structure, this one is too, to be
desecrated most of the time, but I didn't see any column cracking or
shutter falling off today. Isn't that something?

"And yes, I'm cured, of two ailments—in time for what? You can see
the condition Lem's in; it seemed to happen all at once, when we sold
the pig last week. So my resurgence from the drainpipe isn't going to
be much use, and I'd gladly trade it anyway for what brought me up.
Our darling, beautiful Chip . . . You know him well enough, I don't
need to tell you he's not whining now, but you'd hardly recognize his
face. One horror makes a souse of you, another spins you out of it. It
was that hour with him in the hospital that did it, set up the revulsion
that saves me, who've had my life—what insane irony: it was his eighteenth birthday we celebrated at the end of the summer, when we put
a paper hat on his goat and they both jumped the hedge; and there's no
way to return the favor. Nothing can help him, on the physical side,
short of miracle.

"Well, my whirl with the bottle was nasty but short. The other, what shall I call it? unreality, Trotsky's death, had lasted much longer, I still hardly know why. A dream? an illusion? a hope? the idea of a world to be based on reason, in its last spasm? But I think I see it a little better, after today—I mean why that great skull cracking should have taken so many years to move out of my psyche, and I suppose many other people's, into history, where it belongs.

"It wasn't just the end of a revolution and its ideology; that's just according to Hoyle. As I see it now, it coincided with the end of a hell of a lot more than that. You brought up the House of Atreus, when I was going on about all this last fall. They're what the axe came down on, around 1940 if not on any precise day; tragedy itself—the whole material of myth, of meaning. Just as we get so smart about genes and atoms and sending snoop-machines to other planets, we've started this retrogressive mutation of the species, as definite as going from four legs to two only this isn't upward. The new animal: Homo insentiens. Now it's statistics, ballistics, conspiracy theories, theories of crime and everything else, including what you've been talking about, the latest thing in sure-to-kill art traps from Paris. Of course crime is nothing new, but the scale of it is and that changes everything. My grandmother always marveled at having lived through the appearance on earth of the airplane and the telephone. What we've been privileged to see is the morally unthinkable becoming as ordinary as the airplane and the telephone, way beyond what any mind or feeling can deal with. So those faculties atrophy and get ready to fall off the way our tail did.

"That was the spectacle in court today, a good part of it. Nothing that could ever give us a Macbeth, or an Oedipus, or a Captain Ahab, or even Pinocchio. Just that miserable demented blob of a murderer and his nondescript victims, in a three-panel mirror, multiplied more or less to infinity. Our substitute for drama.

"At least . . . But yes, I must be more tired than I realized; forgive me. You're right, this rhetoric of despair is as shoddy as anything else, so seductive, and easy, with just enough validity to make it addictive. I take it back, some of it, with qualifications. It's true that wasn't the whole story, not this round, for a wonder and praise be. And I did feel in communion with another kind of time, in that lovely building, hearing its voice—and oh, it has one!—over all the lunacies and evils chewing away at it. Like that time we stumbled on the two forgotten

children's graves in the woods up the mountain, where the village used
to be, of about the same time, the 1820's; one a baby, one a girl of
sixteen, wasn't it? What mysterious strength it does give, when our past
gets through to us, as I guess some mysticoids think it's trying to do all
the time. Maybe in an ugly city courtroom that defense lawyer would
have sounded more frightening and I'd have disgraced myself, and
helped bring on more crimes. A tall, quick, angry young man, everything narrow about him—shoulders, hips, forehead, set of eyes—feeling very superior to his surroundings and especially to our old friend
Milo Sims, the State's Attorney I think they call him now. The defense
one was going for us hammer and tongs, don't ask me why but it didn't
matter. He had a long chunk of dark oily hair that he'd whip back from
his eyes to emphasize a point. Our next Senator Joe McCarthy . . . Oh
yes I'm sure he'll rise from these ashes all right, I'd bet you anything.
Give him five years."

He had had reason beforehand to think it was all open and shut the
other way, and did set great store by it. The case was much publicized,
a brilliant performance would be a big leg up where he wanted to go
and no telling when another such chance might come. It was well
worth doing without a fee, and it looked easy: an old hick scholar-type
for his opposite number; a judge with an Italian name but so naive he
had no political connections and would have been laughed off the
bench in any other state the young man was acquainted with; the state
anachronism of the two side judges who weren't even lawyers. Better
than all that, of the three who had found the bodies, the only one sure
to be believed was dead. The other two were sitting ducks, with their
histories, and one, the man then alias Johnson, handed him a further
bonus in his first minutes on the stand, being so vague about every
detail of the scene, the jury were bound to wonder on their own what
he was concealing or whether he had really been there at all. When
was it? had the leaves turned? what was the dead girl wearing? how far
from the road? how long between their seeing the car as claimed and
finding the bodies?

The confusion of the witness in all this soon came to look like a ruse
and a damned clever one. Nobody had warned the defender of the
man's training as an orator, which took his scandalous past right out of
the lawyer's mouth and turned it into something like a character testi-

monial—the dark night of the soul came in there somewhere—or that he would arrive in the brand new Cadillac and obviously friendly company of the biggest land tycoon in the region, the Nelco boss himself, of whose favor the young man was indeed practically assured. That was a terrible blow; short of a signed contract it had been in the bag. The two men, of about the same height and a certain similarity of bearing and self-confidence in every gesture and expression, had entered together, as they later left, amid the buzz and bustle accorded to conquerors, like a pair of proconsuls graciously showing themselves to the populace. (Before law school the émigré from the Big Apple and political aspirant had had a course in Roman history.)

Mrs. Palz too, in a more personal way but no less surprisingly, had most of the crowd with her. Not just her own loving and rather numerous family, and not mainly long-hairs and hopheads either. Many were just ordinary conservative natives, a benighted lot that however had to be reckoned with, who had known her and her husband for thirty years and didn't give a hoot about, if they'd ever heard of, "that prime architect of the bloodiest revolution in history, Leon Trotsky, whose household you . . ." Objection sustained; it had seemed worth it ahead of time. He hadn't figured on her sitting so straight in the chair, with head so high, and such a head!—pushing sixty, with strands of grey hair straggling loose but just the same, really, like one of those Junos or Minervas in the history book. He hadn't anticipated that either, or the easy composure of face, voice, folded hands, no matter what was thrown at her. He'd been led to expect quite the opposite all around, except for her not having been to the hairdresser.

The courthouse itself, on what he'd been told was the prettiest village green in Vermont, had misled a number of city-bred minds before his as to their innate certainty of victory in any legal fray. With the somewhat smaller church of the same period in back and another now converted to a grange hall alongside, a rambling white frame green-shuttered inn not much newer on the other side and similar structures in which people still actually lived scattered around, it was a favorite in the Christmas card and calendar trade; a mecca, one would say, not for jurists but tourists and amateur water-colorists in season. Even so, the fair-sized second-story courtroom, in good repair and decently dusted but too infected by the quaintness around to make much claim to the august, was rarely as packed as that day. The balcony, hardly ever used, had had to be opened, and out on ploughed road or lawn deep in snow too an unusual number of cameras clicked unless jammed by the cold.

Inside or out, except possibly in a group of red-nosed neo-Christians demonstrating against capital punishment, far from likely in this case though technically possible, the death feeling that Jim Pace deplored was not much in evidence. As Hannah would tell it, in the "fickle and footloose" collection of relatives and step-relatives of the murdered pair, rancor and the limelight reigned. The TV and other newsmen on the steps during intermission, when they weren't after Mr. Philipson instead, had to beg for tears—"Come on now, can't anybody cry?" The girl's mother in the latest thing in avant-ski garb and raccoon, looking her daughter's age and with a spouse or escort of about twenty-five, was particularly eager to be photographed and wanted to know if they'd make Flash Magazine. The dead boy's older sister arrived on a motorcycle with a mate said to be a second-string jai alai player, who was soon bored and disgruntled at being left out of the pictures and got her to leave before lunch, although they had ridden all the way from Chicago just for the trial. Two young teen-agers, evidently step-siblings of the victims, chatted and giggled until the judge had to call for order; a stepfather somewhere back in the string of rearrangements kept going out to make business calls and apparently also visit the bar in the inn across the green. Another, or perhaps this was one of the long since discarded blood parents, sat alone and except for an air of annoyance at the proceedings, could have been mistaken for the defendant; they were not unlike in age, build, conventional haircut and pudgy, rather somnolent features. However the prisoner, though declared fit to stand trial, was not to take the stand and all that most spectators could see of him was the broad back of his head and now and then his fingers working unhurriedly in the air at chest height, as though on some invisible tangle or braid.

Unreliability of witnesses was to be the line, not any presumption of guilt on their part which too obviously wouldn't wash, yet as the de-fender felt his get up and go being deflated the questions veered more that way; he knew it was a mistake, couldn't help it, there seemed to be strange forces putting the wrong tone in his voice and twist to his words. It had all been so foolproof in the preparation. *They* were smeared with the blood of the victims, not his client; the single blood-stain found in his car, or the car he had been picked up in, had been inconclusive. The attorney would prove that he had not been any-where near the murder scene at the critical time; a bartender over the New York state line was precise in his recollection of him and willing enough to be positive that he had been in the bar at 5:30 P.M., not 2:30; a nut fisherman on the Battenkill, avid to be in the public eye, had also seen him that day and would swear to anything. But even supposing these witnesses should be mistaken as to the exact time of their en-counters, and the defendant should be thought to have been that much farther east before sunset, could he not have had an impulse like that of the discredited minister, to touch that blood, or of Mr. Horton to handle the knife? Could one lend credence to a man so unbalanced as to behave as the *Reverend* (heavy sarcasm there) John Philipson, alias Johnson, had on that occasion? or a woman who not long ago was stopped for drunken driving, and who . . .

Oops: not worth another objection and lost its punch anyway. Largely through the efforts of the Palzes, it had been discovered that the thief of the Boonton Collection had been a failed guru before hitting Vermont; as a failed entrepreneur of stolen local lore, he was now trying his hand as a mercenary somewhere off the coast of Africa. The two cumbrous volumes, of no use and much nuisance to him by that time, were now being proudly exhibited across the road from the courthouse, at the County Historical Society. Ellis Horton must have convinced Thelma that that was the safe and wise thing to do, or perhaps as Brit had suspected, she didn't care all that much any more. She had run in for a peek that morning and was now among the spec-tators in court. It was in her house next to the P.O. that Lem and Hannah had spent their final nights in Boonton.

As to the Johnson-Philipson character, who had himself once served a jail term, in Washington, D.C., was it not correct that in his first statement to the police he had wavered as to whether he, alone of the three with the dog, had glimpsed another male figure near the lament-able scene?

There he put his head in the noose.

"That is correct, and in a sense remains so." It was quite thrilling. An ill-favored recent stepfather of gangland cast, in a loud-striped suit, whipped out a change of eyeglasses and leaned forward in excitement.

The teen-agers were rapt. The defendant stopped his weaving in air, his fingers staying up where they had been arrested; a veteran in his late thirties honorably discharged after incidents not strictly in the line of duty in two Vietnam villages, he had been previously convicted of a remarkably similar homicide in the Adirondacks. Mr. Philipson, no longer alias Johnson (he had made that little amendment with a touch of humor and great courtesy) stood as though in the very act of taking the sins of the world on his broad shoulders, a not unwelcome burden. "At the time, and more vividly for many days afterwards, I saw my own face as that of the criminal. Call this unbalanced if you like . . ." A hoot came from the back of the room, carrying an unpleasant re-minder of some kind; sure enough, it was from Walt Hodge, who had wanted to be there in case anything wrong was said about his friend Brit. But the witness did have a lovely voice and on the whole the listeners seemed duly spellbound, except for one of the side judges, a retired inn-keeper who tapped a pencil rather irritably on the pad before him and turned to whisper something to the judge. The speech would be expanded for the newspeople outside later, with reference to the guilt of all of us in social evils and specifically the Vietnam war, "that helped, if this defendant is guilty, to make him what he is." On the stand the witness could only add, with a playful if still sorrowing little smile, "So yes, Your Honors, in that sense I did almost succeed in seeing another face between the trees, as I believe we all should. This is sometimes called looking for the beam in our own eye."

"Baloney!" cried Walt, and was about to be reprimanded when a fracas broke out in the snow below, loud enough so a short recess had to be called. Everybody was in need of moving around and trying to warm up anyway, the heating system not being quite up to the severe temperatures of that week. A truckful of Boo Boo Sam Dah's on their way to a gathering had been insulted, some said attacked, by the Jesus freaks, although as they loudly proclaimed, far from disagreeing on the capital punishment issue, they scorned the opposing sect for their will-ingness to kill ants and potato bugs. Local townspeople drew near to gape, cracking jokes; skiers homebound or heading north began clog-ging the highway bordering the green. There was talk of a bombscare, but what ensued was a show largely cosmetic, orangoutang versus egg-pate, and sartorial. For a few minutes the stately columns, in their picturesque other-century setting, were backdrop to a confused ballet:

a whirl of beads, placards, tinkling cymbals, white robes flapping and ripping to reveal regular northland winter attire underneath, bright-colored parkas above ankle-length cotton skirts and boots, and flying snow, with only a broken nose or two and quite a mileage of movie film amateur and other as the toll.

Hannah's turn followed ("I think, it may have been before") an acid wrangle between psychiatrists, and was short. Brit had been the only one of the three with a habit of noticing license numbers, she didn't remember how many digits of that one he had reported (the sheriff filled that in, it was three). Etc. The insinuation now seemed to be that the three of them, the walkers with the dog, might have had some compelling reason to go to that spot at that time, and further, might indeed have seen another male figure there whom they had some interest in protecting. The white-haired old music-lover Milo Sims handled that nonsense, and also got Hannah's "drinking problem" out of the picture if not out of the record, in some way she didn't bother to follow. "I was in quite a saintly state of ubiquity—go ahead, it's not murder we're laughing at—roaming the world and time looking for the lost treasure: *grief.*"

She hadn't wanted Lem to go to the trial but loyalty to her required it. He was sitting in front of Walt, looking much aged and shivering in the heavy parka, always before in March worn for sugaring or its preparation, that he would travel in. They were to leave for Europe the next evening, after the night in New Haven, unless the witnesses should have to stay over but it was becoming clear that that would not be necessary.

Those few minutes on the stand, she related, were the only time she was facing the defendant. She got no impression of the homicidal or anything else from the flabby, commonplace face, until some laughter in the courtroom caused him to turn around with a sudden beginning of a smile, as though pleased to discover that the show he had been watching was worth it. At that, catching sight of the Palz married daughter with her young husband's arm holding her close against nerves and general distress in the occasion, the prisoner again stopped his peculiar finger motions, his hyperthyroid eyes took on a gleam of ecstatic appetite, and he let out a half-smothered cry, something like "EEEK!" or "Whee-ee!" like a child's cartoon Indian on the warpath.

After a break for more psychiatric deliberation, the State's Attorney,

known to hold some quixotically level-headed views on the treatment
of the criminally insane, began dropping his air of the seedy backseat
observer and driving to the crux. He had at some point, presumably
apropos of the Russian Revolution and its various architects, gotten
some smiles among the jury and elsewhere by remarking that his own
youthful addiction to the racetrack for instance would not, he supposed, have any bearing on his testimony if he had had the misfortune
to come on the scene in question. The effects of such shock were well
known to be various and often prolonged; in that sense these witnesses
were to be seen as subsidiary victims; the two still alive had willingly
testified and deserved the thanks and sympathy of the court. The de-
fender thereafter saw fit to drop certain items. But his case and the
rosy future depending on it were lost anyway, through nothing to do
with Mrs. Palz or Mr. Philipson, or Brit Horton either, with which last
name the attorney finished hanging himself if he hadn't before. A
boner, blurted out in an angry tiff with the prosecutor, which snapped
Hannah out of her reveries, she had no idea just when or in what
connection; something to do with whether a dead man's character
might be allowed as evidence even if his deposition couldn't be.

"A man of high repute, we hear, in his tiny arena"—giggles from the
Boonton contingent and more smiles in the jury box—"but of a family
tainted with insanity."

This brought quite a jolly little uproar and a shout, "Hey, Leona,
ain't you goin' to speak up?" Walt again, of course. But she just sat
listening intently beside her new friend Thelma Nesbit. The way it was
generally figured, it was an attack of homesickness toward Christmas,
along with fierce mourning for her brother Brit, that had cured her;
she had suddenly tired of her double identity, quarreled with Harriet
Two, and apparently decided she had done all she could for the FBI, a
bunch of ingrates anyhow. Back home, she kept all the shades pulled in
front toward the road, upstairs and down, would only look out back
toward the pastures and sugarbush and was too busy to do much of
that, as with Louise Horton moved away to live near a daughter upstate, Leona and Thelma had gradually taken over the bakery business
and were enjoying it thoroughly. Now they were planning a trip to
Florida together, the first away from their home state in either of their
lives.

The proprietor of the hardware store who had sold the hunting knife on the morning of the crime had been very busy that day and couldn't swear that this was the purchaser. What had stuck in his mind was just the customer's jacket; he saw all kinds of weird jackets every day but that was a new one on him—sort of sateen like most of them, bright blue with a big gold serpent and the words in gold . . . Must he say them? He must. He blushed and said the words so low, the prosecutor had to repeat them himself: FUCK ME I'M WIDE OPEN.

He held up the jacket, found on the defendant in the blue car. On cross-examination the other lawyer would whip out three identical jackets; they were the most popular thing nowadays, you could buy them practically anywhere and see them on practically anybody. His three had not been worn.

The New York State bartender and the foolish fisherman were quickly disposed of. Dosie Willett, in size and looks the star of the show, who had been a town joke from childhood for his slow wits except at the accordion and inability to remember names and faces, nevertheless would not be budged this time, although he always let his wife speak for him at Town Meetings when necessary and had never before had to open his mouth in front of so many people. However, his vexation of spirit seemed to have lifted, now that the unholy incident was about to be wrapped up one way or another. The defendant had gone berserk over his not clearing the road fast enough to suit him, so he had climbed down from his grader to have a friendly word with him and though he might forget a face (grin there, in response to one from the entire balcony) he had been struck by the man's gold wristwatch.

Then came the keeper of the fire tower, the Tolstoy-worshipper, and his girlfriend of that season, reconciled or not, it was hard to tell. The blue car had come by, they'd thumbed for a ride into Boonton and the driver, smiling, had come almost to a stop before slamming the accelerator down again. They had seen the jacket, soiled in front and at the armpits, and the face. Later, in the crowd on the steps, the young man was heard saying no, he wasn't afraid for his life, not that way, and if he had been he'd have testified anyway. "It could just as well have been us two, if we'd come down half an hour sooner. There're enough murdering maniacs around without me lying to help another one get out there. One thing I don't sell is myself." He didn't elaborate on any offers for that.

Lem and Hannah would hear the verdict, Guilty, first degree murder, on the car radio on the way to New Haven. Life without parole that would be, for the second such episode; they had gathered that much in the legal maze. But old Milo, the friend for whom they had put together their first Debussy "spoof," hadn't told them what power the judge or anybody would have to get the murderer shut up as crazy when he'd been declared sane. "And the angels weep," Lem murmured with his first smile of the day, dry and rueful, and Hannah knew he was referring to a favorite ikon he'd come by years before, that was now in storage.

It was a small apartment Claire Nolan lived in, in a dingy building just off-campus, in such contrast to her other, Vermont setting, it made them feel half a world away from Boonton already, though they had visited her there often before with no such sensation.

"I hadn't thought about that enormous vase, in Coyoacán, for years. It was in the diningroom. I was sitting facing it, with my back to the courtyard, about ten in the evening, long past dinnertime, chatting with some of the household—secretaries and perhaps one of the bodyguards. The Old Man and Natalia had gone out, I don't remember where though the possibilities were few and acting on any of them would have made for the usual fuss. The vase, of many colors, was on a broad shelf half way up along the wall.

"All of a sudden, with nobody near it, it teetered to one side, and then back the other way, and at the same time I had a fit of nausea. As you know I never drank much of anything, even wine, until that loathsome period last fall, so it wasn't that. I looked around the table and everyone was staring just the way I must have been. For a few seconds the vase, a rather valuable one probably, was swaying wildly, so was the room but nothing else was that breakable, and by the time we could come to our senses and try to hold it, it was over. That's the only earthquake I've ever been in, quite a small one as they go.

"It's funny, I don't remember the designs that were really on the vase; it takes on what it needs to. And stranger still, I'm not positive it didn't crash to smithereens, but I think that by some miracle it didn't. Anyway as I've been seeing it today, it never does quite topple. Of course, earthquakes have always been taken as symbolic, at least I guess they have, it would seem hard to miss. Still, if I'd been through one in an ordinary house I don't suppose I'd be remembering it quite this way.

"Lem! what is it? Yes, darling, I know, I'm coming to bed right away. Did you remember your Simenon for the plane? . . . You know, we never would have butchered that pig. We were saps about her, even after she went rampaging through Leona's parlor a few months ago.

"Yes, Chip talked to us a little, not about what happened though, we'll never know much about that. And when we left he asked us, very lovingly, not to come again. He said if we wanted to send him some poetry—Keats and Yeats and Rimbaud he mentioned—that would be nice, there wasn't any in the hospital. Except for that, he just wanted to be thought of as an animal that got hurt in the woods, long ago. That's the company he said he felt best in."

The hitch at the Mt. Akatuck airport was probably imaginary. Some character had been seen loitering around the waiting plane and Pace went into one of his spells of fright. He'd had them off and on since the attempted kidnapping; it had done something to him, being tied up in the trunk of his own car and then having the car wrecked besides. He just didn't feel as invulnerable as he'd have liked, it was like having the ocean come up to his door, so insisted on having the Cessna thoroughly gone over. Hence the extra night at the shanty as he called it, where he would have to forgo the party he could have had in different company. He'd thought at first that the minister might go for that kind of amusement, nothing holier than thou in that case, but he was about to get remarried, to a stylish dame he'd been engaged to once before a long time ago, and might be too old or not the type anyway.

So Jim Pace discovered the luxury of disinterested conversation instead. Fantastic. For once he had a friend who really understood things, in depth, and didn't want anything from him either. The bit of finagling on getting his pilot's license restored had been Pace's own idea and didn't count, because he felt better with his new friend at the controls than flying himself. Keen, competent, never jittery; get a kick of breeze or downdraft between the mountains and he was right on the ball. As he was in other ways. On the platform too, people said. Pace hadn't heard him perform that way, until the little affair in the courthouse, but there'd been a big turnout in Worcester he'd heard about, at a university or something, and just after the story was in the papers about his daughter's suicide out in Michigan. Got quite a play that did, on TV too, because of the father's recent splash and comeback, maybe a little more than Pace's daughter would get. He didn't begrudge that, was proud to be friends with such a man, of vastly more education than himself and who could swallow his grief and hold forth to a cheering audience only two days later. No wonder he'd been appointed to that fine church and his office waitingroom, where Pace had picked him up a couple of times, was jammed with young people after him for counseling.

The realtor felt, to his great surprise, that he could use a little of that himself, especially on one small matter he hadn't yet managed to mention, another reason to welcome the holdover although it obliged them both to make a number of phone calls about important business the next morning. Pace even had to change air tickets to a night flight, for the ski trip to Gstaad he was taking with a young lady he called his secretary. Yes, you could really talk to the man; he'd listen; even about the unsatisfactory date with his own ex-girlfriend, now known as Penny Fried, who'd apparently led Pace on just to get a ride to New York. Went to the hotel with him all right but clamped up on him at the worst moment—"Jesus, it actually hurt!"—and then railed at him the rest of the night or what felt like it. Social this and that; the works. A regular fem lib fiend she turned out to be. To all this the once and now newly famous counselor and man of God merely nodded, sitting by the fireside, at the scene of the drama that had drawn them together, they being the two survivors, unless you counted the young cripple, who had also figured in that girl Penny's tirade in the hotel bedroom. Couldn't tell if she was mad for him or at him the way she carried on; both by the sound of it. John Philipson pulled at his pipe, looking neither surprised nor aggrieved nor even particularly interested, beyond the demands of courtesy and the general human dilemma. It was as if the whole romantic runaway bit and its epilogue had been someone else's story.

"And then the weirdest thing, a new one on me. When I woke up she'd left a note and a five-dollar bill, said it was all she could spare then for her share of the room and dinner and she'd send me the rest when she got a job. And by God she did. Sent a money order from San

Francisco about a month ago. For crying out loud!" After a pause for mystification, and to see if his guest would care to elucidate out of his far better acquaintance with the female phenomenon in question, he went on: "I paid a little more than I really had to for the Holloway place—the old lady lost her shirt last year, on some theatrical bummers—so I guess now she'll be able to help with the rehabilitation stuff. I'm trying to get my insurance to do something on it too. Lousy luck that was, and could just as well have been one of us that got it." He poured himself a second stiff highball at his makeshift bar, in the corner that had been the Banks matrimonial bedroom. The minister was still nursing number one, the most he ever took. "Still, I can't help wishing it had happened some other way if it had to, not rescuing *me.*" His laugh was short and self-conscious, quite uncharacteristic. "Of course when you look at so many other young guys now, you can see maybe that bullet saved him from worse. Like those nuts out there on the green today. And that boy Chip always was a dreamer; no practical sense; could easily have drifted that way. Boy, if a son of mine ever . . ." He didn't see much of his two sons and what news he got of them wasn't too good; besides this might stir up thoughts of his friend's recent family tragedy.

John Philipson mused into the diluted stuff in his glass, mouth pursed, his large frame comfortably relaxed in the canvas sling-chair that by itself seemed to dispel all history from the house. "We can only undermine our own usefulness by trying to take on the guilt of the world . . ."

"You seemed to be taking on quite a bit of it in that speech today."

"Oh in that sense, certainly. But that's not fabricating guilt in what's only a matter of luck. Brit too. He meant well, and I guess it's lucky for you he did, but let's face it. He was too old, and had heart trouble already. He got in the way."

"Well . . ." This was the moment, if ever, for the little item Jim Pace had thought he might use the counselor for the disposition of, but they were distracted just then by a terrific racket in the attic. Rushing up the narrow stairs, not much better than a ladder, they found a mouse caught by one paw, thrashing and banging the trap on the floor. "Hey, these are great floorboards. Real oldtime chestnut, and look at the width of them! I'm going to rip those out and use them in one of the chalets. You might not believe it but I can nearly double the price just for one feature like that." The mouse gave piercing squeaks and banged itself a few feet away from them. "I've never been up here before." He turned his flashlight away from the rafters and onto the only non-structural object left from Banks days, a ragged and filthy old horsehair mattress speckled with mouse droppings. "Have to get that dragged out, they're nesting in it." Bang bang, then quiet; the mouse must be exhausted. Pace laughed, in his normal healthy way, not like a few minutes before. "Hey, whadda you know, that must be where Walt Hodge tried to kill himself, with a whole bottle of pills I think it was, back last fall. This house has sure seen some good stories, you can say that for it, though I'd just as soon have been left out of one of them."

"Me too. But I'd say this one"—he pointed to the remains of the mattress and was surprised by his own sudden grimness of tone and by the mere fact of the recollection causing it—"had had a wrong ending." Pace, his face in darkness, must have been surprised by such a sentiment from one of his calling. The mouse went into a new spasm and seemed in danger of flopping itself out of reach, to keep them awake all night. "Of course I don't pull for suicide. Only that one might have been a public benefit." He felt bruised all over his body, thinking of the highschool parking lot and how he arrived in it. An outrage really, and now that he had been forced—by a mouse!—to remember it, he realized, before wiping it out of mind again, that the outrage had been unique in his experience. His mother had never slapped him; his war, if reprehensible, had involved no hand-to-hand combat or anger; never had physical violence filled him with such righteous loathing as now looking at that mattress.

"Oh I guess he's pulled himself together, as far as a halfwit can. He was kind of rowdy in court today but he looked sober." The full tactlessness of this Pace couldn't know. "There used to be a lot of drink and incest and suicide around these hills. It's a good thing we're getting another element in." He tore a shred from the mattress, grabbed the mouse, trap and all, in it and downstairs threw the whole package out the front door into the snow. He poured a last nightcap. "There's just one thing, Phil, I'd like to ask your advice about. I guess you'd say psychological advice, if that's the lingo in your trade."

"It'll do. Shoot. What is it?"

"It bugs me a little. Oh, not too much, not to lay awake over. Certain things just can't be helped, no sense crying over 'em." He got up, paced a few yards, changed to another chair. "Getting cold, isn't it? But I guess it's too late to bother with the fire again. Lord, those Bankses must have been tough. See, I got these electric heaters in and that gas floor furnace over there so I could open out this fireplace, you have to have that for demonstration, in ski country. All they ever had, for these Vermont winters, was one of those cheap stoves, with the pipe stuck into the chimney here. For the whole house. Must have done plenty of bundling under those conditions, and it's true the old boy was some stud, I used to hear. Well, what I started to say . . . But it's nothing to bore you with, to hell with it."

"No, please go on." Exercise of his skill flooded the counselor with warmth, dead fire and Vermont winter notwithstanding. The ugly reminiscence in the attic vanished deliciously.

"It's just that . . . Well, I had to do something a few months ago I'd rather not have. Nothing much, considering the stakes, and I mean a whole lot of public good, along with a few pennies in my pocket, which I never underestimate." He flashed the well-known, good-natured smile. "Brit Horton had what he called his woodlot, twenty-seven acres that came to him from way back in the family, separate from his house lot."

"I know. I heard him talk about it."

"Then you know the location, and that we had to get a right of way, for my road off the new town one, or make a big detour for about another hundred grand. Stubborn old bastard he was, wouldn't listen to reason. If it was just me personally . . . But I have to play ball with the big boys to some extent, you know what I mean." His listener didn't, and would rather not. "They're getting their fingers into real estate all over this section and they don't play for peanuts. So, well, to make a long story short, I got a couple of my guys to slip the old deed book out of the town records one night and do a little work on it. Some job. The deeds were all handwritten in those days. Of course they had to strew things around, make it look like an ordinary job. You probably heard about it, and how they found a whole bunch of papers and other record books out back in the swamp next morning. Luckily a string of town safes around the county were being looted then, for cash, along with all the other break-ins, so it looked all right.

"Actually it was kind of a masterpiece. Never been done before that

I know of. Just a few words, you know, an old stone wall here and an old tree there, but the damn thing dated from 1820 so you can imagine. I had to fly a fellow up from Texas for that side of it; an expert; did it right here in this room and it was back with the other stuff in the swamp by six in the morning. The family copy had been lost a hundred years ago, like most of them."

Branches creaked beyond the black, unshaded little windows and an owl gave three hoots, close enough so the two men snapped around, then sank back with a smile at their foolishness. A slight crust had already formed on the latest snow, so the mouse and its encumbrance hadn't fallen through and they could hear it squeak faintly from time to time.

"I'll say this. I did him a favor he wouldn't do himself. I've doubled the value of that acreage for him; Louise is left a lot better off. Everybody along the road will be. So why should I even feel like telling you about it, can you tell me that?"

John Philipson gave him a fairly straight, long look, one he well knew the effectiveness of; people could be counted on to either squirm or blossom under it, depending. His voice, however, was unjudgmental. "We can't turn wrongs into rights, can we? But I don't suppose it would be bugging you so if he hadn't put himself out for you afterwards, that night here. Isn't that right?" Pace made a noise allowing as how it might be and that the fact was unpleasant to him, he'd like it to go away. "But I've never known human motives to be clear-cut and simple, actions either." Buzz buzz buzz; the Boston to Albany; no, wrong time. It seemed to be a great babble of voices, including his own. Must be the courtroom, but they were from farther back too; his wife, mother, brother, daughter, son couldn't have been there that day, could they? why of course not, at least two of them were said to be dead. And now as the voices subsided he felt a terrifying weight beginning to press on him, a leaden ceiling slowly lowering, something he seemed to have experienced once before; it was associated with a strange glow over some valley or other and with some kind of strange ripply music too. He forced himself to go on speaking. "You did, after all, have the option of taking your loss and delaying your whole project a year or two, or whatever it would have meant. For that matter you could have chosen way back to be a poor man and not out there changing the world at all."

"Well, there are degrees in these things. And personal friendships, they figure. This is hard to say but well, I guess I was really fond of Brit, more than I realized, and kind of admired him. And I owed him something too. Not just that night here. From way back, when I was young . . ." The rest came much harder. "He let me tag along on a fishing trip, to Quebec, when I was sixteen. And lent me fifty dollars; all the cash he had in the world, pretty nearly; for the first land I ever owned."

This time it was Philipson who had to pace a little, before taking a peculiarly rigid stance facing one of the black windows. The light inside was low, so that what he looked at was not so much a reflection as a ghostly negative of their two figures and the interior scene on a forbidding waste of snow. No, there were three figures; he distinctly saw and recognized the third one, smiling and at ease in the chair he had himself just vacated. Furthermore that whole version of reality, room and all, seemed to be slipping away into the total black void of which the snow was only an antechamber. He reached to hold it back and was surprised when his fingers bumped into glass.

"Have you ever thought of going to a Tibetan monastery, for the rest of your life?" No answer; flabbergasting thought. "I have. Quite often. Like right now."

He went back to his once more unoccupied chair, a rather hard one to lean forward in but he didn't feel like reclining at the moment. "There's one saying, or command, of Jesus that seems hard to apply to the present-day world of action, say business or government, without proposing that it grind to a halt altogether. That is, 'Go, and sin no more.' He said it to a woman caught in adultery, considered a sin at the time, not to anybody in your position. But he did say some pretty harsh things about the rich and as we say, successful. Most great religious teachers have. You can talk that way from a desert, or the sidelines. Historically, the church has usually straddled that fence; they haven't often been out there flaying the mighty if it could be avoided. That's how the institution has survived, to be the only lasting power for good in our era."

"You some kind of Jesuit? I seem to remember my mother talking about them."

"No, no." He laughed, with constraint and no look of cheer. "Just a poor simple-minded Protestant, hoping not to get left too far behind."

A branch cracked, almost like a gunshot that time, then there was a heavy whir of wings close by the window, followed by a screech and scuffle beyond the front door. So there was one gone mouse, and probably one cross-eyed owl, with that hardware attached to its dinner. The minister suddenly yearned for his new city apartment and the still handsome Althea waiting for him in it. An odd sensation of disgust, that seemed to be at both his host and himself, had crept upon him; there might have been something wrong with the shrimp.

Pace must have been having similar thoughts."Gives me the shimmies, as my mother used to say, this godforsaken hill, in all this goddam snow. And all those diamond drills out there"—he flung an arm toward the winter wonder of stars—"a size and voltage for every cavity, ever think of that? not giving a damn about *us*. When I think of all those poor suckers buying the shit I'm dishing out for them!" He hadn't said that as part of the counseling session but the thought came at once; he had seldom said anything like it before and then only in bed. He couldn't have foreseen the effect of it this time. "What did you say? Are you feeling all right?"

"I said a fine trio we make."

"Trio? Who's the other one?"

"The man on trial today, of course." It was almost a whisper. "The murderer."

"Oh come on now . . ."

"You probably couldn't see his face where you were sitting. He was laughing. At me. So I guess he's not completely insane." However, he pushed off the great leaden weight once more and sank back into the somewhat abandoned position called for by those devilish modern chairs. "To get back to your problem, what you did to Brit obviously stinks. That's what you wanted to hear, isn't it? And you've got a fourteen-karat heel *and* faker telling you so. You're only one of those things as far as I can see. And at least you're admitting it. Don't worry, you'll do worse before you're through. The world stinks, and we're in it."

That cleared the air. Pace smiled, suddenly feeling, he had no idea why, much rejuvenated. He slapped his friend on the shoulder. "You're a great guy, Phil. I don't know how you do it. You've given me a new lease on life."

The older man—how much older? five years? six?—had just been struck by the awareness that he wouldn't be needing this particular friendship any more, after the next morning's flight. "And I can return the compliment, Jim, in all sincerity."

In flannel pajamas they watched themselves on the eleven o'clock news, not nationwide but wide enough, in color and not far from lifesize, the set being the latest thing on the market, with an aerial that in daytime made the little farmhouse look upside down and in all ways incongruous. They both came over as amiable, just solemn enough for the occasion which wasn't a funeral after all, and generally impressive, in their fur hats and collars, descending the courthouse steps in a group that included the white-haired prosecutor—actually there was a little more focus on him—and others less conspicuous. Other brief shots were of the ruckus outside earlier; the foreman of the jury, a perky old lady schoolteacher, saying she wasn't at liberty to say anything but felt they'd done right; and a family of happy hikers on the Long Trail, at a different spot and season from those in the case.

The most stirring bit might have been the sequel to the minister's reply in court, about the other face between the trees. But as he came on clearing his throat for that, the screen became a home aquarium in frantic distress; faces intermingled and deliquesced, vertical streamers of eye-splitting light raced sideways. Pace fiddled peevishly with the dials. "These goddam manufacturers, can't make anything that'll last a week any more. Same as that fool ice-maker over there. Wait'll you see this though, this is a honey. Automatic vacuum cleaner. I had it put in just to try it out for the next condominiums." He pressed a button by the chimney. Amid a roar fit for a Concorde, the hair on their heads was whipped upright, their pajama pants and tops puffed to the breaking point, glasses crashed, papers flew like bats and a duststorm blasted them from every part of the room at once. "For Christ's sake!" They stopped coughing and were able to rinse out their eyes eventually. "Damn thing, it was working all right the other day."

However, they had both been clearly identified before the other malfunction, the "outstanding New England realtor" as among the spectators, and the witness Reverend John Philipson as the nationally prominent preacher and former civil rights activist, one of those who had chanced on the murdered pair during a period of "retreat" in Vermont. There were some smiles of a different caliber elsewhere in Boonton after the program, and in a few houses a thought for the

young unknown dead. In this one all was serene, until Philipson began
to mumble in his sleep, something about a vision and blinding light and
then about the mouse. The words "Save him!" and "Set him free!"
came out quite distinctly; maybe it was the murderer as well as the
mouse he wanted to set free.

Pace dozed off, to be snapped awake again by loud groans, and that
time his friend was on his knees by his couch, beating at his temples
with both fists and crying out, "Help! my God! help!" But before his
roommate could think what to do, the crisis had drastically changed.
The sufferer sprang to his feet, unlocked and threw open the front
door, letting in an icy blast that would give them both pneumonia in
short order, and with no appearance of either anguish or chill took a
few steps out in the snow. By the time Pace had fumbled for his coat
and galoshes to go after him, he was on his way back in, positively
chortling.

"Oh hello, Jim, did he wake you up too? I'm sorry, I must have been
dreaming. I was seeing some kind of miscreant out there, nothing like
that young gang but he looked somehow familiar, I can't think who it
was. An old blabbermouth. Got what's coming to him anyway. Had his
foot caught in a trap, beaver trap maybe, and was all tangled up in
something like a parachute. Squealing like a stuck pig. A great big bird
with a sort of Chinese face just came and carried him off." He was still
chuckling as he got back in bed.

Pace needn't have been nervous about the next morning's flight. He
was the one with the runny nose at breakfast; his guest was in fine
shape, and didn't remember having had any dreams of any kind.

So off to the butterfly view, of the planet's shape and profits and
pleasures, and its peculiar relation to the sun that causes such white-
ness over some parts at regular intervals; while the empty Brit Horton
and Palz and Holloway houses, and Doc Macklin at his seasonal weekend routine of broken legs, etc., quickly receded, and late-starting
skiers continued to speckle the highways all across New Hampshire,
along with ordinary humans-in-motion, shoppers, poets, rock stars, Tartars, fleers from one thing and another or just everyday rabbit-types

getting somewhere from the usual somewhere else; in which flow, later
in the day and somewhat to the south, were Lem and Hannah Palz in
a Connecticut limousine, headed for Kennedy. The driver noticed in
his rearview mirror that they weren't hopped up as even such elderly
people were apt to be on the drive in. Looked more like passengers the
other way, when it's all over and mostly nothing to write home about
though of course they'd have written plenty just the same. The old
man—well, really not all that old—looked especially wrung out in
spite of his robust outdoor air, more than you generally get in Connecticut these days, and the muscle he'd shown, like a much younger
man, heaving the baggage in. Poor-type baggage, not a new piece in
the lot. Maybe somebody just died in the family or it was bad news
they were going to in Europe. With her glove off, his not, she held his
hand all the way in, and tried to start some talk or sneaked a look at
him sideways now and then, but he'd only nod or murmur and keep
staring ahead. Even the shape of Manhattan from the bridge, on such a
rare clear day too, didn't get him; mostly it was just business travelers
at it all the time who were past raising their eyes for that. She was
mopping her eyes with a Kleenex some of the time, maybe worrying
about her wrinkles; his mother got like that about crying after she
turned sixty, said it ruined your skin to have unhappy thoughts.

But then just before the air freight area something happened. Must
have been something she was thinking about that made her giggle like
that, not loud or so it changed the sad look much but it did take the
years off her, brought a real sweet kind of zany brightness to her eyes
and spun her husband right out of that gloomy trance he'd been in. He
turned to her with the nicest smile, probably asking what was so funny,
and she must have said she'd tell him when they were in the air. For
the few minutes left in the limo she just rested her still smiling and
permanently corrugated cheek against his parka-padded shoulder and
his ungloved right hand reached for hers, in sign of return from his
dark wanderings wherever it was, farther than planes would ever go.

The driver was curiously cheered by the sudden development and
felt like a fool for it. They were nothing to him, all he knew of them or
would ever know was the name on the ticket, but it felt important,
somehow his own life (how dumb can you get?) looked a little more
promising because of it and he actually managed a gruff goodbye as
they trundled off.

Jim Pace, with what felt like the beginning of a sore throat, and the young lady who was or wasn't a secretary were just half an hour ahead of them in the sky but First Class.

And on the cheapest transatlantic night flight, in a window seat, a few days later, Margo Philipson sat with a little boy not yet three years old on her lap, saying, "No, your Mommy can't come to you any more, but Granny's going to stay with you. And maybe on a beach some-where we'll find your uncle Robbie and he'll take you in his arms and show you all kinds of seashells and wonderful things . . . And before that we'll visit Lem and Hannah, they're going to love you too, in a little house somebody's lent them, in a beautiful country, in the south of France. With a wild kind of garden you can run and play in, with mimosa and a pear tree they told me. Of course there won't be any pears on it this time of year but . . ."

"I want to go home!"

Looking down at the tear-smudged face pressed to her chest, she noted a certain resemblance to his maternal grandfather, in the fine straight nose and lift of forehead, but the cheekbones were wider and the eyes brown; that was good.

"Yes. Pretty soon. When our money runs out. And then Granny'll go to work."

"Like Mommy? in her office?"

"Well, no. I'd like to . . ." Help people? the blind for instance? Oh, fakery. Her lack of training for anything struck her dreadfully. "We'll find something, that will do some good to somebody, somehow. There are lots of things people need. Like food, and clothes." The boy was suddenly sleepy enough so she could croon on, to herself, without its troubling him. "Like books, and trees, and flowers. Like loving some-body. Like behaving decently." She settled the child on the other seat with his head on her lap and snapped the seatbelt around him, as though guarding him from multiple harms. "Hush now. Go to sleep. It's going to be a very short night."

Indeed her own eyes had scarcely closed when the morning stir began here and there in the crammed cabin, a bustle of thoughts really more than of bodies; a waking, even in those who had not slept, to the various practical and mental challenges however slight about to rear up at them. Oh dear it was such relief getting up in this thing away from it all and now here we go again. She raised the window shade and there was such a sight as she had never imagined and that even Walt could not have seen, since he'd never been up in a plane. Even so, he'd understand, he'd be the person to try to talk to about it. Another sunrise, that's all it was, but of such wild imagination of color on the clouds below and such scale and manner in its tremendous clarities, it was like having the greatest symphony orchestra playing inside your rib-cage. Silly goose, she told herself, for bumbling with words when such wonders could simply be; words not yet at home in her mind even, only dating from her recent friendship with the Palzes. There had been no music but the family Gilbert and Sullivan in that other life, and not even that in the earlier one, of her childhood; she had only the foggiest idea what a symphony was. Now, as to the pyramids and the thought of skiing a while back, she felt passionately drawn to that adventure. Mozart, Beethoven, Monteverdi—yes, she'd start there, they would bring that heavenly event around the plane into a language her heart could grasp. If she worked hard at it, she prudishly reminded herself. Never mind if she'd never catch up with Hannah and Lem, she'd be happy to just keep learning from them.

How much, how much there was to love, and to learn! and with the thought, dizzying as the sunrise, tears for her daughter could at last break forth, like a cry of agony, like a prayer. The glory outside turned to nothing through that shower. Yet it was almost more than she could bear not to wake the little boy and say, "Look, my darling, look! It's your first sunrise over the ocean, the very first of your whole life!" But she knew she must let him sleep. They had a long, confusing day ahead.

In Vermont, half way between Boonton and Waterville, Walt Hodge was just then plunging coatless into the night and a fierce late-season snowstorm, out of his bride-to-be's cozy and noisy little house. For footgear he had on only a pair of thin old carpet slippers. It was the eve of his wedding day, and the face and name of Margo filled him to bursting. Lord forgive me, I done everything I knew how for You but I can't get hitched up with another woman, even for You I can't, You shouldn't have asked that of me, Lord. A passion of thirst seized him. Nothing in the world but the angel mother whiskey, untasted so many months, could ease such pain. He'd heard the snowplough down on the main road, he could bash the pickup through the snow that far, and did, while voices that must have been calling from the doorway were lost in shrieks of wind. Several miles from town, the near-zero visibility was further confused by an eerie glow that might have issued from the big trailer camp nearby but seemed to him of less earthly origin. He could just make out the end of the road leading to the tumbledown shack he and Margo had visited together. The thirst had left him, and left an enormity of shame to compound his misery. He thought the light was trying to lead him up across the field, and if he followed it the answer to all questions, or at least the main ones, would be revealed. He rammed the car into a snowbank, and struggled across a stone wall and up the swirling hill until his feet were numb as two rocks and the deceiving light had vanished. He fell face down in a drift, had no interest at all in trying to get up, and was so quickly covered in the blizzard, it was several days before the body was found.

Poor cuss, they said, fell off the wagon and went on another toot. Just what everybody'd expected all along.